cocoa beach Boardwalk

SWEENEY HOUSE
BOOK 2

CECELIA SCOTT

Cecelia Scott

Sweeney House Book 2

Cocoa Beach Boardwalk

Introduction To Sweeney House

The Sweeney House is a landmark inn on the shores of Cocoa Beach, built and owned by the same family for decades. After the unexpected passing of their beloved patriarch, Jay, this family must come together like never before. They may have lost their leader, but the Sweeneys are made of strong stuff. Together on the island paradise where they grew up, this family meets every challenge with hope, humor, and heart, bathed in sunshine and the unconditional love they learned from their father.

For release dates, preorder alerts, updates and more, sign up for my newsletter! Or go to www.ceceliascott.com and follow me on Facebook!

Chapter One

Erica

Erica Sweeney-Armstrong woke as a mother for the first time to a startle of fear and worry, an ache of self-doubt, and one sliver of hope no brighter than the light of dawn slipping through the plantation shutters.

That was normal, wasn't it? Fear, worry, doubt, and hope? All new mothers felt that way, didn't they? Of course, they were afraid the baby might be hungry, or worried she didn't sleep through the night, or doubted their ability to care for an infant. And surely that flicker of hope grew into love almost instantly.

But none of these feelings felt "normal" because the child she'd agreed to foster and adopt was not a baby in a bassinet, fulfilling Erica's dreams after battling infertility. Instead, her daughter-to-be was a shy, lanky eleven-year-old with stringy dark hair and narrow shoulders set in resentment and fear.

Jada Perez was an entire person, with a name, a back-story, a personality...a past. How could Erica possibly be a mother to a kid who'd been raised already by someone else?

Someone else, she reminded herself, *who was a recently convicted felon facing twenty years in federal prison for armed robbery, drug possession, and reckless endangerment of a child.*

That was the sum total of what she knew about the woman who gave birth to Jada, ostensibly raised for eleven years, and signed away all rights to custody before being incarcerated.

Erica shifted on the bed, sneaking a peek at Will, who slept soundly. Her husband, to no one's surprise, had been a rock of strength and optimism from the moment the agency representative had arrived with Jada the night before. Will had been, well, *Will*—calm and rational and unfazed.

Erica? So fazed. She let out a soft whimper, hearing that voice way in the back of her head.

This wasn't what I wanted.

She didn't let Jada know that, of course, because if Erica was disappointed, she couldn't imagine how brokenhearted that little girl was right now.

After months in and out of foster homes, Jada had no clue where or how she'd live to adulthood. Her only hope was a program called "foster care adoption" that Erica and Will had happily signed up for in anticipation of finally getting a baby.

Well, not a *baby*. A child. And now she had one, so she'd better quit wallowing in what-ifs and get up and be a mother. And not just a foster mother with the full intention of adopting. And certainly not a foster parent who took the six-month release clause.

No, not Erica Sweeney-Armstrong. Not a NASA rocket scientist who never met a problem she couldn't solve. Not a woman who finished what she started and excelled at everything. So she would excel at this, too... wouldn't she?

Well, not by thinking about herself, but only Jada. She didn't know if she could love Jada like a daughter yet, but she sure could ease some of the pain that kid must be suffering right now. The rest would come. She hoped.

Was six a.m. too early to start?

No, not at all. Maybe Jada was sleeping peacefully, but more likely she was a ball of anxiety who needed to know she was safe and secure.

Erica's chest tensed as she slipped out of the bed and tiptoed into the hallway, more

nervous to talk to this little girl than she was to put her next mission on Mars.

With a sharp inhale, she wrapped her hand around the door handle and slowly pushed it open, craning her neck to see into the guest bedroom, praying there was going to be a sleeping girl under the puffy comforter, home and happy.

The comforter had slipped to the floor, along with half a dozen pillows. And the queen-size bed was completely empty.

"Oh." Erica put her hand to her mouth. Had she run away? Had she sniffed out Erica's disappointment last night and simply couldn't stand the idea of living here?

"Hi." The tiny, mousey, barely audible voice made Erica jump, and she whipped around to see Jada in the hall behind her. Her messy locks hung over her face, her slender frame covered in a faded, oversized T-shirt that nearly reached her knees.

She looked...utterly helpless and lost.

"Oh, oh my gosh, sweetie." Erica puffed a breath of relief, leaning against the wall. "You scared me. What are you doing up so early? I was just coming in to check on you."

Jada looked up at Erica with eyes that were unimaginably big and dark and full of...fear? Distrust? Confusion? Whatever it was, the emotions ran deep and they hurt. Erica *had* to remember that.

"I just..." The words were barely audible as she stepped past Erica into the room. "Went to the bathroom."

"Oh, okay. Good. I'm glad you're making yourself at home." Erica smiled, stepping into the room and clasping her hands together in front of her.

Should she have said that? Maybe it was too soon for the "H" word. This wasn't home to Jada, not even close.

Jada didn't respond, but walked back to the bed, lifting the comforter from the floor and practically burying herself in it, knees hugged to her chest protectively, her eyes narrowed as if to silently say, *"You can leave anytime."*

Erica had to remind herself that this was literally dawn of Day One. There was a long journey ahead and plenty of time for mother-daughter chats.

But she couldn't resist at least trying to take a brick or two from the wall around Jada. She had to start somewhere.

She took a few steps to the bed and sat down on the edge, debating placing a hand on Jada's arm but deciding not to. Physical contact seemed like maybe a Day Two thing.

"Do you need anything?" Erica asked. "Anything that would make you more comfortable?"

Jada just shook her head, a messy black wave sliding to cover her delicate face.

"Look, I..." Erica let out a breath, trying to meet Jada's gaze even through the hair. "I know this is a lot for you right now. I can't even imagine how you're feeling. Scared, frustrated, anxious...all of that is completely valid. Do you..." Erica dug for anything that could possibly get Jada to talk. "Have any questions?"

The girl looked up at her, her lower lip quivering a tiny bit. Classic deer-in-headlights—or an eleven-year-old girl who had just been ripped away from her only family member and dropped into a big, unknown house with a couple of strangers.

Give it time, Erica.

"How long am I going to be here?" she asked in that thin, ragged voice.

Would it terrify Jada if she said *forever*? Or did she need to hear that? Erica had no idea. "Well, honey, I don't know what Miss Abigail told you when she brought you here, but—"

"They never tell you anything at foster homes," she said softly. "You gotta, you know, figure it out."

Erica nodded, hating how hard that must have been for this kid. "I promise you this," she said. "There's no 'figuring out' necessary. I will tell you everything because..." She gave a soft laugh. "That's kind of who I am. And I'll answer any questions. As far as how long you'll be here, well..." She gave in and put her hand on the comforter, feeling the slender leg under it. "I'm hoping a very, very long time."

Jada's eyes flashed a little as she inched out of Erica's touch. "Yeah, uh-huh."

"You don't believe me?" Erica guessed, hearing a note of doubt in the girl's voice.

"I just..." She shrugged. "A lot of people do this for, you know, money and—"

"No!" Erica sat up straighter. "We're not professional foster parents, Jada. Will and I wanted a...child. We want to be parents more than anything. I promise you that."

Jada just stared at her, something clicking behind those midnight eyes, but Erica wasn't sure if she got through.

"I'm here for you, okay?" Erica said quickly, reaching for the girl. "Will and I both are. In fact, I'm working remotely for two weeks, so I'll be home all the time to help you get settled in and be there for you. Whatever you need."

"What's 'remotely'?" Jada repeated the word, confusion knitting her eyebrows together.

"Oh, of course. It means I can do my job right here, at home. I'm an engineer, and they usually aren't crazy about work from home over at the space center, but they made an exception for me. For *you*," she added brightly.

"The space center?" Jada asked, the first flicker of real interest. "That's cool."

"Oh, it is! Maybe I can take you there sometime."

"'Kay." She nodded.

"So, you always up this early?" Erica asked as she stood, not really wanting to leave yet.

"Sometimes," Jada said.

After an awkward beat, Erica picked up one of the many decorative pillows Jada had discarded onto the floor. "Guess these are overkill, huh?" She chuckled. "Guest room stuff. But we'll make it your room. We can paint or..."

Wait. Too much.

Erica took a step backward. "First things first. Breakfast? I make a mean Belgian waffle. Do you like those?"

"I...I guess. Like an Eggo?"

"Oh, so much better. Why don't you...brush your teeth and come on down for the most incredible waffle you've ever had? How does that sound?"

Jada nodded again.

"Okay." She backed out of the room with a cheery smile. "See you downstairs!"

She left the door open when she walked out, pressing her hands together as she headed down the stairs. On the way, she suddenly tried to see this home through Jada's eyes. Was it just a cold, monstrous, contemporary suburban home in the guarded, gated neighborhood of Riverside Palms? Or could it be *her* home?

Maybe. It was up to Erica to make this Jada's home, no matter what it took.

She could do this. She had to do this. She could get past the initial shock, show that girl what real love looked like, and be a mom.

There was no turning back now. Jada wasn't the rosy-cheeked, button-nosed newborn that Erica pictured in her many baby fantasies, but she was hers. And Erica had never met a challenge she couldn't conquer, even a bashful pre-teen who didn't really want to be here.

Chapter Two

Sam

Samantha Sweeney sat on the back deck of the cottage, inhaling the beauty of Cocoa Beach, taking in this little slice of paradise that she, once again, called home. Beyond her, the Atlantic Ocean splashed onto the shore, sparkling in the sun, and the familiar songs of the birds echoed through the air.

Was it wrong that she was already procrastinating the start of her work day? Well, who wouldn't? Yes, she had a great new job as an admin in her brother's ad agency, and she loved the work and the sense of independence. That was a new feeling for a soon-to-be-divorced woman who'd never had a real paycheck in her life.

But this was...so *nice*.

The job was terrific, but moving back to this cottage—and the inn her mother ran that was attached to it—was the real balm on her wounded heart. Any strides she'd made in the last six months were due to this cottage, this beach, this air, and this life.

After learning her husband was cheating on her—and now in love with someone else and having a baby and living in her old house—Sam had followed Taylor's advice and moved back to the property where she'd grown up. She might only be twenty-four, but her daughter was smart, and so was this move.

It had even been amazing for Ben, Sam's sixteen-year-old son, who'd struggled so mightily when his parents separated and filed for divorce. Rough for a while, but he was recovering, despite the serious car accident he'd been in recently. Ben was on the mend, physically and mentally.

Icing on the cake, she got to be close to two of her siblings, including her sister...who became a mother last night.

"Yikes," Sam muttered, pulling out her phone. She still had a few minutes, so she texted Erica for the third time, dying to know how it was going with the almost-teenager who'd landed in her lap.

Knowing Erica, they were already bonded, having mother-daughter coffee time, and planning to slay the world Erica-style. Still, she'd appreciate a text back.

"Oh, you haven't left for work yet."

Sam turned at the sound of her mother's voice, a little surprised to see Dottie Sweeney completely dressed for the day, carrying a few notebooks and magazines, and... was that a ring of paint samples in her hand?

"I'm driving myself and can get there by nine-ish," Sam explained. "Is that what I think it is?"

"Yes, it is!" She swung the paint samples on her finger. "I can't wait, Sam. I remembered I had these up in a closet from when we repainted the upstairs hall of the inn. I was hoping to start picking a...palette? Isn't that the word designers use?"

Sam smiled at her. "You're diving right into this reno-vation, I see."

"Why not?" She reached for Sam's hand. "I'm so excited, my head's been spinning all night. Now that I've made the decision to renovate Sweeney House, I simply can't think of anything else. Same for you?"

"I *want* to think about it," Sam said. "But...I have to work all day, all week. When I told you I'd help you with the project, I meant it. Then I woke up and remembered I have a real job. And it's not renovating our one-of-a-kind ten-bedroom family jewel." She made a face. "Think it's too soon to ask for a vacation? A sabbatical? An extended leave of absence to become the Joanna Gaines of Cocoa Beach?"

Her mother laughed, the sound music to Sam's ears. After a year of grieving the loss of her beloved Jay, Dottie had become a ghost of her former vibrant and energetic self.

But since Sam's arrival more than a month ago, Dottie looked brighter. There was a gleam in her eyes and a sparkle in her smile. Her silky gray curls fell around her face, which still looked dang good for seventy-two.

"The fact is," Dottie said, "your boss is your brother, and my son. You could ask John to cut your hours if you have to."

Sam moaned. "I don't think he's going to love to see me walking out at two every day," she said, picking up her phone to check to see if her sister had texted back. "Have you heard from Erica? I'm dying to know how she's doing."

"I'm sure she's doing fine. Shocked, but fine," Dottie said. "Erica doesn't back down from a challenge."

"True, but that was the stunner of the century when the adoption agency lady pulled up to the party last night with an eleven-year-old. Definitely not what Erica was expecting."

"No, but it shouldn't matter." Dottie shrugged. "She wanted to adopt a child and Will told me they knew this was a possibility. I trust Erica to love that child like her own, and we're here to help." She rattled the ring of paint samples. "And renovate."

Sam laughed. "You are on a mission, Dottie Sweeney."

"I am!" She leaned forward, her eyes sparking. "Sam, this renovation has given me new life and purpose! And you made it possible."

"My future ex made it possible," she joked. "But I still love the idea of investing my divorce gains into Sweeney House. And, Mom..." She took her mother's hand. "I love seeing you this happy again. Wow."

Dottie gave her a warm smile. "Part of the fun is doing it all with you, Sam. I feel like this is an opportunity you and I have never had."

"Because I ran off and married a jerk." Sam put her lip out. "We did miss a lot, Mom."

Dottie flicked it off, as if the years they were at odds just didn't matter anymore.

"Water under the bridge, honey. Today's a new day and we have a thrilling project. I want to line up our vendors and pick colors and have a plan for each room! I want to rip up that carpet in the hall and meet with an architect for the new restaurant—brilliant idea, by the way—and, oh, I was thinking maybe some of the windows could be replaced. And then I want to—"

"Whoa, hold up there, Mom. I am literally gone forty hours a week. You can't do all that alone."

"No, I can't. But you..." She wrinkled her nose. "Yeah. Five-month vacation." She sighed and fell back on the chair cushion. "I guess I got ahead of myself."

"No, I love your enthusiasm. I feel it, too. I'd rather renovate than administrate, but..." She shrugged and dared a look at her phone. "I'm going to be late for that, too."

Dottie just nodded, placing the paint chips on top of a copy of *Southern Living* that she'd brought out. "I understand."

Sam regarded her for a moment, feeling pulled in two directions. The job, which she'd been so thrilled to get at her brother's firm...and the renovation, which brought such life back to her mother. It hadn't been an easy decision to change the inn that had Dad's fingerprints all over it.

"We'll figure it out, Mom," she said. "It might just take a little longer. But I can make some calls from work."

"And I can do some things on my own," her mother agreed. "I was thinking about the antiques and furniture. Are we getting rid of all of it?"

"I'm sure there will be some things we can preserve and repurpose," Sam said. "I bet we could find someone who does that. You know, repaint, resurface, revive them. Will probably knows someone who can do that."

"Thank you for caring about them." Dottie smiled, giving Sam's hand a squeeze. "And thank you for even wanting to take on this work when you have a new job."

"Believe me, I'd rather renovate. Is that awful? John pulled strings to get me that job and I really feel I owe him more than a month. But *this* job, Mom..." She turned to see the side and back of Sweeney House, taking in the faded blue paint and slightly fogged windows. The roof was old, too, and she knew the inside had such unreached potential. "This job is huge."

For a long moment, neither said a word as they looked at each other, thinking about how they could do what they wanted to do.

"And we have Will to help us," Dottie said, giving voice to those thoughts. "He's a construction manager, as you know, and promised to handle a lot of the work."

"In between his other jobs and a new not-baby." Sam smiled. "Yes, Will can help, but I'm still a little worried about the amount of physical labor and time."

"He can bring Jada anytime, you know," Dottie said. "I'm a good grandmother."

"Good?" Taylor unexpectedly breezed onto the patio in a T-shirt and sleep pants, a half-peeled banana in one hand, coffee in the other. "You are a fantastic grandmother! Best in the business, I'd say."

She leaned over and kissed Dottie's head, then looked at Sam, her dark brown waves sliding over toned shoulders. "And, yeah, you're a pretty good mom. Why aren't you at work, by the way? It's almost nine."

"Because I'm going to quit."

"*What?*"

"I'm just kidding. Sort of." Sam slid over on the sofa cushion to make room for Taylor. "Grandma and I are just realizing that we may have bit off way more than we can chew with the inn reno."

"What do you mean?" Taylor asked, taking a bite of banana.

"I mean it will take a ton of time and energy and organization, and I'm putting all of that into my job at Coastal Marketing."

"Right, that makes sense. A renovation of this scale could definitely be a full-time job, I can't imagine the amount of work that goes into it," Taylor agreed. "So, you have two jobs now and I can't even find one," she muttered, shaking her head. "Amazing."

"Oh, Taylor." Dottie leaned closer to her granddaughter. "There are dozens of bars and restaurants all over this town. Surely someone is looking for a sweet, wonderful addition to their staff."

"I don't want to bartend anymore, Grandma." Taylor pulled on the banana peel and rolled her eyes. "The very thought of mixing a whiskey sour makes me nauseous, to be perfectly real with you guys."

Sam sighed, feeling for her daughter, and not just for the job hunt. Sam had to remind herself that her daughter was nursing a broken heart after the enchanting surfer boy she'd been seeing had to leave suddenly and return to his home in Hawaii for a family emergency. Taylor had really fallen for the kid, and his departure had left her girl tender and blue.

As if sensing her mother's pity, Taylor waved a dismissive hand. "I'll be all right. Go enjoy work. Like, now, before you don't have to quit because you got fired."

Sam pushed up on a sigh. "I love this job," she said, probably trying to convince herself as much as the other two. "The agency is fun and I even reconnected with Annie Hawthorne, my high school buddy, since she's an accountant there. But..." She stole one more look at the inn. "I want to dive into that remodel and not come up for air."

"It wouldn't pay anything," her mother said.

"I'm not as desperate for money now that Max gave me that big pile from the Guilt Fund. And we'd have so much fun, Mom."

Her eyes grew misty with affection. "We would, Sam."

"We'll just have to take it slow and work hard on the weekends," Sam said, picking up her empty coffee cup. "I gotta run. Fly, actually. Is Ben awake? I don't want to leave without saying goodbye."

"He's dead to the world," Taylor told her. "I think sleep is the best thing for him while he recovers."

Sam nodded, torn again. "Will you tell him I wanted to kiss him goodbye?" she asked Taylor.

"Of course, but I'll get a Ben Parker eyeroll."

"And I'll make him breakfast in bed," Dottie said. "He really loves that."

"You're a doll, Mom. Thank you. I'm off." She blew a kiss to both of them, grabbed her bag, and headed out to the rental car her insurance company had given her after Ben totaled her SUV last week.

Pulling out onto A1A, she took a deep breath and thought about exactly what she could say to her boss and brother, having no idea what direction to take this next step.

Chapter Three

Taylor

As Taylor walked along the beach, splashing the ankle-high water with her feet, the same question played over and over in her mind: Was she pathetic?

She was going on twenty-five, completely jobless, living at her grandmother's cottage, and one hundred percent single. Not to mention the fact that she was looking out longingly at the waves of the ocean, as if Kai Leilani, the only guy she'd ever really fallen for, was going to surf all the way from Hawaii back to Cocoa Beach and sweep her off her feet.

To her disappointment, though, the ocean was quiet and still, and Kai was thousands of miles away. And Taylor was a medical school dropout who'd spent the last six months pouring drinks, flirting for tips, and going home to her cat.

Okay. Maybe she was a little pathetic.

But she was so much happier here—or at least she had been, until Kai left. Taylor hated that the actions of a boy influenced her mood whatsoever. She had vowed to never get attached to a man, and somehow, over early mornings on the beach and secret kisses and laughs and deep conversations...she'd gotten attached.

Nonetheless, even with Kai gone and her heart a bit bruised, Taylor was still over the moon to be in Cocoa Beach. Despite her own ups and downs with Kai, she'd seen a switch flip for her mom, who was her best friend in the world and deserved nothing but joy.

Not to mention the fact that she was a rock-solid hour away from her sad excuse for a father and his new girlfriend and their baby-to-be.

Talk about pathetic. If anyone deserved that title, it was Max Parker.

"Yo, Tay!" The surprisingly deep voice of her brother, Ben, caught her attention, and Taylor turned away from the water and looked back at the cottage.

He stood on the deck, leaning on a pair of crutches that he'd been using to get around since the accident. Waving his hands like a maniac, he shouted to her again. "Whatcha doing out there? Moping?"

Taylor rolled her eyes and jogged up the sand to the cottage, hopping up the wooden steps onto the deck to join her brother. "I'm not moping, I'm *thinking*."

"What, are you Socrates?" He laughed as they sat down on the two chairs that looked out over the beach.

"I don't know. Was he a med school dropout with no talents or passions or direction in life?" she quipped.

"Stop feeling sorry for yourself," Ben shot back, clearly having none of Taylor's beachside pity party. "You sound like Mom did when we first moved here."

"But look at her now," Taylor said, waving a hand. "She's *overflowing* with passions and purposes and new things to care about. She doesn't even have time for them all. Can you believe she's considering quitting the agency?"

"Seriously?"

"So she has time to help Grandma renovate. And you know, Ben, when she talked about it, I saw real passion in her eyes. She was good at that kind of stuff, too. Remember how beautiful our house was in Winter Park?"

"Beautiful until Dad…" He swallowed the rest. "Anyway, I get it. You want passion. I mean, you had Kai. You were passionate about him. Not that having a crush is, like, a hobby or anything, but still."

Taylor eyed her brother. "Your little brush with death sure did make you forthright, kiddo."

He lifted a shoulder. "Am I wrong?"

She sighed, knowing full well that he wasn't wrong at all. Ever since they'd arrived in Cocoa Beach, she'd been enchanted by the dreamy professional surfer, and hadn't given too terribly much thought or time to anything else.

But now he was gone, and it was time to start figuring out who Taylor Parker really was. She wasn't the surgeon that her father so desperately wanted her to be. She wasn't the wife and mother that Sam had been with such grace and strength. She sure as heck wasn't a bartender.

"I'm just so useless right now."

"Oh my gosh, seriously?" Ben groaned and rolled his eyes. "Taylor. Get out of the dumps. This whiny crap doesn't suit you at all."

She shot him a look. "Coming from the person who

spent six months isolating himself and staring at a video game screen and refusing to talk to anyone?"

"Yes," he said without hesitation. "Coming from that exact person, actually. The one who realized what a waste of time it is to sit around and be sad. I know Kai left and it sucks, but you're Taylor Parker. You make the best out of everything and you're hilarious while doing it."

Taylor rocked back and forth on the old, worn-down Adirondack chair, an unexpected ache pressing on her chest.

Ben was right. She'd done enough wallowing. She'd only known Kai for a month, after all. It was starting to get depressing, and borderline embarrassing. It was time to pick up the pieces and be the same strong, feisty, fearless girl who quit medical school to stick it to her father and convinced her mom to come here and start a new life.

She turned to Ben, smiling. "You're right, Benny boy. I think your concussion actually made you smarter."

"Not how that works," he said on a laugh. "But... thanks. I just, I don't know. I feel like I'm seeing stuff so differently now. Not to sound like, well, Socrates about it, but I feel like I got some major perspective."

Taylor let out a breath and studied her brother, her mind viscerally remembering the day of the accident.

It had been a terrifying, stressful, adrenaline-fueled blur, but she'd gotten her and Sam to the ER outside of Orlando, waited to find out if Ben was even okay, and then, for the sweet little cherry on top, had to see her Dad.

What a day it had been. But Taylor knew, however

horrifying it was for her, it had to have been ten times worse for Ben.

She set her chin back down on her knees and watched the waves crash onto the sand. "So, I totally get it if you don't want to talk about this, but...were you scared? Like, when it happened?"

Ben glanced at her, his eyes flashing with the memory. "Honestly? I don't really recall much. I remember hydroplaning, and cursing. Loudly." He laughed a little. "And then I woke up in the hospital, confused. I saw you and Mom and I realized how freaked out you guys were, and I felt terrible. That was about it."

Taylor shivered, shutting her eyes. "I'm so glad you're okay."

"So am I," he said softly. "So, take it from me. Life's too short and fragile to mope."

"Words from the Reformed King of Moping himself."

"I told you, I'm a changed man. What can I say?"

The two of them laughed, and Taylor leaned back in her chair, looking up at the sky as the warm afternoon sunshine baked into her skin. "Okay, then, Wise One. Tell me what to do with my life. Advise me. Guide me. Philosophize."

"I don't know..." He puffed out a sigh and ran a hand through his hair, which unfairly stayed shiny even in this insane humidity. "You said Mom was probably going to quit, right? The admin job at Uncle John's agency?"

"Yeah." Taylor frowned. "But knowing Mom, she will not have the guts to let Uncle John down by quitting. He went to the mat to get her the job, and there's a decent amount of responsibility. I doubt she'll just bail. It's not who she is."

"Why don't you take her spot, then?" Ben asked nonchalantly. "Boom. Problem solved. Everybody wins."

She snorted. "Yeah, like I could run the office admin at an ad agency. I don't even really know what happens at ad agencies. They make ads, that's it. That's the extent of my knowledge."

"So what? Mom didn't have any experience."

"But..." She tilted her head, thinking about that. "True, but..."

"But what?"

"But...it's not a bad idea there, kid," she said on a laugh, sitting up. "In fact, it might be genius. She could waltz right into Uncle John's office with a replacement, and then she wouldn't feel bad about it. And I'd have a job."

"Now we're talking, Tay. If he gave the job to Mom, I'm sure he'd give it to you. You've even got a college diploma, which Mom doesn't. Plus, Uncle John *lives* to help out the family. He's that guy, always bringing everyone together. He'd probably love to have the next generation of Sweeneys in his office."

Taylor didn't know too terribly much about her mom's relatively new position at Coastal Marketing, but the more she thought about it, the more it sounded like something she actually could definitely do.

"It's mostly organization and technology. I'm not bad at either one," she said, thinking out loud.

The whole marketing and advertising thing would be

a learning curve—considering she'd majored in Biology in undergrad—but she'd pick it up.

"You know what, Benny? I love this idea!" She leaned over to give him a hug.

"Ow!" he shouted, drawing back. "Broken rib, remember?"

"Oops! Sorry." She ruffled that obnoxiously silky hair. "Okay, I'm off."

"Where are you going?"

"To change the world, Socrates!" She laughed as she jogged onto the sand, her heart light for the first time in a week. Really light, like there was hope and maybe, just maybe, some passion. "Well, to change mine and Mom's, anyway!"

"You're weird," he called from the chair.

"Yep. Good to have you back, Benny!"

Taylor had been to Coastal Marketing a couple of times before, so she knew to head straight up to the third floor as soon as she walked into the lobby.

The building was right on the beach, with huge windows that looked out on the oceanfront view. It was a heck of a place to work, and the possibility of coming here every day sent a chill of excitement zipping up Taylor's spine.

Would Mom go for the idea? Probably. Had she already talked to John so he was looking for replacements? Highly doubtful, but still, Taylor didn't want to waste one second. She had to march right in there and, at the very least, throw her hat in the ring.

She took a deep breath when she reached the frosted glass doors with Coastal Marketing etched in them. This was perfect. This was a real job, at a real company, run by her very own uncle.

She hoped.

"Hey!" At the front desk, her mother looked up from her computer keyboard, wide-eyed, when Taylor walked through the door. "To what the heck do I owe this pleasant surprise?"

"Well..." Taylor straightened her back, wiggled her brows at her mom, and walked closer to lower her voice. "I want to talk to you about something."

Sam drew back. "Is everything okay?"

"Oh, yeah. More than okay." Taylor sucked in a breath. "Did you quit yet?"

Mom looked positively pained by the question. "No, Tay. I don't think it would be fair to John for me to walk out on—"

"Well, you should. And..." She held up her hand to hold off arguments. "Hear me out. If you quit *with* a replacement right behind you, ready to take your job, and it's someone Uncle John knows and loves? That wouldn't be so awful, would it?"

Sam sat up, her brows knitting together with intrigue. "And who would that be?"

"This girl right here," Taylor said, tapping her chest.

"You? Seriously?"

"Mom, I think I'd be great here. It's exactly the type

of position I'm looking for. It's a starter, and I'm eager to learn and grow and move up. And you can teach me everything."

"Taylor, that's..." Sam shook her head slowly, laughing with disbelief. "That's actually brilliant. I can't believe I didn't think of that."

"I didn't, either. Ben did."

"Wow." Sam leaned back in her chair, studying her daughter. "That concussion made him smarter."

"That's what I said!" Taylor laughed. "So, you think I can take your spot? It could work?"

"I think..." Sam looked up at Taylor, smiling. "That you will absolutely thrive here. And I'm so proud of you for taking the initiative and coming here, Tay. I'll talk to John."

"Thanks. I really want this. I'm done moping."

"You know..." Sam bit her lip, a smile pulling at her face. "I think I am, too."

Chapter Four

Imani

Imani Sweeney pressed her hands onto the cool, hard quartz countertop in the kitchen and shut her eyes tightly. She took a slow, deep breath, digging for the grace and composure that was normally so effortless for her.

She'd been a full-time mom for fifteen years now, from the day Damien was born. And she'd loved every minute of it. Sure, there had been challenges. Tears, stress, worry, frustration…but none of it ever really *got* to her.

The work was hard, but so rewarding to do everything imaginable for her three beautiful, amazing kids and, of course, her husband, John. They had a wonderful family—some would even call it picture perfect.

The house, the kids, the big SUV, the man who ran his own business and the wife and mom who never, ever missed a beat.

But today? That beat felt like it was about to be missed. Badly.

"Mom!" Twelve-year-old Liam's voice broke Imani out of her thoughts, and she turned around and silently begged for patience.

Now what? "What is it, hon?"

"Finn's birthday party is on Saturday, at that rock climbing place. You can take me, right?" He looked up at her with a big smile and hopeful eyes.

Finn's birthday party? How could this possibly be the first time she'd heard about this?

Imani thought for a second and walked over to the huge, messy, terrifyingly full month-long calendar on the wall of the kitchen.

"Uh, let me look—"

"No, she can't take you, Liam," Damien said matter-of-factly, without even looking away from the TV where he was rapidly pressing buttons on a controller, playing a video game. "I have my basketball summer league semifinals on Saturday, and Mom and Dad both promised to be there. Right, Mom?"

"Yes, yes. I know you have a basketball game..." She glanced at the calendar again, the different pen colors and highlights all starting to blend together in front of her. "I see that on here."

"So you'll be there, right?" Damien asked.

"No, she's taking me to Finn's party!" Liam insisted, his young voice rising.

"Liam, I didn't know about Finn's party," Imani said slowly, keeping calm. "I did promise your brother we'd be at his game, though. Maybe a friend can take you—"

"Wait, Saturday?" Ellen, Imani and John's youngest at nine years old, raced over to her mother with wide green eyes and her dark curls falling all over her painfully adorable face. "Mommy, you said we could go ice skating this weekend. You promised!" She whined out the last word at a pitch that made Imani's ears hurt.

"Well, we'll have to push that to Sunday, El. It looks like your brothers have a lot going on Saturday."

"No, Mom," Damien called into the kitchen, still glued to his incredibly loud video game, the electronic music of it hurting Imani's brain. "Sunday is the beach cleanup for my volunteer hours, remember? You said you'd come help out. Mr. McKay already has you on the list, and I need those hours to get into a good college."

"No!" Ellen shrieked. "That's not fair! Mommy, you said!"

The familiar squeeze of stress gripped Imani's throat, and she took a deep breath and looked at each of these children, each more stunning than the last.

She and John had created three brilliant, energetic, mixed-race miracles who she couldn't physically love any more if she tried.

But, holy cow, they were exhausting, and their little young lives were so incredibly busy.

Imani supposed that's what she got for raising three social extroverts who loved activities, sports, friends, and doing *stuff*. All. The. Time.

Sometimes she wished just one of them wanted to stay at home in their room. But not these Sweeney kids. They were nonstop, and Imani's life was spent hauling her SUV up and down A1A and obsessively managing the nearly impossible schedules.

"Okay, okay." She held up a hand. "Just give me a second, you guys. We can figure this out. Your dad will be home on the weekend, so maybe he can take you to the party, Liam. And Dame, I'll watch your game."

Damien shrugged. "Okay."

"What about ice skating?" Ellen asked, her voice quivering.

"Ellen, you can't even go ice skating here." Liam squinted at his little sister, his face twisting up with confusion. "We live in Florida."

"It's called Space Coast Iceplex and I saw it on TV, so I know it's real!" Ellen shouted.

"Ellen, lower your voice," Imani said with a hand to her daughter's shoulder. "Liam, stop being rude. Space Coast Iceplex is definitely real. Your father went there as a kid."

"See?" Ellen turned back to Liam and stuck her tongue out, making a face.

Imani ignored it.

"Why don't you go ice skating next week?" Damien, who'd inherited the steady, conflict-hating, peacemaking gene from his dear father, suggested. "It's summertime, you can do whatever you want on the weekdays."

"She's at ballet camp next week," Imani explained, doublechecking that on the calendar, written in pink marker, which meant it was for Ellen. Blue was Damien, and green was Liam.

"Ballet camp!" Ellen exclaimed, instantly jumping into pliés and pirouettes, flying around the kitchen.

"You're still coming to the beach cleanup then, right, Mom?" Damien's voice echoed through the room, but to Imani, it sounded miles away.

Beach cleanup. Sunday. Volunteer hours. Basketball. Ice skating. Finn's birthday party.

Imani clenched her jaw and pressed her forehead against the calendar, begging for her normal ease and composure that had somehow started to fade away.

Motherhood had become her entire life, taking over every minute of every day. When she wasn't driving the kids around, going to their events, or helping them with homework, she was worrying about them. Thinking about them. Wondering where Damien was going to go to college or how John was going to handle the day Ellen wanted to start dating.

But lately? She'd been feeling swallowed up and erased in the hectic, delicate world of being a full-time mom.

"Mom! Did you hear me?" Liam asked, bringing Imani back to Earth once again.

She pulled her face away from the calendar, pushed her long braids back behind her shoulders, and looked at her son. "No. What is it, Liam?"

"I asked if I could have a phone. All my friends are getting them. Please?"

She opened her mouth to respond, but didn't get a word out.

"No way, Liam," Damien answered. "I didn't get a phone until I was almost fourteen. Right, Mom?"

"Not fair!" Liam insisted.

"I want a phone!" Ellen chimed in.

"Mom, I can explain why I should get one now," Liam continued. "I have a list of reasons."

Imani closed her eyes, her heart pounding.

"Can we go to the Verizon store?" he asked. "Maybe tomorrow?"

"Mom's taking me driving tomorrow to practice for my license test," Damien said. "And you're too young for a phone. Isn't he, Mom?"

Suddenly, Imani was stricken with dizziness, and the world seemed to shift and swirl and spin under her feet.

She couldn't handle it anymore.

"I'm going upstairs," Imani announced, turning to walk out of the kitchen and head up the long staircase.

She could hear the confused questions echoing from her kids in the living room, but she ignored them, her palms sweating and hands shaking as she walked into the bedroom, closed the door, and flopped down on their luxurious bed.

Forcing herself to take slow, deep breaths, Imani managed to calm down from the stress and anxiety. She slid down and sat on the floor, reaching underneath the bed for an old, plastic bin that was latched shut.

She yanked it out, wiping a layer of dust off the top of the bin and unclipping the latches before taking the lid off.

The very first thing in the pile was a printout of an article, a feature piece on the best resorts and restaurants in French Polynesia.

She smiled at the faded paper, memories flooding back to her as she ran her thumb over the name of the author underneath the title.

Imani Tucker

Wistful nostalgia rocked her to her core as she thought back on her years as a successful travel writer, bouncing around to different countries all over the world, staying in the most beautiful places imaginable.

She could still smell the air of Tahiti as she skimmed through this article, remembering the deep, cerulean blue of the ocean, the salt in the air as she stepped out on the deck of her over-the-water bungalow.

Oh, those days were something. Filled with excitement and newness and the constant thrill of adventure.

Imani dug through the memory box, pulling articles from travel books, magazines, and websites that all had her heart, soul, and experiences poured into every word.

A piece on the best hotels in Lyon, France. Oh, she had loved the French food. The sweet smells of croissants on every street corner... Just the thought made her heart squeeze with sentiment.

She pulled out another paper, this one a feature piece on one of the most magnificent places Imani had ever stayed: a small, quaint, wildly upscale hotel in Positano, Italy called the Eden Roc. She laughed to herself, remembering how she had gotten sick on that trip, and the staff came up to her suite and served a five-course meal with a white tablecloth, right on her balcony.

Imani studied the faded, glossy pictures of the vine-covered terraces and colorful, postcard views from that Southern Italy tour.

Before her life was soccer games, packed lunches, and birthday parties, it was...this. An endless itinerary of exotic, picturesque, mind-blowing places that she wrote about for *Fodor's* travel guides.

Sure, being an established travel writer had been brutally hard work and deeply exhausting, and certainly had its lonely days. But right now, as Imani grazed these old books and sank deep into the memories, it was hard to recall anything but how wonderful that life was.

It had been a fabulous season of her life, but like all seasons, her life had changed. And she loved this life, with this incredible family. She did. But...that one tapped into a whole different side of Imani, and she missed it.

She missed being the woman who got on those planes and trains and boats. A fearless, independent, successful woman, impressive and established and...*free*.

Now, who was she? She lived for her family and bent over backwards for her kids. As it should be. But...her gaze fell on the picture of the Eden Roc.

It hadn't been just the travel and exotic places. She'd had a purpose, a plan, a paycheck. Now she had...the schedule of three small non-stop humans.

For the first time in fifteen years, she ached for her old self...and that hit her with another unexpected wave of emotion. A black splash of guilt in her chest that made her cringe just realizing what she was thinking.

How would John or the kids feel if they knew she was up here reminiscing about her life before they were in it?

The very thought of it hurt her heart.

With a new conflict and turmoil nagging at her, she packed up the box, shoved it back under the bed, and got up.

"Mom? Where are you?"

Duty—and Ellen—called, and there was no more time for living in the past. She had to figure out how to be in three places at once this weekend, and do it with the effortless poise that seemed so hard to come by these days.

Chapter Five

Erica

S hopping. Every eleven-year-old girl on the planet loved shopping, right?

Erica finished firing off her last out-of-office email and shut her laptop before heading upstairs with determination and optimism. A shopping spree was just the thing to at least catalyze the process of bringing Jada out of her shell.

Especially since she'd shown up with nothing but a small, worn-out backpack. Poor thing.

It had been a full three days since the arrival of this new and unexpected addition to the Armstrong family, and Erica wasn't even certain Jada had spoken more than three *sentences* since she'd gotten there.

As much as she was unsure and worried and definitely in over her head, Erica was certain she would be able to make strides with this little girl. She had to. They were adopting her, after all. She just needed something—anything—to make her feel like a mom.

And what better place to start than the mall?

"You ready to go?" Erica asked cheerfully, tapping her knuckles on the outside of the guest bedroom door.

"Okay," came the tiniest mouse voice from the room.

She pushed the door open gently, finding Jada sitting in the corner holding an old, raggedy-looking stuffed rabbit, bent over a notebook and scribbling something with a pencil. Instantly, Jada straightened, closing the notebook and sliding the rabbit under the bed.

"You're going to love this," Erica cooed, gesturing for Jada to follow her out of the bedroom. "We'll get you all sorts of clothes or toys or books or shoes...whatever you want."

Not that she was trying to buy Jada's love or anything. Okay, maybe a little. But, despite her best efforts to be patient and understanding and deeply sympathetic to everything little Jada had been through, Erica was getting desperate.

She had to open up soon, right? Erica and Will weren't scary people, although Jada looked at them like they were from another planet.

To her, she guessed, it felt like they were.

"Let's get rolling." Erica waved her hand toward the garage as Jada followed her down the stairs and through the door, climbing into the back seat of her SUV.

As she made the short drive to the mall, Erica filled the silence with chatter and rambling. She'd learned quickly that Jada was a big fan of one-syllable answers to any and all questions, so Erica decided she'd just talk and talk until Jada eventually had something to say.

But, by the time they arrived at the mall, *eventually* had not come yet.

It was okay. She would keep trying.

"So, where do you want to start?" she asked brightly

as they walked through the main entrance into the
Merritt Square Mall. Erica, of course, wanted a plan. "It's
not the fanciest mall in the world, but it's definitely got
what you need. Maybe one of these days we can make
the trip over to Orlando and hit up Mall at Millenia.
Now, *that's* an experience."

Jada just nodded, wandering ahead a little bit to look
at the fountain in the middle of the foyer.

"How about Gap?" Erica asked, stepping next to her
and standing side by side. "Is Gap still cool? New pair of
jeans, maybe?"

Jada looked up at Erica, those mysterious and beautiful and deeply complicated brown eyes studying her. "I
like dresses."

No three words had ever given anyone as much joy as
those just did for Erica.

She spoke. And not only did she speak, she expressed
something. Something tangible, something about herself.
Something that Erica could work with.

It was a microscopic start, but a start nonetheless.

"Dresses!" She clasped her hands together, looking
down the long concourse of the mall. "I bet we can find
you some dresses."

They walked side by side past the rows of stores, and
Erica was careful and cautious not to overdo it too soon or
freak Jada out.

Calm, chill, normal day at the mall with her kid.
That's all it was.

"Are you, like, a pink and flowery girl? Or more of a"

—she waved a hand—"neutral tones, low-key kind of girl?"

"I don't know," Jada said softly, shaking her head. "I never really bought clothes before."

"Oh." Erica sucked in a sharp breath, the reminder of where this child came from hitting her hard all over again.

The realization only made Erica want to shower her with even more clothes and gifts. Not to win her over, but to show her she deserved it. To give her a happy childhood that she'd clearly had to miss out on for all these years.

Suddenly, Jada stopped in her tracks, turning to face a mannequin window display at Old Navy.

Erica stopped walking and stepped over to join her. "Do you see something you like? We can go in here, if you want."

Jada nodded, pointing at a purple and yellow sundress on a girl in an advertisement who looked about her age.

"That dress?"

She nodded again, with a little more certainty this time. Her long dark hair bounced around her face, but Erica could still see her eyes peeking through it.

"Come on!" She gestured for Jada to walk into the store. "Let's find it for you."

Jada moved slowly through Old Navy, staring at each display and touching all the different materials of clothes, as if she'd never been in a real clothing store before. She seemed mystified.

Erica's heart practically cracked in half, and she wanted to buy her the whole store. But, she didn't want to overwhelm Jada any more than she already was, and she also didn't want her to feel like a charity case.

She wanted her to feel like, well, her daughter. Whatever that looked like.

"You can pick anything you want. And I think we can find that dress you like." Erica leaned down to get closer to Jada's level, giving her a grin. "There's a section for your age in the back, they have tons of stuff. Want to check it out?"

Jada nodded again, and Erica swore she saw something that could maybe be interpreted as a smile.

As she watched the girl slowly walk over to the "tween girl" section of Old Navy, she felt a glimmer of hope worm its way through her chest.

This could work out. This could be good. This could be everything that was supposed to happen. And, no, it certainly wasn't the visual Erica had imagined for raising a child, but some things in life just couldn't be planned out, despite Erica's best efforts.

As Jada pushed through a rack of colorful dresses, Erica whipped her phone out to shoot a text to Will, who was on-site overseeing the construction of a new housing development on the mainland. She saw a few texts from Sam, and made a mental note to reply when they were done shopping.

Made it to the mall. Going well, I think. She's a little bit less terrified, so that's progress, I suppose. See you at home for dinner later!

Erica quickly put her phone back in her purse and focused her attention on Jada, who was timidly running her fingers over the yellow-and-purple dress.

"Oh!" Erica hurried over to stand next to her by the clothing rack. "You found it! Here, I'll grab your size, which I'm guessing is extra small, and we can get you started in a fitting room. Pick out some other stuff," she encouraged, looking at another rack to their left. "There's some cute skirts over here."

"I think..." Jada said quietly, looking up at Erica and pointing at the purple dress in her hand. "I think I want that one."

Erica laughed softly, not sure how to interpret Jada's vague assertion. "I know, honey. If it fits and you like it, we'll definitely get it."

"So...that's the one I pick." Jada rocked back and forth on her toes, never holding eye contact for more than a second or two.

"Jada, you can..." Erica thought for a second. "You can pick more than one."

Jada just stared at her, her lips pressed together like she didn't know what to say or think or feel. "I can?" she whispered, the words barely audible.

"Of course!" Erica exclaimed, clinging hard to this opportunity to make Jada happy and give her something that would show her love and comfort and...joy. "Dresses are the thing then, huh? Let's find you some more."

Jada smiled—this time, a real, clear, unmistakable smile. With teeth and everything. "Okay."

An "Okay." A smile *and* an "Okay."

Erica had had a lot of victories in her life—mostly big ones. MIT, the job at NASA, getting promoted to head aerospace engineer on the Eagle Launch...but this little, tiny victory felt bigger than them all.

They rummaged through the whole section at great length, and Jada picked out about ten dresses and a few shirts and pairs of colorful summer shorts to try on.

As they looked, the ironclad guard walls of fear and trepidation that Jada had around her started to maybe, possibly, come down the smallest bit.

"All right..." Erica laughed, holding about nineteen hangers on her arm, which was starting to seriously ache. "Ready to do some trying on?"

Jada nodded and headed to the back of the store to the fitting rooms, even with a little bounce in her step.

"Here you are, my dear." Erica slung the pile of hangers onto a hook on the wall of the dressing room. "I'll be right out here on this bench. I expect a full fashion show. No skipping, even the duds. I want 'em all."

Jada laughed the tiniest bit, and then quickly caught herself. Like she wasn't allowed to laugh or was scared to.

Erica stayed in the chair, watching Jada come out in every little variation of cotton dress, summer T-shirts, and even a jean skirt that was unbelievably cute. By the fifth or sixth outfit change, Jada had even pushed some of her hair behind her ears.

"Oh my gosh!" Erica clasped her hands together, smiling at yet another adorable dress, this one pink with blue polka-dots, loose and comfy around Jada's slender frame. "Another winner. Add it to the 'yes' pile."

"Um..." Jada ran her hand through her hair, twisting her foot on the ground. "There's already a whole bunch in the 'yes' pile."

Erica had never seen a girl fight so hard *not* to have clothes bought for her, but it was sweet and endearing and also kind of heartbreaking.

"Thank goodness, because we've got to fill that closet in your room with something, right?"

Jada just swallowed, gave another quick smile, and turned back into the dressing room. She soon came out in her original clothes, and said that was the last dress.

"Amazing. You're a supermodel in the making," Erica teased, gently moving past her and picking up the extensive, wildly colorful, and fun "yes" pile.

She wrapped her arms around the clothes and headed straight for the register at the front of the store, nodding for Jada to follow her.

As the cashier rang up each item, Erica looked down and watched Jada.

Her eyes followed the clothes, one piece at a time, her gaze wide and captivated.

Erica wondered if she'd ever even been to an Old Navy. There was so much she didn't know about this girl. Her girl.

"Okay, ma'am..." The Old Navy cashier tapped some buttons loudly on a keyboard. "Your total is a hundred and eighty-four dollars and sixty-seven cents. Cash or card?"

"It'll be card," Erica replied, inserting her credit card into the machine.

She looked down at Jada again, whose jaw was slack like she had just seen a ghost. "That's a lot," she whispered.

Was it? Erica had hardly even registered the dollar amount, her mind was in so many other places.

"Well, you need clothes, girl!" She nudged Jada playfully, took her card back and grabbed the bags of clothes before heading back into the mall.

"Um…" Jada stopped in her tracks.

Erica halted and turned to face her, angling her head to study the girl's constantly mystifying expression. "What is it?"

"Th-thank you. A lot."

She felt a smile spread across her face, and held onto Jada's gaze for as long as the girl would allow it. It wasn't a hug, but it would do.

"You are very welcome. You hungry? I think Will is bringing us dinner, but I smell an Auntie Anne's soft pretzel with our names on it. I won't tell if you don't."

"Okay." Jada nodded and smiled again, and the two of them headed to Auntie Anne's, ordered cinnamon sugar pretzels, and sat down at a bench by the big fountain.

"So," Erica said between bites of sweet, buttery goodness. "You got all kinds of new stuff, huh? Lots of options for first day of school outfits in August. I know we're over a month away, but…" She lifted a shoulder and smiled. "I always loved planning my first day of school outfits."

Suddenly, Jada's face darkened and her eyes flashed,

and a nearly visible darkness seemed to cloak her out of nowhere.

Her lip began to quiver as she lowered her pretzel slowly, clearly and suddenly upset.

What was going on? What could Erica possibly have said that changed her mood so drastically?

"Jada, what is it? What's wrong?"

"No." Jada shook her head furiously, her hair falling in front of her face, making it utterly impossible to try and search her expression for an answer. "No...I can't. No."

"You can't what?" Erica asked, trying to cling to the tiny bit of victory and progress that seemed to be slipping away from her as quickly as it had appeared. "What's going on, sweetie?"

"I can't...go to school." Jada just shook her head some more, hiding behind those cascades of hair. "Please," she added weakly.

She couldn't go to school? Why on Earth not?

"Oh, Jada." Erica pressed a hand to her heart.

Of course she would be scared to go to school. It was a brand-new place, brand-new town, brand-new family, new house, new *life*.

However intimidating and overwhelming this whole thing was for Erica, she had to always remind herself it was a thousand times worse for Jada.

"I know all of this is so new and scary and crazy." She offered a sweet smile. "But you're going to love the school, I promise. It's where I went to school when I was your age, and my brother and sisters went there, too. It's really going to be—"

"No!" Jada insisted, her lip quivering. "I-I can't go. I'm not going."

Oh, boy. Well, people always said that parenthood was one challenge after another, but what did they say about taking in an eleven-year-old who had a heart-breaking past and had been through God-knew-what-kind of horrible times?

Erica was at a complete loss as to why the mention of school shut Jada down so completely, but she couldn't help but feel drained and defeated as they left the mall and headed home, and the girl didn't speak another word.

"I DON'T KNOW, Will, it was like she just…flipped a switch." Erica shook her head, pacing back and forth in their oversized bedroom, running a hand anxiously through her thick hair.

"Babe, hey, whoa…" Will Armstrong, as calm and cool and reassuring as a human could be, walked over to his wife and placed two unwavering hands on her shaky shoulders. He was fresh out of the shower, with damp hair and sweatpants on. "Deep breath, okay?"

Erica inhaled sharply and let it out, shutting her eyes.

"It's been three days. Three. Days. Three days since she was thrown into a weird house with weird people and no clue what was going on, how long she'd be here, or what we are like."

"Are we weird people?" Erica asked, a hint of laughter breaking through her stressed-out tone.

"To her? Yes, I would assume so."

"The good kind of weird, though, right?" She leaned closer to her husband, pressing her forehead against his chest. "The endearing kind?"

"The best kind." He kissed her forehead, keeping his lips pressed there for a long time, giving her a chance to fully and completely melt into the arms of the one person on Earth who made her feel okay with not being in control.

"It was going well, though. It really was." Erica pulled away, sighing with confusion and defeat. "She was...smiling a little. And she liked trying clothes on, and shopping, and she even thanked me."

"Our girl has manners. That's a start." Will winked at her and headed over to the closet to pull a clean white T-shirt on.

"And then we got pretzels, and everything seemed good. She wasn't exactly, you know, a chatterbox, but it was fine. And then she just...wham. Shut down. Lights out. Walls up."

"Well, what did you say to her before that?"

"I mentioned her starting school here in August. She's supposed to be going into sixth grade." Erica shrugged. "I rambled something about picking out her first day outfit from the clothes we'd bought. And then she just kept saying no, and insisting that she wouldn't go to school. She was adamant."

"Huh. Maybe she's had a bad time at school in the

past or something." Will shook out his wet hair and furrowed his brow, as puzzled as Erica was, but not nearly as broken. "Well, hon, I think you're going to have to accept that bringing this girl into our family isn't going to be a linear thing, you know? Some days will be good, and some will be not so good."

"But will it always change minute to minute like that?"

"I don't know. We don't know her yet. Hey." He took her cheeks in his hands, getting a little closer. "Give it time. I know, patience is a challenge for you."

"*Motherhood* is a challenge for me."

"Want to try and go talk to her right now? Together?" he suggested.

"I don't know. She might want to be alone. I don't want to freak her out or bombard her..." Erica glanced down, feeling completely clueless as to how to approach any of this.

"Erica. She's our daughter now. We can't be scared of her."

He was right. Jada had enough fear for all of them, anyway.

She walked side by side with Will down the hallway, and gently knocked on the door to the guest room, which was latched shut.

"Hey, kid." Will leaned close to the door. "Mind if we come hang out for a second?"

Nothing in response, but Erica could have sworn she heard a sniffle. Was Jada crying? How was Erica already screwing this whole thing up so royally?

"Come on." Will nodded, jutting his chin toward the room.

"Okay," Erica agreed with a hushed voice.

Will slowly opened the door, and he and Erica quietly walked into the bedroom.

Jada was curled up on the bed, holding that same stuffed rabbit from earlier. She had its floppy, worn-out ears pressed against her face, which was damp with tears.

"Jada, sweetie." Erica walked over and sat down on the edge of the bed. "What's wrong? Is this still about the whole school thing?"

Will stood next to Erica. "We promise you, you're going to love it, and there's nothing to be afraid of. It's a great school, and—"

"No, I can't go!" Jada reluctantly looked up from the stuffed animal, her sad eyes rimmed with red.

"Why not?" Erica asked, glancing at Will, then back at Jada. "Can you...can you tell us why you can't go?"

Jada sniffed and wiped a tear from her cheek, keeping her gaze locked downward at the bedspread. "Because I can't do that stuff. I can't do what other kids do at school and I'm not ever going to be able to." Her voice shuddered with another sob.

What did she mean she couldn't do "that stuff"? What stuff? School? Socializing?

"What, um..." Will sat down on the bed, too, studying Jada with the slow and steady patience that always kept Erica calm. "What do you feel like you can't do?"

"Like reading and math and stuff." Jada mumbled her words into the stuffed rabbit, refusing eye contact more fervently than ever. "School. I'm not...I'm not like that. I can't do that."

Reading. Could Jada not...read?

Erica exchanged a quick look with Will, whose eyes flashed with sadness, but he quickly turned back to Jada.

"You don't know how to read?" he asked, his voice cloaked in kindness.

Erica wasn't so sure she could have maintained that tone. But that's why there were two parents in this equation.

"I can kind of, but I'm not good at it. I'm the slowest reader ever. And I'm really bad at math and everything else. Like, really, really bad." Jada shook her head aggressively and chewed on her bottom lip. "I can't do school."

"Have you ever *been* to school?" Erica asked slowly, furrowing her brow as she studied the girl in front of her, who clearly had way more layers than your average onion.

Jada just shrugged her skinny shoulders and wiped her face with her palm. "Sometimes. But Mom would always take me away after a few weeks or whatever. I never stayed, because we always had to move. Or stay in, you know, one of those shelter places. And me and Mom talked a lot in Spanish, but in school they only talked in English. So I never learned." She looked up, her big brown eyes gripping Erica's heart. "I never learned any of that. I can't go. Please don't make me go."

Erica leaned back and took a deep breath, trying to process this new and unexpected development.

"Don't worry," Will said to Jada. "We're not going to

put you anywhere that you don't feel comfortable, okay? I know it's scary and weird, but you can trust us."

"You can." Erica nodded. "I promise."

Jada just gulped, hugging the bunny tighter to her chest and staring straight down.

One day Jada would realize this was all for the best, but now, this was very, very hard.

"We'll let you get some rest." Will pulled the comforter over her shoulders. "See you in the morning?"

Jada nodded.

"Goodnight." Erica smiled and gave a little wave. "Sleep well."

She and Will turned to leave the bedroom, and flicked off the light switch on their way out.

"Erica?" Jada's timid voice caught their attention, and they both turned around in the doorway.

"Yeah?" Erica asked eagerly.

"I had fun," Jada whispered. "With the shopping."

Erica nearly swayed. "I had fun, too."

On that, they shut the door softly and walked down the hallway to their bedroom. Erica knew Will had to be feeling as stunned and worried as she was by what they'd just found out.

"What are we going to do, Will?" Erica flopped down on the bed. "She's so scared and shy and broken. If she can barely read...how are we going to just throw her into sixth grade? It'd be cruel, and she'd never stay caught up. Not to mention she'd probably hate us forever."

He lay down on the bed next to her, running a hand

through his hair and staring up at the ceiling. "We could homeschool her for a year or two, get her up to speed."

"Honey." Erica rolled onto her side and looked at her husband. "It took a lot of explaining and nearly a miracle to get Roger to even let me have these two weeks of working from home. I could never homeschool her. I'd lose my job."

Will puffed out a sigh. "I know. Plus, it's so important for her to socialize and start making friends with kids her own age. Especially because it doesn't sound like she's had much of that...ever. She needs to feel like a normal eleven-year-old, you know? I really believe that."

"I know, I couldn't agree more. We have to help her."

"We will help her."

"We can tutor. The rest of the summer, right?"

He nodded. "I'm good with that. She's a bright girl. We'll get her up to speed, or close."

"Plus, she's already bilingual. That's an advantage, although to her, I imagine it doesn't feel like much of one right now."

Erica thought about what it must be like for a girl who spoke mostly Spanish at home to try and read English and understand teachers when she was hardly ever even in school.

"Math, too. Everything, I guess." Will shook his head. "Poor kid."

"But you know what, Will?" Erica felt a smile pulling at her cheeks, as a new sense of optimism started to rise in her chest.

"What?"

"It's *school*. It's a lot of school."

"A ton of school, yeah."

"Yes, a ton of school. But *school*, as you know, just happens to be my specialty." She winked.

"She said humbly," Will teased.

Erica sat up, grinning at him. "I can do this. I can teach her. If anyone can show someone how to excel in school, it's me."

"I do believe in you, and I absolutely think you can help her a lot." He leveled his gaze. "But let's worry about surviving before we worry about excelling, okay? It's all right if she doesn't immediately jump onto the honor roll."

"I know that." Erica crossed her arms.

"Do you?"

"Yes." She bit back a laugh, falling into her husband's embrace.

Erica was self-aware enough to admit that she had never envisioned herself raising a child who wasn't, well, on the honor roll. But she knew she couldn't push her obsession with academic success onto Jada.

She was too fragile. She needed love, not motivation.

"I'll start tomorrow. I'll get books and worksheets and study guides and I'll teach her. Every day, all the time."

Will looked at Erica for a long time, his blue eyes glistening a little. "You already love her, don't you?"

She let out a sigh. "I'm really trying to."

Chapter Six

Sam

It was truly a night for celebration. John had agreed to hire Taylor, as long as Sam trained her, and they would start that next week. After Taylor was up to speed, Sam was free to renovate to her heart's content.

And her heart *was* content. The move to Cocoa Beach continued to bring her healing, peace, clarity, and that elusive fresh start at life. But to her, the most wonderful gift she'd gained by coming home was the relationships with her family.

After spending twenty-five years married to a man who drilled it into her head that family was a nuisance and a problem and *their* relationship was the only one that mattered, Sam had found a new kind of freedom and joy in reconnecting with her siblings and mom.

Along with Dottie, Imani, Erica, and Taylor, Sam headed over to Cocoa Beach's classic local watering hole, Sharky's Sea Shack, for fruity frozen cocktails and a heaping dose of family girl time.

As they walked up to the beachside, tiki-style restaurant, Sam suddenly remembered what had happened the last time Taylor was at this very spot.

"Oh, Tay," she whispered, drawing her daughter

closer. "I just remembered this was where Kai said...good-bye. Do you want to go somewhere else?"

"Pssh. Please." Taylor waved a dismissive hand. "I'm totally fine, Mama. Moving on to bigger and better things. Besides, where else in Cocoa Beach can you get a piña colada with whipped cream?"

"Probably literally anywhere," Imani teased, walking next to them as they headed around to the back deck, which overlooked the ocean.

Taylor shot her aunt a playful look, and they stepped over to a high top in the corner of the deck. The back patio of Sharky's was decorated with twinkling vineyard lights all strung overhead, and little tiki torches with casual mismatched furniture added to the familiar charm of a favorite hangout spot.

The warm, salty breeze billowed through the air, lifting Sam's long dark hair around her face and surrounding her in the comfort of home.

As they chatted about Taylor's new job and ordered drinks to toast her, Dottie beamed from one woman to the next. "Nothing makes my heart happier than seeing all my family getting closer and helping each other. I'm sure John is thrilled to have you on the team."

"I'm excited!" Taylor said brightly, nodding her head. "My first big-girl job, I guess, but I'm ready to learn. I'm so glad it's not in an operating room." She curled her lip, making Sam relieved that Taylor had decided to abandon her plan to follow in Max's footsteps, which so totally didn't suit her.

"You're going to be amazing." Sam grinned at her.

"Besides, you're learning from the pro," she added with a self-deprecating snort. "You know I run a smooth ship."

"Hey, you crushed it at that position."

Sam rolled her eyes. "John held my hand and Annie walked me through every technological issue imaginable. And math problem. You'll be way better off from the jump."

"Where's Erica?" Dottie asked, craning her neck with a worried look on her face, trying to spot her youngest daughter, who had been lagging behind on the walk over here.

"Preoccupied, I imagine." Sam sighed, wondering how her darling control freak of a sister, who planned her life down to the minute, was handling her newly upside-down world.

She hoped tonight would bring a chance for Erica to open up with the rest of the women and share how the past week had been with her new daughter. They were all there for support and love, because even brilliant, determined, unstoppable Erica would need a soft place to fall every once in a while. Especially right now, Sam imagined.

A few minutes later, she came rushing in.

"I'm coming. Sorry, you guys." Erica smiled and sat down between Sam and Dottie, quickly putting her phone away. "I was just texting Will to see how it's going at home."

"Ah." Dottie nodded. "He's home with Jada tonight, yes?"

"Yes." Erica let out a breath, looking a bit jittery and

nervous. "Bonding time. It worked out well that we all wanted to get together tonight, because Will has been wanting to have some quality time with her. Evidently, she's never seen a single Marvel superhero movie, so he's going to show her some of his favorites."

"Oh my gosh, cute." Taylor held her hand to her chest.

"Yeah, she seemed excited. Well, Jada's version of excited, which is basically just not silent and terrified." Erica slumped back against the chair, looking out over the ocean. Let's see if he can make more progress than I have."

Sam could see stress and worry written all over her sister's face. The Sweeney sibling whose life was always the most together—or tied with John for that title—had quickly become the one who was the most lost.

Except maybe Julie, John's twin sister, who toured the country in a van with her boyfriend and teenage daughter, Bliss, playing gigs with their band. But Julie was *literally* lost, not figuratively. Or at least never settled. And she, by far the most distant member of the grown Sweeney family, liked it that way.

"Do any of you ever hear from Julie?" she asked, leaning in to the group. "Sorry, that was completely out of the blue. I was just wondering about her."

"Some texts here and there." Dottie glanced away, lifting a shoulder. "She seems so happy but, wow, I do miss her."

"Same for me, here and there but she's so busy and... adventurous. It's hard to hold her attention for very long,"

Erica answered. "I miss her too, though. I wonder how Bliss is doing," she mused.

Imani shook her head. "I certainly haven't heard much. I do see her Instagram, though. She's all over the place."

"That she is." Sam chewed her lip, having forgotten that the topic of long-lost Julie was not a super happy one. "Anyway, what's new?"

Tracy, the woman who had to have been working as the manager at Sharky's for twenty years, came over with their drinks.

"Sam Sweeney, I must say..." While she served, Tracy leaned down next to Sam. "So, you were right when you warned me off doctors."

Sam lifted a brow and looked at her, remembering their conversation about Tracy's new man a few months ago. "Didn't work out, huh?"

The other woman rolled her eyes. "He didn't quite understand the concept of monogamy."

"Yep. Been there, sister."

"But, honey..." Tracy leaned back and gave Sam an exaggerated study from top to bottom. "You are looking fine as heck! Glowing, girl!"

"Isn't she?" Taylor added sweetly, shooting her mom a quick smile.

"She's radiant," Dottie agreed, beaming at Sam with pride and a knowing look.

Sam felt her cheeks warm, and she pushed some hair behind her ears and waved a hand, laughing. "Please,

please. Keep 'em coming. God knows my microscopic self-esteem can use all the help it can get."

"You look better though, Sam." Erica smiled at her. "A lot better."

Drinks in place, Tracy crossed her arms, looking at each of them. "You Sweeney women are all stunners. Look at this crew. And you, Miss Dottie! I hear talk y'all are giving Sweeney House a li'l makeover. Is it true?"

Dottie laughed softly, sharing a look with Sam. "We are. Sam and I are doing a full renovation together. That's one of the many things we're celebrating tonight."

"Goodness gracious, I can't wait to see how it comes out. Place truly is a Cocoa Beach gem, isn't it? But wow, that's a big project."

"That it is." Sam smiled wistfully and held her mother's gaze. "We have each other. And Erica's husband, which helps."

"Oh, yeah, cute construction guy. I know him."

Erica laughed. "Is that his street name?"

"Should be." She winked. "All right, I'll leave you gals to your celebration. Holler for the next round!"

"So, speaking of the reno." Erica turned to Sam. "How is that going? Will says you guys have some cool ideas, nothing unmanageable."

"Yet," Sam quipped. "We've got plenty. But come on, Erica. Please tell us how it's going with Jada. I'm not going to sit here and talk about floorboards and antique restoration and paint color when you have this mega life change going on."

"She's right," Imani added, raising her brows. "We're invested, and we want to help you."

Erica's brow furrowed and she shifted in her seat.

Taylor sighed, giving Erica a look of kind understanding. "You mentioned you feel like you haven't made a ton of progress? I mean, it's still so new..."

"I know, I know." Erica smoothed down her ponytail with both palms, leaning her elbows onto the wooden table. "I have to keep reminding myself of that. Because I want to just snap my fingers and make everything perfect, you know? I want to just flip a switch and bam." She snapped her fingers. "I'm her mom, she's my kid, Will's a dad, everyone's happy and good and normal. And it feels right. I want it so badly to feel *right*."

"Oh, Erica. My dear Erica." Dottie shook her head slowly, giving Erica an adoring glance. "Never were a huge fan of 'trusting the process' as they say, were you? Patience—not your strong suit."

Erica shrugged and laughed a little.

It was true. Sam could remember from the time Erica was five years old, she mastered everything. Quickly. Video games, sports, Scrabble, and school? Forget it. Erica would spend the summer reading the textbooks for classes she hadn't taken yet, so she could already be ahead of everyone else.

"You?" Sam gave a sarcastic gasp, nudging her sister playfully. "No, never. You're completely fine not being instantly perfect at something."

"Ha ha." She stifled a laugh and rolled her eyes. "I

know, patience is definitely not my strong suit, and I like to be good at things. Sue me."

"But this isn't just 'something,' sweetie." Dottie leaned across the table and squeezed Erica's hand. "This is an adoption."

"How's Will doing with it?" Imani asked.

"He's a natural dad, so he's doing okay. He's got way more patience than I do, and he doesn't worry a tenth as much. His attitude is that in time it'll all be okay, but I'm just not convinced."

"Parenting is hard," Dottie said. "You learn on the go. Heck, I'm still learning as I go, and I'm seventy-two."

"It's not just..." Erica shook her head. "It's not just parenting, which in and of itself is completely new to me. It's parenting...her. A girl who I know nothing about. Who has a past that doesn't involve me. Who won't say more than three words at a time. Who might never, ever trust me or love me or feel like my daughter. And..."

She swallowed, clenching her jaw a little, pausing as they all leaned in with silent support.

"We have some challenges we didn't expect," she continued. "Like, she's terrified to even go to school and I'm putting together a curriculum to homeschool her for a month before it starts."

"Ooh," Taylor said. "That sounds like a fun summer."

The others chuckled, but not Erica. "It's not fun, but I can't let her go into sixth grade and get wiped out because she can barely read. It's..." Erica groaned and dropped her head into her hands, clearly having needed this girl time more than anyone else. "Look, I don't know how to connect with her, plain and simple. I do know school, and she needs some help in that area. I'm hoping that will be a turning point for us. Is it fun?" She glanced at Taylor. "No, but I'm doing my best."

The "oh, honeys" rolled out from everyone, but it was Imani who leaned in, her dark brows knitting together as she looked at Erica.

"What you're doing is wonderful and brave and probably the hardest thing you'll ever do in your life," Imani said. "And, I might add, not always the most rewarding."

"And we're here for you, Aunt Erica," Taylor added, sipping her drink. "I'd be more than happy to hang out with Jada if you ever need a sitter or just, I don't know, a cousin friend for her."

Erica brightened a little. "Taylor, you're too sweet. Thank you."

Sam tried not to beam too hard with pride in the young woman she'd raised, and focused on her sister. "We are here for you, and please just give it time before you spiral down a rabbit hole. You and Jada won't have the bond of genetics, and you won't have the bond of having raised her from a baby. That's true, you know that. But Erica, think about the kind of unique bond that you and Jada *could* have, you know? She could love and trust you in an entirely different and very powerful way because of what you are doing for her."

Erica sat back and took a sip of her drink, considering this.

"That's a great point, Sam." Imani pushed her long braids behind her shoulders. "Jada will always know that you *chose* her. You made the decision to give her this amazing, loving, safe, happy life, and she knows what her world was like before you came into it. She's going to love and appreciate you even more once she grows and opens up. Of course she's not going to trust you yet. She's eleven and terrified and completely out of place. When she's old enough to understand what happened, it's going to bond you in a way that nothing else ever could."

Erica looked around the table, her eyes a little misty. "I haven't really thought about it like that, to be honest. I'm so wrapped up in all the things I'll never have with Jada, I hadn't even considered the things that we could share that normal mothers and daughters don't get to share. You're all such amazing moms. Well, not you, Tay. Not yet, anyway."

They all laughed, and Taylor lifted her drink, shrugging sarcastically. "Hey, anything can happen, right?"

Sam flashed her a look.

"For real, though." Erica smiled. "I'm surrounded by some seriously incredible moms. I'm really lucky."

Imani sighed, looking down at the table for a second, her expression darkening.

Dottie must have also noticed the sudden shift in energy in her daughter-in-law. She put a hand over Imani's and patted her. "Imani, dear, are you all right?"

All attention went to her, and she forced an awkward laugh and waved a hand. "Oh, yeah, I'm totally fine. Really."

Erica gave her a *get real* look, flicking up a brow.

"Hey. What's wrong, sister? I just spilled my emotional guts out. It's your turn."

Imani shook her head. "I don't want to make it about me. I'm fine."

"Please, for the love of all that's holy, make it about *anyone* but me," Erica urged.

They all moved their focus right onto elegant and flawless Imani, a sister and daughter by marriage, but every bit as loved by the Sweeney clan.

"You said..." Imani pressed her lips together. "That I'm an amazing mom."

"You are," Dottie interjected, without hesitation.

"Yeah, no question," Sam added, thinking about how Imani was probably the most composed, serene mother she knew.

Her kids worshipped her, John adored her, and she really had it all figured out. At least it seemed that way to Sam.

But as Sam had learned so brutally from the unraveling of her own life and "perfect" family, things were most definitely not always what they seemed.

"Lately, I..." Imani inhaled sharply, looking out at the ocean, the moonlight illuminating her delicate profile. "I haven't been feeling like such an amazing mom, to be honest with you guys."

"What?"

"How?"

"Imani..." Sam angled her head. "What's going on?"

She chewed her lip and thought for a second, looking more and more distressed by the minute, an unusual expression for Imani Sweeney. "Normally, nothing bothers me. Nothing gets to me. I have three insanely active and busy kids, and I'm in the absolute throes of being a mom. I've always felt so calm and relaxed and my kids are great and my marriage is great and...I've been happy. But recently, I've been getting so caught up in being a mom, I feel like I've really, truly lost myself. Any semblance of my identity outside of that family has completely disappeared. I miss it. I miss...who I used to be."

All of the women looked at her as words of sympathy and support fell over the table.

"So, Erica," Imani continued, giving a dry laugh. "I'll one up you on the guilt train. I have been thinking about my old career. A lot. And...missing it. A lot. How's that for horrible?"

"Oh, Imani." Sam shook her head slowly. "It's not horrible at all. I felt so lost being nothing but a mom that I'm overwhelming myself with new passions and projects trying to figure out who the heck I am on my own. At least you know who you are."

"Do I?" She huffed out a sigh and looked skyward. "Because I feel like being a mom and constantly running around and worrying about this school project or that sporting event or whatever it may be...I feel like it's somehow *erased* me."

Although her situation was entirely different, Sam could certainly relate to the feeling of losing oneself in motherhood.

But Sam had never had a career of her own, never

had a job. She had never been or done anything besides raising kids.

Imani, on the other hand, had an impressive career as a travel writer. And even though Sam saw Imani as one of the most grounded and self-assured people she knew, she could certainly understand how her sister-in-law might miss her exotic and exciting and independent past.

"It probably doesn't help that you had, like, the coolest job on the planet." Taylor raised her brows and grinned at her aunt. "Sorry, but it's true. I totally get how you would miss it."

She smiled. "The other day, I almost had a full-on breakdown. It was like everyone needed something from me at the same time, I was expected to be in five places at once, the calendar was a wreck—oh, it was awful. And you know what I did?" She chuckled, shaking her head as if she couldn't even believe it herself. "I went upstairs, and I shut my door, and I looked through all my old clippings and articles. Relived all those trips and places and moments. Romanticized the crap out of them, for sure. But I ached for that kind of independence and freedom. And I love being a mom! But, dang, it's been a little rough lately."

"You know..." Erica lifted a shoulder, clearly happy to have the conversation focus on someone else's problems instead of hers. "You wrote for *Fodor's* and traveled the world and had all these amazing experiences, and you couldn't do any of that with kids. But you could always go back to work. Work is important, too. I mean, you'd have to pry me out of the Space Center to get me away from my job. And I'm a mom now, too."

"Oh, no." Imani dismissed the idea, flicking her hand. "I could never. I'm just musing. My kids need me. John would crumble without my constant handling of everything for them. I mean...I couldn't."

"Well, sweetie, I don't know." Dottie glanced at her, leaning forward to chime in. "Don't be so quick to shut it down. If you're feeling lost and, as you put it, 'erased,' maybe doing something for yourself could be a path to consider. Even something small. John's a grown man. He would support you."

"I can't switch up on my kids like that." Imani bit her lip. "I have to put them first, always."

Sam looked at her, relating to that very notion all too well. "You can't put them first if you yourself are feeling so hollow. You owe it to yourself to be rejuvenated and excited and maintain some kind of identity outside of all that. Trust me." She looked at Taylor and grabbed her arm lovingly. "Not that my kids aren't my greatest joy in the world, because they are. But I wish I had listened to the voice in my head that told me I wanted something more. I wish I had listened to it years ago."

Imani just let out a breath, looking straight ahead and stirring the remnant of what started out as a Bahama Mama in a plastic cup. "I don't know, you guys. That's crazy talk! I mean, I haven't worked since Damien was born, and..."

"So what?" Taylor nudged her. "You wouldn't be traveling all over creation like you used to, but you're a writer! You could definitely freelance. There's stuff all over the internet and social media now, blogs and podcasts and newsletters. They'd love to have you on as a writer."

Erica waved a finger at Taylor. "She's right, you know. You could work as much or as little as you want. It doesn't hurt to just put some feelers out there. You really should consider that, Imani."

"Absolutely," Sam chimed in. "And you could start right here. It's a tourist town. There are all kinds of travel books and websites about Cocoa Beach. It might be home to us, but it's still a huge travel destination."

Dottie nodded. "You should look into it, Imani. And I know John will back you one hundred percent. And if he doesn't..." She arched a brow. "You just send him to me."

Imani laughed, shaking her head as her mental wheels started visibly turning with possibilities.

"Freelance..." she repeated slowly. "I could think about dabbling a little, seeing what I could find locally. I think if I just had something, even something small, that was for myself, it would make me feel a whole lot better. Y'all really are the best." She smiled and looked around the table.

"I second that." Erica lifted her glass. "I feel a thousand times better just having talked to you guys."

"See?" Dottie grinned, touching Taylor's arm with one hand and Imani's with the other, stretching her arms out wide, as if she wanted to climb across the table and hug the whole group of them. "This. This is what I live for."

They all laughed and shared a little moment of mushy family love, something that Sam had been missing for so long, she knew she'd never get tired of it.

"Now if only we could get Julie here," Erica said on a laugh. "Then we'd have all the Sweeney ladies on one island."

Dottie blew out a breath. "That'll be the day."

Some more time spent chatting with her sisters, daughter and mom and another round of cocktails later, Sam hardly noticed her phone buzz with a text.

When she pulled it out and checked it, she saw Ben's name, so she quickly turned away to read the message, feeling suddenly sorry for not having checked in on him at all since she'd left the cottage.

After all, he was only two weeks past his accident.

But Sam was able to breathe a sigh of relief when she read the text, which was just him asking her if she'd go to an orientation at his new high school on Monday.

She sent a quick text back saying, *Of course*, and then resumed time with her female family.

Sam still had a long way to go, sure, and she was not without her bad days. But they were fewer and farther between, and every morning she woke up excited to work on the reno plans and be with her family.

It occurred to her that for the first time since she'd moved back to Cocoa Beach, she didn't feel like her life needed any immediate fixing.

And that felt good.

Chapter Seven

Taylor

Taylor wondered—for a brief, fleeting second—if marching into Coastal Marketing last week and confidently asserting that she wanted to take on the role of office manager might have been biting off a little more than she could chew.

She and her mother had spent hours in here yesterday, since they'd decided the training should happen on a Sunday when the place was quiet. There would be a learning curve, for sure, but at least she knew where the client files were, and Sam walked her through all of the departments, helped her set up a work email, and generally made sure Taylor wouldn't completely blow her first day.

As she breezed into the lobby of the office building, she glanced down and admired her outfit choice one more time—white cotton pants and a soft, floral blouse. Summery, professional, and cute.

She felt her ponytail swinging back and forth behind her as she headed into the elevator and up to the third floor. As soon as she walked into the lobby and put her purse in the front desk drawer, she caught John's eye.

"Taylor!" He waved, quickly finishing up a conversation in the design team corner of the office before heading through the maze of desks and cubicles to greet her at the front.

"Good morning, Uncle John." She smiled widely, not sure if she was supposed to shake his hand or something. She opted for a wave. "I'm ready to roll."

"Hey, everyone!" John turned and called loudly over the entire office, which quickly came to a hushed silence. "I want to introduce you all to my awesome niece, Taylor. She's going to be taking over as administrative assistant and office manager here at the front. Be nice to her and share your knowledge."

"It's great to be here," Taylor said, glancing at all the faces throughout the open room full of cubicles, monitors, and sample ads posted on the walls. "Hopefully, I'll have a chance to meet you all individually in the next few days."

The room echoed with greetings and pleasantries before everyone turned back to their phones, computers, and work.

"So." John pressed his palms on the tall counter in front of Taylor's new desk. "Did Sam get you up to speed?"

"Well, I know where the breakroom is, how to make coffee, and that if Mr. Wittington from Sunshine Toyota calls, you definitely want to know about it, no matter what you're doing." She grinned. "Right?"

"Even if I'm in the bathroom," he joked. "Same for anyone from Blackhawk Brewing, our newest client."

"Yep, I heard about them," she said.

"Sounds good. Your mom picked up on everything pretty quickly, but if you have any questions, just ask, well, anyone. Or me, of course."

"Okay, awesome." Taylor nodded and looked at the desk, which was exactly like she and her mother had left it yesterday, neat and ready for her to start.

"Thanks, Uncle John." She smiled at him, brushing a loose strand of hair behind her ear. "I really, really appreciate this."

"Of course." He gave a reassuring nod. "We're family. And that's beside the point, because I do think you're going to thrive in this role."

"I hope so."

"Listen, I've got a meeting to get to, so if you want to just go ahead and familiarize yourself with the computer software, the office, meet people...just make yourself at home, okay? Play around with it all. It'll take about five minutes and people will start asking you to make copies, file, and completely reorganize some client profiles."

With that, he headed back to his office and Taylor slipped into the swivel chair, running her hands along the cool surface of the desk, nerves and excitement buzzing through her.

"Okay," she whispered, pressing the power button on the desktop computer tower below her. "Here we go."

For the next hour, she answered the phone, which seemed to ring at least once every minute or so, and got comfortable with the software. In a quiet moment, she slipped into the kitchen to grab coffee.

She definitely knew her way around this particular

area, since her mother placed a high value on getting coffee and taking a break. As she loaded the Keurig with a K-cup, a couple of people walked into the room.

The man and woman, who both looked to be around John's age, said hello to her and introduced themselves as Melissa and Craig, who worked in online marketing.

"I know, I know," Craig said, sounding frustrated, shaking his head as he continued their previous conversation. "It's absolutely the worst, isn't it?"

"The worst," Melissa agreed, nodding. "I mean, the videos work on Instagram and Facebook. But now, every client wants their content posted on gosh darn TikTok," she practically spat the words, sounding majorly irritated.

Taylor's ears perked up, as she was an avid TikTok user, on-brand with her generation. She didn't post much, but she'd certainly spent enough time lurking and watching videos to figure out how the whole app worked by now.

She stepped aside as her coffee finished brewing, and slowly reached for a packet of sugar, shaking it with her fingers.

"It's just such a different beast, I swear." Melissa put her own K-cup in the machine and placed a mug underneath it, leaning against the countertop while her coffee poured.

"Well, you can't use the same piece of content." Craig shrugged. "So the entire thing has to be reconfigured every time, and it always ends up terrible. The client's never happy."

"Yeah, well..." Melissa took her coffee and blew on it,

cooling off a bit of the steam. "We can't exactly tell them no, can we? They are TikTok happy."

"TikTok this, TikTok that." He groaned. "Everyone wants TikTok now. I can't keep up."

"Who could?"

As they made their beverages, Taylor had to practically bite her tongue not to dive into their conversation.

She knew it was her first day, she had no clue about the marketing industry, and she was hired to work the front desk, not give her two cents on social media advertising and content creation.

But, still... From what it sounded like, their issue had a super easy fix. And wasn't it the right thing to just let them know?

"Um, sorry, I'm totally eavesdropping," Taylor said on a nervous laugh, tightening her grip on her coffee cup. "But did you mention having an uploading problem with videos on TikTok?"

"Yeah." The other woman smiled kindly. "We aren't exactly familiar with the interface, and even though everyone here is pretty internet savvy, keeping up with social media trends and technology has given us some serious roadblocks lately. It never stops changing."

"Especially all the TikTok stuff," Craig chimed in, sipping his coffee as he shook his head. "Our Facebook, Instagram, and Twitter content creation is top notch. But of course, now it's something new."

"It's always something new," Melissa sighed.

"Well, not that it's in any way my place to offer suggestions to you guys, but if you make a video that's specifically created for TikTok on their user platform, you'll be able to save it to your drive, remove the watermark with editing software, and upload it to Instagram as a reel."

"Remove the watermark..." Craig nodded slowly. "That makes sense. And you can use the same video then?"

"Yeah, if you created it on TikTok, just make sure the resolution stays intact when you save it, but it should. The dimensions for Instagram reels and TikTok videos are the same, but Instagram doesn't promote videos that still have the watermark because TikTok is a competitor, so they want things that appear as original content."

She looked from one to the other, but both people were a little speechless as they stared at her.

"Is that, um, all there is to it?" Melissa asked.

"Well, TikTok won't allow a direct upload, so I would use the TikTok software to create the video in the first place and then export it. It seems counterintuitive, but that's actually what a ton of influencers do to keep their content consistent on all the different social media platforms."

Taylor swallowed and realized she'd probably just completely overstepped her admin bounds, especially considering the fact that it was her literal first day and her job was to answer phones and manage schedules, not give advice to the marketing team.

The two of them looked at each other, and started to slowly nod.

"That..." Craig laughed, shaking his head a little. "That makes so much sense. Wow."

"Thank you!" Melissa lifted her mug in a mock toast. "Good to have a millennial in the office," she joked. "Craig, let's get started on that and see how it fares for our very particular client who is sure their next million in revenue is coming from TikTok."

"It could be," Taylor said. "The influencers are powerful on that site, and I openly admit to a slight TikTok addiction—mostly cat videos—so I've picked up on a few things."

"Thank you." Melissa said. "So, don't be a stranger over at the ad department, okay? If you can help our stuff go viral, we don't care about qualifications."

"Design team would probably love to talk to you, too, about the changing content trends on TikTok. They're always tracking them." Craig arched a brow at Taylor and gave her a knowing smile. "Something tells me you keep up."

She shrugged. "A little."

"It was great meeting you, Taylor, and thanks for the assist." Craig smiled and waved as he and Melissa took their coffee mugs and headed out of the breakroom.

"Great to meet you, too!" Taylor said cheerfully, leaning against the counter and sipping her coffee.

She couldn't help but wonder what she could do if she got her hands on their social media accounts. Buffed with followers and backed with a likely hefty advertising and promotion budget, Taylor could get their content on trend and following the constantly changing fads of TikTok and social media in general.

Clients' content and advertising videos would go viral if they used trending sounds, concepts, memes, and ideas. Not to mention if they were able to get some branding and sponsorship deals with big-time influencers. Or even small-time influencers, for that matter.

Taylor's mind raced, and she smiled to herself as she headed back through the office to her spot at the front desk.

Even though it had only been an hour, Taylor suddenly sensed she was in the right place.

Chapter Eight

Imani

I mani scanned the words on the computer screen over and over again, her heart racing at the very thought of making this a reality.

Twenty to twenty-five total hours of work...

Completely local...

Small online blog-style magazine featuring hidden gems all over the Space Coast and other parts of Florida...

She took in a deep breath as her eyes fell to the big blue button at the bottom of the website page.

Freelance Writers, Apply Now!

It was just a small, part-time gig, right? A cute travel website called *TravelBee*. How bad could it be? Imani could just write a few pieces for this travel site, get her work fix without even having to leave town, and be done with it. Then, this "working again" bug could be out of her system and she would go back to being a mom.

No harm done. To anyone. It wasn't like she was jetting off to another country or writing an immersive European piece that would take a year to research.

It was right here, on the Space Coast. Small-time writing without the travel. She could totally do that.

Imani chewed her lip as she read over the qualifications and requirements for about the tenth time. She knew she was wildly overqualified for a writing job like this. In fact, she'd bet that when someone at this travel site saw her resume, they'd pounce.

"Hey, hon!" John's voice echoed through the house as he shut the inside door to the garage.

Imani smiled and stood up, turning to see him walk in the door at 5:23, like every day.

"Hey, you." She reached out and gave him a long kiss, wrapping her arms around his tall frame.

Imani's mind buzzed with the possibility of taking this freelance writing job, but she didn't want to instantly bombard John with this idea the second he walked in the door. But she did want to talk to him about it, and soon. Mostly because she couldn't think about anything else since she'd found the job listing.

"How was work?" She joined him on the sofa, where he'd already plopped down and kicked off his shoes.

"It was good. Really good, actually." He untucked his button-down shirt from his khakis and leaned back into the pillows, feet up. "Taylor's first day at the front desk, and everyone already likes her."

"Oh, that's wonderful," Imani said cheerfully. "She's going to thrive in your office."

"I think so." He cleared his throat and ran a hand through his hair. "It's good to have some youth around the place, too. All of my original hires just aren't as hip as they used to be, myself included."

Imani chuckled, playing with John's hair. "I think you're very hip."

"Well, thank you, but I sure don't know my way around the social media apps like the kids these days. Speaking of..." He glanced around. "Where are ours?"

"Damien is over at Travis's house. He's staying for dinner but I'll pick him up later. Liam is at his piano lesson at Mrs. Georgia's down the street. He rode his bike. And Ellen is—"

"Daddy!" Ellen shrieked and hurried down the stairs, running straight to her beloved father.

"—right here," Imani finished with a laugh.

Ellen climbed up onto the couch and situated herself between the two of them.

"How's my girl?" John kissed the top of his daughter's head, ruffling her wild, curly hair.

"Good." She grinned and giggled. "I'm hungry."

"I can start dinner in a minute, but I wanted to talk to Dad first," Imani told her. "So maybe get yourself a little snack, sweetie. A *little* snack."

Ellen headed over to the pantry, bouncing on her toes as she scanned the snack selection for something that Imani hoped fell under the category of "little."

But her brain was way too preoccupied to worry about Ellen's snack choice right now.

She turned back to John and took a deep breath, feeling a smile that she was unable to hide pull at her face.

"What is it?" he asked with a curious laugh. "You look like you've got something on your mind."

Oh, did she ever.

"Yeah, um..." She swiped a braid behind her shoulder and leaned closer to him. "I do, actually."

In their seventeen years of marriage, John had always been predictable. In the best way possible. He was steady, reliable, and unchanging, and Imani could usually guess what his reaction, opinion, or analysis would be on just about any topic.

But right now, Imani truly had no idea how he was going to react to the declaration that she wanted to go back to work.

Ready or not, she was about to find out.

"Okay." She glanced at the kitchen, where Ellen was sitting at the countertop, eating a granola bar, completely entranced by the game she was playing on her iPad. "This is going to sound a little out of left field, so bear with me."

"Oh, boy." He laughed affectionately. "All right, hit me with it."

"John, I..." Imani shut her eyes for a second and took a deep breath. "As you know, I haven't been feeling completely like myself lately—"

"There's been a ton going on with the kids," he said kindly, placing a hand on her arm. "I know how crazy everything has been this summer."

"Well, yes, it...it has. But it's more than just stress and busy schedules." She looked over at Ellen again, to make sure their daughter was out of earshot and not paying attention.

John frowned in confusion, angling his head as he studied his wife. "What do you mean? What's going on?"

"Lately I've been..." She lowered her voice and held his gaze. "Feeling like I've lost myself. Feeling like I've become such a mom that I'm not anything else anymore."

"Imani." He reached out and ran a gentle hand across her cheek. "You are the most wonderful woman I know. You're incredible. And you happen to be an amazing mom, but that doesn't mean that's all you are."

"I know, I know." She toyed with a loose thread on a throw pillow. "I've just been feeling that way. I seem to have gotten lost in the shuffle somewhere, John. Swallowed up in their lives, so much so that I don't have one of my own. It's really been affecting me."

"Honey." He gave her a concerned look. "I know you said you've been overwhelmed, but you never told me this before."

"Because if felt silly or...fleeting. Plus, I didn't want to put more on your plate. I know how hard you work. And I always pushed these thoughts and feelings aside, assuming they'd go away."

"And have they?"

She shook her head, looking up at him. "No."

"Well..." He inched closer, wrapping an arm around her. "Maybe it's time for your favorite bubble bath and a glass of wine? I'll stay with the kids while you escape to the home spa."

"John."

She had just enough disdain in the word that he sat up.

"Okay, okay. A real spa? A weekend away with a girlfriend or one of my sisters?"

Her eyes shuttered at how far off he was. "I want to go back to work." The words tumbled out, and Imani instantly drew back and held her breath, knowing that was most definitely not what he had in mind.

"You...oh." He cleared his throat, raising his eyebrows and nodding slowly as he attempted to process the statement. "You want to start working again...*now?*"

In that one word, she heard all she needed to know.

"Now" could be translated into, *When we have a teenager and two soon-to-be teenagers who all need constant attention, guidance, help, love, transportation, meals, and the seriously involved mother they are accustomed to?*

"Do you think that's a good idea?" he asked, taking his feet off the ottoman to sit at the edge of the sofa. "I mean, where is this coming from?"

Yes, she did think it was a good idea. Because she needed this, as much as her kids needed her.

"I know it sounds insane, but hear me out, John." She squeezed his hand. "There's a small travel magazine looking for a writer to highlight the Space Coast, specifically Cocoa Beach. I wouldn't have to go anywhere, it's all freelance, so I could decide how much or how little I want to write for them, all totally small scale. And I just think it would...it would give me the little boost of independence and identity back that I need so badly. I can write for this one magazine, and be done with it. Out of my system, back to full-time mom-ing."

She paused, waiting to read his reaction.

"Imani, I don't..." He leaned forward, pressing his

elbows into his knees. "I don't know about this. I mean, I know how you are with writing. Once you dive into a project, it takes over your whole life."

"It's one article," she added quickly. "A couple, maximum."

"Honey, I know you." He turned to her. "It's going to be double that, because that's how you are. You're going to want to do everything at the highest level and you're going to put your heart and soul into it. And, believe me, I adore that about you. But...the kids. They need you. I need you. I just don't know if this is the right time for something like that."

Her whole chest tightened with all the unspoken arguments she didn't want to present. This was exactly the response she feared. She didn't want to argue with him, but needed his support.

"I know, I know," she said. "But I promise you, I can manage it. The kids are still top priority, all the writing is done at home, and it's not like I'm going to be traveling. I mean, unless you count a couple trips up and down A1A."

He gave a mirthless laugh, clearly less than thrilled about this proposition. On one level, she understood. She was a dedicated stay-at-home mom, and he worked a lot, so having her fully devoted to the kids was a good thing for them.

John constantly leaned on her to make everything come together flawlessly, and for fifteen years, she had been. And she'd been happy.

But Imani was certain that the kids would not be any

worse off if she took this job. She knew that, but John didn't.

"Is it going to stop here?" he asked her plainly.

She frowned. "What do you mean?"

"Is it really going to be one and done? Because once you start writing again, once you get your hands back on your career, I just don't see you giving it up again so easily. You're going to want to go bigger and better. And believe me, if that's what you really want, then I don't want to stop you. It's just..." He pinched the bridge of his nose.

"No, I'm not. I just want...something, John. Something that isn't soccer games or science projects or ballet classes. Something that is *mine.*"

He nodded slowly, holding her gaze. "Okay, hon, I understand. I really do. You give everything you have to this family. You deserve to feel fulfilled, I just...I thought being a mom was enough."

"It *is* enough," she insisted, a sudden pang of guilt hitting her gut. "I don't mean to say it's not enough and I don't want to sound ungrateful. This family is everything to me, you know that. I just..." She drew in a shuddering breath.

"Hey, hey." John wrapped his arms around her, pulling her close and kissing the top of her head. "It's okay, I understand."

"You do?" She looked up at him.

"Yes. I don't want you to feel lost or erased or anything less than your wonderful self. If doing a couple of freelance pieces for a local magazine is going to bring you the fulfillment that you're missing, then I'm all for it."

"It's just something for me, you know? Everything I do is for the kids or you—and I love it. But I'm missing myself sometimes."

"Then you have my support." He punctuated that with another soft kiss on her hair. "And if you need me to pick up any slack with the kids, I'm here for anything that comes up."

Imani's heart swelled. "And now I know why I love you and married you, John Sweeney."

"I love you, too."

With John's blessing and a sense of total peace and calm around the decision, Imani headed back over to the computer. There, she clicked Apply and sent in her resume, along with a sample of her work—a piece she wrote on Mykonos, Greece—and a cover letter.

This was good. This was the right thing. And even though John was hesitant at first, he'd come around. And he would see that this wasn't going to affect the kids or their family at all.

And Imani, for the first time in a long time, was doing something for herself. And she needed that.

Chapter Nine

Erica

This particular Saturday morning was bright and happy and full of endless possibilities. Erica had already texted her boss and told him she would be out of commission for the weekend, and planned on spending it with her family.

Not the usual style of Erica Sweeney-Armstrong, who was readily available for work at all hours of all days, because space exploration was truly a twenty-four-seven industry. But today, her phone was off, her automated out-of-office email was set and ready to go, and she was fully focused on her family. And, more specifically, on the newest member of that family.

Will had left early to go over to Sweeney House and show Dottie and Sam the reno plans he'd drawn, so Erica decided to bring Jada there to get some more quality time with the family.

She'd tried to spend an hour a day on "school stuff" but Jada was beyond not interested, and Erica didn't feel like pushing it. But blueprints and floor plans had a lot of potential for sneaky math lessons. Real world applications were better than worksheets anyway.

"So, remember the first night you got here and you

were dropped off at that cottage on the beach?" Erica asked Jada as she drove down A1A, heading toward Mom's house.

"Mm-hmm," Jada mumbled.

"And you met my entire overbearing and insane family?" she joked, glancing over at her, hoping to catch a glimpse of a smile.

"Yeah." Jada curled up against the window, staring out at the palm trees and buildings and glimpses of ocean in between. "I remember. They were nice."

"Good. I'm glad you think so." Erica smiled. "Well, that big building next door to the cottage, that's an inn called Sweeney House. My mom owns it and runs it. You remember her, too?"

"Dottie," Jada said softly, nodding.

And maybe one day, "Grandma," but...baby steps for now.

"That's right," Erica said. "And Dottie, along with my sister, Sam, and a little help from Will, is renovating and remodeling the whole inn. All ten rooms, and all of the common spaces. I think they're even adding a full kitchen and dining room and..." She laughed and waved a hand. "Anyway, it's really an exciting project. So I thought we could go over there and hang with them and maybe come up with some cool ideas for the inn. Sound like fun?"

"Okay!" Jada nodded her head, and almost showed a glimmer of enthusiasm.

And maybe a little fraction lesson or a reading comprehension passage here and there wouldn't hurt, Erica thought to herself.

"All right, here we are. The beach." Erica pulled her SUV to a stop in front of Sweeney House. "Smell that ocean air, huh?"

Jada hopped out of the car and squinted in the sunlight, shielding her eyes from the blinding brightness. She was sporting one of her new sundresses, this one pink and blue with big, tropical, floral patterns.

Erica knew that Jada was still staggeringly shy, so being around the family was a lot for her. But she had to get used to it, and once she got to know them, she'd surely adore them as much as Erica did.

"Hey, you two!" Will came jogging out of the lobby of Sweeney House, beaming at them.

"Hey." Erica accepted his hug and added one of her own. "We want to help with plans!"

He crouched down to Jada's level and gave her a high-five. "Is that right?"

Jada laughed a little and shrugged, but she didn't shy away or hide, so that was...progress. Maybe.

"Come on in. Dottie and Sam and I are just working on the new layout. Looks like we're going to be taking out a few walls and expanding the downstairs."

"Wow, this is turning into quite the project," Erica said, walking side by side with Jada as they followed Will into the inn.

"Yes, but worth it," he said. "It's going to really take the whole place to the next level. It's so outdated, in aesthetics and functionality." He leaned closer to whisper, "Wouldn't ever have had the nerve to say that to Jay, by the way."

She laughed, knowing how invested her father had been in every aspect of Sweeney House. "And you'd have been right not to, but I do think he'd love nothing more than seeing Mom this excited and happy."

"Dottie? She's over the moon, and so is Sam. The place is getting an overhaul, because everyone wants that B&B feel now," Will continued. "And they expect a little luxury even on the beach."

"That makes sense. I'm so excited to see how it turns out. It's going to be weird seeing it different. Nothing at Sweeney House ever changes. Ever."

"Well..." Will glanced at her. "It's about to."

They walked into the lobby, which was comfortable after a lifetime of living next door. But if she took her own filter and familiarity out of the equation, she could see just how tired, faded, and in need of a makeover this place really was.

As a kid, it was just a place of joy and love. *But that was because of Dad*, she mused. He had his hands on every inch, and his essence was so deeply infused in it, the very scent of the rooms could bring her to tears.

Despite the nostalgia and the memories, she was thrilled for her sweet mom, who needed this change as much as the building itself.

"See that desk?" Erica pointed to the front desk, where Jeanine, the clerk who'd been with Sweeney House since Erica was a kid, sat with a phone pressed to her ear.

Jada nodded.

"When I was around your age, I would sit there and

do all my homework after school, because my parents were always here, working. And when no one was looking, I'd get on the computer and play like I was a fancy businesswoman. I'd fake phone calls and click the keyboard and everything."

Jada actually giggled at this. "Why would you do that?" Jada asked softly.

"I don't know." Erica shrugged as they headed into one of the back offices to the small meeting room. "I guess I wanted to pretend I was important."

"Are you important now?" Jada looked up at her, interest in her dark eyes.

Erica thought about the question, tipping her head as she considered the most honest answer. "I guess to some people I am."

Was that a good thing? Erica had no idea. But her newly adopted daughter was curious about her, sort of, so that had to be a positive thing.

"Look who it is!" Sam popped up from a conference table where she and Dottie were studying a computer monitor. "Baby sister here to correct all of our math."

"Hello, hello." Erica laughed and hugged her sister, then walked over to give Dottie an embrace as well. "I'm just here for moral support. And maybe a tiny bit of math. Just a little." She winked at Jada.

"Jada, honey, how are you?" Dottie asked, beckoning her into the conference room.

"Good." Jada kept her gaze cast to the floor, staying close to Erica. Almost like she…trusted her. Felt safe with her, even a little bit.

The tiniest victories were still victories, after all.

"They can show you the masterpiece." Will pointed with clasped hands toward the hallway. "I'm going to go make some phone calls to general contractors I know in the area, see how soon we can get the ball rolling on demolition and construction. You'll need permits, so prepare to wait for some things."

Dottie waved a hand. "Oh, William, I'm not worried. You'll make it happen."

"I'll do my best." He stepped toward the door. "Let me know if you guys need anything."

Erica turned to Jada and gave her a big grin. "Want to see?"

Jada nodded and craned her neck to look at the computer screen as Sam turned it around so they could get a good look.

"So." Sam pointed at the drawing on the screen, which was a three-dimensional rendering of the lobby and downstairs area of Sweeney House. "This is how it's currently set up. But we're going to take out"—she pointed to a thin line on the screen that separated the sitting area from the main lobby—"that wall, and open all of this up for a sizable dining room. We can do breakfast, brunch, even host small private events. Fantastic, right?"

"Amazing," Erica agreed, glancing at Jada to see if she showed any interest in this at all. "What an incredible change, and a new revenue stream for Sweeney House."

Erica took a step closer, frowning at the on-screen blueprint. Was that wall structural? A load-bearing issue could cost a fortune, but she decided to leave those questions to the contractor. She was here as family, not as an engineer.

"Can't you just picture it?" Sam looked up, her eyes bright with anticipation. "Morning coffee, fabulous, homemade omelets, a sunny pale orange color on the walls. White tablecloths, or maybe that cool light, organic-looking wood. Won't that be fabulous?"

If the ceiling doesn't fall down, Erica thought with a smile. "Wow, you're decorating already, huh? Have you even laid out the square footage yet? Considered code and permitting with a gas stove and a kitchen?"

"Killjoy," Sam teased, looking at Dottie for backup.

"We have your husband for that," her mother said. "And Sam to make it a showplace."

"You know what? That's a good plan," Erica said, gently easing Jada closer to the computer. "Hey, Jada, see this room here? The one that Sam wants to make a dining room?" She waited a beat. "With orange walls?"

"*Pale* orange," Sam shot back dryly. "Think peach or...maybe..." She glanced down at the table and read something. "Tangerine sunrise. I like the sound of that. Good enough to eat."

But Jada didn't smile; she was intent on the computer screen. "That one? Without the line for a wall?"

"Yes!" Erica said, excited. "Do you know how to figure out the area of this room?" she asked gently.

Jada looked up like she'd asked her to build the room, not compute square footage. "The what?"

"The area, like how many total square feet are in that

room. I'm sure Sam and Dottie know, but I can show you how to calculate it, if you want."

"Seriously?" Sam arched a brow. "You're being serious right now?"

"Yes. The area of a room is absolutely critical in a renovation plan, obviously."

Sam leaned closer to Jada to whisper, "Not as critical as the wall color, or curtain selection. If you want a *real* lesson, it's that curtains add texture to any room, and they should pull your accent colors in with your base colors to make it feel finished." She gave a smug look. "I heard that on HGTV last night."

"Oh!" Dottie held her hands together. "Did I tell you we're going to hire a full-time chef?"

Sam inhaled dramatically. "I can already smell the croissants."

"Guys," Erica said. "I'm trying to show Jada how length times width works."

"No, you're trying to bore her to death," Sam fired back with a playful glance. "Jada, when we paint, can I count on you for some help? Erica will approve it as art class."

Jada smiled at the joke while Erica gave up on math and plopped down next to Mom. "So what about all the antiques?" she asked. "Have you guys decided what you're going to keep yet?"

"Oh, that's a whole project on its own." Dottie shook her head. "And I'm afraid my poor old soul has got just too many fond memories of each and every piece in this inn. I can't bear to part with anything."

Erica put a hand on Dottie's arm. "I know this has got to be hard for you. You and Dad designed this whole place from the ground up."

"It's true, and there are some things that haven't been easy. And some things I haven't even bothered to think about because I know it's going to hurt. Like the clock." Dottie sighed and lifted her shoulder as she referred to the massive, ornate, and not-functioning grandfather clock that was Jay's family heirloom, and a major eyesore, in the lobby of the inn. "But it is time for a new start. I'm hoping that a lot of the antiques can be restored and made into more modern, you know, contemporary versions. And we could keep them in some of the rooms."

"I think that would really help preserve the character of the inn," Sam added.

"I love that," Erica said, turning to Jada who still stood a few feet away. "You know, there are some really old pieces of furniture that my parents collected, all antiques, which means they are over a hundred years old."

"Wow, cool." Jada looked around. "Like what?"

"Well..." Erica thought for a moment. "There's a bed frame upstairs that my parents got at an antique shop, and it was made in the year 1902! How many years ago is that, do you think?" She tried to play it off cool and casual.

Obvious? Too obvious? It was just some friendly everyday math.

"Um..." Jada's expression darkened instantly, and she frowned. "I don't...I don't know."

"The real question," Sam interjected with a wink. "Is should we repaint it? And what color? Or just refinish and polish the wood…"

"Come here, Jada." Dottie got up and waved a hand, gesturing for Jada to follow her out of the back office. "I want to show you some of these antiques we're talking about. You haven't had a chance to get a full look at the inn. There's wonderful history here, and not just Sweeney family history, either. Cool stuff with stories and life."

"Okay." Jada was hesitant, but she followed Dottie down the hall.

As soon as they were gone, Sam turned to Erica with a *get real* look. "Drinking game! Take a shot every time Erica tries to sneak a school lesson into a conversation."

"I'm just trying to, you know, help her."

"By making her do word problems on the sly? You want her to run screaming from the room?"

Erica sighed, leaning way back on the conference room chair. "I know, I know. I'm just trying to teach her some academic stuff before August. I told you how behind she is."

"I know it seems bad, but she'll be okay, right? I mean, she'll catch up. It's sixth grade. Even I passed it."

Erica pressed her lips together and shook her head, glancing through the doorway to make sure Jada was long out of earshot. "I'm not so sure. I don't…I don't think she can read at even, like, a second-grade level. And forget math. She's so discouraged, she just says she's not even going to go. It's like she was never given a fair chance. It breaks my heart."

"Oh, hon." Sam's expression softened as she looked at her sister with sympathy and understanding. "You're going to figure out how to navigate this, I promise."

"I don't know." Erica puffed out a breath and held her palm to her forehead. "I don't want to just sit her down and make her do schoolwork. That's so...cold."

"Just make it fun," Sam said.

"Easy for you to say. You're fun. I'm a rocket scientist."

"Exactly," Sam said. "You went to MIT, for crying out loud. Who better to tutor her? Just chill and make it more fun than, you know, the square footage of a room."

Erica laughed softly at how right Sam was, but her smile wavered. "You make it sound easy. You make motherhood *look* easy. I feel like she's going to hate me if she fails, and hate me if I teach her."

"She won't hate you for helping her, she'll be grateful. Just keep it a little less, you know, structured."

Erica nodded, considering that.

"And trust me, all kids act like they hate you for a minute or two. Give it enough time and she'll realize how much effort you've put in to help her and give her a chance."

"I can't, Sam. I just...I want her to like me so badly."

"I know that."

"Like, look at you and Taylor." Erica gestured at her sister. "You two are actual best friends. More than mother and daughter, even. Taylor worships you. I want to have that so bad, but it seems impossible. And I feel like if I sit down and try to go all teacher mode on her, she's going to feel patronized and think I'm the bad guy."

"Okay, well, first of all, she's eleven, so I don't think she even knows what feeling patronized is. I'm also not entirely sure I do."

Erica smirked and rolled her eyes.

"And second of all, Taylor and I were not always the way we are now."

She cocked her head. "What? Yes, you were. You and Tay are inseparable."

"Oh, Erica, not even close. When she was in middle school, right around Jada's age, she thought I was a literal jail warden. She actually told me that."

Erica drew back. "Taylor? No way."

"She hated me for a while there. Despised me."

"But why? You were the best mom, and Taylor would be the absolute first person to say that."

Sam lifted a shoulder. "Now she would, because she's twenty-four and has some perspective. But when she was eleven or twelve, some things happened, and we had quite a rough patch."

"What happened?"

"Well, I thought she was hanging around with the wrong kids. She got into a friend group with these girls, Allison Crofton and Bethany Morris. I just..." Sam wrinkled her nose at the memory. "I didn't like those girls. They whipped around the neighborhood in their parents' golf carts, never wore shoes, snuck around with boys. They were bad news."

"Yikes. No shoes? How awful." Erica gave a dry laugh.

"I suspected worse, especially with the boys."

"Eesh, yeah. I get that." And Erica would be the same kind of mother. She hoped. Although she couldn't even get Jada to do a math problem, so who knew what she'd be like in a few years. "What did you do?"

"I told her she wasn't allowed to hang out with them anymore. Period. End of discussion."

"Whoa, authoritarian," she teased.

"It was, a little bit." Sam smiled at the memory. "But I told her they weren't real friends, they were going to get her into trouble, and she couldn't see them anymore. And that was that."

"And Taylor got upset with you?"

"*Upset*?" Sam snorted and looked at the ceiling. "You would have thought I'd cut off her right arm. She screamed and yelled and didn't talk to me for days. Maybe a week. Slammed her door and pouted in her room, the whole middle school bit."

"How did you deal with that?" Erica asked. "Didn't that hurt you?"

"Of course, it destroyed me. But I stuck to my guns because I knew I was doing the right thing. And at that time, in that situation, it was more important to be her mom than her friend."

"Wow." Erica exhaled deeply, a new level of admiration for Sam growing in her heart.

"And then," Sam continued, "when Allison and Bethany were kicked out of school for hiding drugs in their lockers a few years later, Taylor came home and hugged me harder than she ever had in her life."

"Oh, good. Not for them, but for you." Erica sighed, wondering if she'd ever get a hug like that from Jada, if she'd ever be appreciated for discipline or teaching or *anything*. "You're a well of wisdom about this stuff, seriously. I'm such a rookie, Sam."

"Hey." Sam placed a gentle hand on her sister's arm. "You're doing a great job. And you know, if she ends up hating you, she always has her fabulous Aunt Sam. Who would never, *ever* make her do math problems in the summer."

Erica groaned and gave her sister's arm a jab. "You're the worst, you know that?" She jutted her chin out toward the hallway. "Come on, let's go see what they've gotten into."

Sam and Erica headed to the second floor, where they found Dottie and Jada standing in front of a solid oak dresser in one of the empty suites.

Erica seemed to recall her dad telling her that he and Mom had snagged the piece at an antique show in Miami, and it was such a find.

"What are you guys up to?" Erica asked, walking over to join her mother and Jada.

"I was showing Jada this chest of drawers," Dottie responded with a wistful smile, her gaze locked on the old, worn-out piece of furniture.

It was a reddish-colored wood, with some stains and markings and a fair amount of wear and tear. The brass handles were loose and hanging a bit lopsided, and the color had been washed out from decades of sunlight and exposure.

Dottie leaned back, rested her hands on her hips and looked right at Jada, who reached out and gently ran her fingers along the corner of the wood. "So, my granddaughter here and I are just trying to figure out what the heck to do with this guy, aren't we?"

Erica held her breath at the word *granddaughter*, tense as she watched Jada for a reaction.

She didn't seem to noticeably recoil or flinch or, no surprise, speak up, so Erica took it as another tiny victory.

Goodness, she loved her mother for the way she treated Jada. Like the little girl had always been there, and was a natural part of this family. No weirdness or dancing around or euphemisms. Maybe that's what Jada needed. To feel normal.

How was Dottie so effortless in that way?

Oh, she had a lot to learn from these amazing mothers around her.

"Well..." Sam walked up and placed her hand flat on the top of the dresser. "Whatcha think, Jada? We're puzzled and could use some fun ideas. And, as much as I love my dear darling sister, she's not really the creative type." Sam looked over her shoulder and sent a loving grin to Erica. "But I've got a feeling that you are."

Erica raised her hands and drew back, shaking her head. "I can't argue that. I can tell you how to take that dresser apart and put it back together with tongue and groove joints, but please don't ask me to decorate it."

Jada looked at the dresser, then up at Dottie with

those big, doe eyes. They weren't quite as hidden behind her hair as they had been a week ago.

"Um…" Jada spoke softly, and everyone tuned in to hear what the little woman of very, very few words was going to say. "Maybe you could make it blue. With clouds on it. To match the sky." She pointed to the big window above her, which was trimmed with white wood.

Blue with clouds on it. Not sure dear old Dad would approve of that particular choice for an antique piece, but the whisper of enthusiasm in Jada's voice made Erica smile.

"Well!" Dottie gasped with delight, clutching a hand to her chest. "I think that sounds like a fantastic idea!"

"You do?" Erica whispered the question.

"Absolutely!" Dottie practically sang the word. "The whole point of this renovation is to breathe new life into old things, you know? And I think our newest family member here…" She placed a hand on Jada's shoulder. "Is the perfect person to think outside the box on how to revitalize these pieces. And she has done just that."

"Wait…" Jada drew back, pushing some curls out of her face and staring up at Dottie. "Really? You…you liked my idea?"

"Liked it?" Dottie laughed. "It's the best idea anyone's had so far! Everything is always 'paint it white' or 'refinish the wood' or make it modern or contemporary or in style. But you think we should just…How did you put it again?"

"Match the sky?" Jada said softly, a glimmer of hope in her sweet little voice.

"Match the sky." Dottie nodded. "I love it, and it's decided. This chest of drawers will match the sky."

"Seriously?" Jada asked again, this time a full-on smile taking hold of her face, and she turned to Erica, beaming. Or, well, the closest thing to beaming that Jada seemed to be capable of at this point. "You're going to do it?"

"Heck, yeah, we are," Sam chimed in, shooting Erica a wink. "And if you want, you can help us paint it."

"And some of the other pieces," Dottie added. "I think you might just be the visionary we've been missing."

"Wow!" Jada giggled, her smile the widest Erica had seen it. "Cool!"

"That is cool." Erica looked at Sam and Dottie, feeling emotion tug at her heart. "It's very, very cool."

Dottie gave her a nod and a knowing smile.

"Hey, everyone." Will's voice grabbed all of their attention, and they saw he stood in the doorway of the suite.

Erica wanted to run right up to him and tell him that Jada giggled and smiled and showed some level of joy, but she held back.

Normal. That's how Jada needed to feel. Not like an animal at the zoo that was being observed and studied and fawned over.

"Good news." Will gave a thumbs-up. "Just talked to a buddy of mine, Ethan, who restores, paints and refurbishes antiques as his side hustle, and he's really good at it. Best in the area."

Dottie grinned. "Will he do blue with clouds?"

"He'll do anything," Will said.

"It's my idea." Jada stepped forward, her voice a little less quiet than usual.

"Yes, it was," Erica added quickly, locking eyes with her husband so they could relish this moment of victory silently together.

"Well, that's..." He ~~locked his gaze with Erica's, then~~ beamed at Jada. "That's fantastic, Jada. Great to have you on the job." He added a high-five that was as natural—and beautiful—as anything Erica had ever seen. "You'll love this guy, Dottie. He's all about preserving the integrity of the piece, but"—he patted the dresser next to him—"bringing everything back to life. And, God knows, this guy needs a little of that."

"And can he paint the sky on the dresser?" Jada added a tentative smile. "That's my idea," she repeated, clearly loving the feeling of contributing and being a part of a family, something Erica knew was entirely foreign to Jada.

"He can bring your ideas to life, kiddo."

"I love it." Dottie laughed softly. "When can I meet him?"

"He's actually on his way now, if that's all right."

"What?" Sam smiled, looking at her mother. "That's great. Thank you, Will."

"Of course," Will said. "He was in the area when he called me back, so he said he'll stop by and take a look at some of the antiques and furniture pieces and see if you guys can come up with some stuff together."

"Definitely."

Will nodded, holding Sam's gaze before slowly looking over at Erica. "You guys want to take a break and go down to the beach? Jada, there's a boogie board in the garage at the cottage that has your name on it."

Her smile reached her eyes and brightened them. "Sure."

"Let's do it." Buoyed by the response, Erica walked with Will down the hall and over to the cottage.

The whole walk, Erica replayed the last few minutes. Jada had never had a family—not one like this, anyway. As much as it had to be intimidating and foreign to her, she was now a part of it, and Erica's family was nothing short of amazing—as they just proved.

Erica had obsessed over every single small victory with Jada so far, but today? The smile on her face and the excitement in her voice? Today felt like a *big* victory.

Chapter Ten

Sam

"That was really sweet of you, Mom." Sam looked at Dottie as soon as the two of them were alone in the suite again. "I know how much it means to Erica that we're including Jada and treating her like part of the family."

"Sam, honey." Her mother looked at her, a twinkle in her eye. "She *is* part of the family."

Sam nodded slowly, taking a deep breath as she ran her hand across the top of the antique dresser that would soon be painted blue with clouds, courtesy of her new niece. "It's nice to see her coming out of her shell a little bit, you know? Erica is so stressed about the whole thing."

"Well, that's what Erica does. She stresses. But then... she succeeds."

"Greatly," Sam added with a snort. "And I have no doubt that this will be a typical Erica Sweeney-Armstrong success story."

Dottie perched on the edge of the king-sized bed, her fingers trailing over the wrought iron headboard that had seen better days. No doubt she'd want to save it, but maybe this antique genius who was on the way could do the work.

"So, this Ethan guy." Sam sat down next to Dottie, brushing the thick white lace comforter underneath her legs. "Sounds like a good option, right?"

"Yes, I think so. His name is familiar, but I don't remember how I know him. But he can certainly give us an estimate, maybe show us samples of his work. And if something can't be refurbished?" She shrugged. "Then we'll get rid of it."

"Mom." Sam shot her a look. "You're telling me that you're going to be willing to part with *any* of the old furniture that you and Dad bought together?"

Dottie let out a soft sigh and shut her eyes. "I am going to. Of course, I'd like to repurpose and reuse as much of the old stuff as we can, but I truly am committed to giving this place an entirely new life. If that means some goodbyes, then...so be it." She reached out and grabbed Sam's hand, giving it a loving squeeze. "It's a new chapter for both of us."

That it was.

"Knock knock." An unfamiliar man's voice echoed from down the hallway.

Dottie and Sam both stood up and walked to the doorway, peering down the hall to see a tall, broad figure striding toward them with full confidence, as if he owned the place.

"Ethan Price. You must be Dottie Sweeney." He notched his head.

"I am." Her mother headed toward him, looking up— way up, since he was over six feet—and frowned. "Have we met, Ethan?"

"Actually, no. But your, uh, late husband brought a few pieces to the shop in my garage and we got on really well. I was sorry to hear of his loss."

"Oh, thank you."

Sam noticed her mother visibly soften at the mention of Jay, so she stepped closer to get a better look at the man. And that didn't exactly hurt. Sandy blond hair, just long enough to fall around his forehead, framed a tanned and handsome face with the perfect amount of scruff on his angular jaw.

He might be in his mid-forties, but he wore a white T-shirt and jeans the way a younger man would, like he was born in that outfit.

"Hi," he said as he noticed Sam and gave her a flicker of a smile. "Ethan Price. And you are…?"

"This is my daughter, Samantha," her mother said. "She's my partner in crime here for this renovation."

He nodded. "Samantha." He reached out his hand and shook hers, holding it long enough for her to notice calluses and a firm grip. Clearly, this man worked with his hands all day.

"And it's just Sam. Hello, Ethan. Thanks for coming out so quickly after my brother-in-law called."

"Like I said, I've done a little work for Jay and I've always wanted to see the inside of this place." He glanced around. "I can practically smell the history in here."

"And the dust, I'm sure," Sam quipped.

Ethan angled his head and glanced around at the décor. "Could use a facelift, probably. But hey, that's where I come in."

"How long have you been refurbishing antiques?" Dottie asked.

"Oh, my dad did it for years in our garage growing up, and I picked up the bug." He ran a hand through his hair. "I love finding weathered furniture and bringing it back to its original glory. It's so much better than all the generic modern crap that everyone buys now."

"Well." Sam raised her brows and gave a soft laugh. "You won't be finding any generic modern crap at Sweeney House."

"And..." Dottie lifted her finger. "We fully intend to keep it that way. But most of our furniture does need some upgrading. Plus, we're remodeling the entire downstairs."

Sam leaned forward. "And all the finishings. And floors. And the outside. And did we mention there's a cottage next door?"

"A full renovation?" Ethan smiled and nodded his head, his eyes flickering over to Sam. "Bold. I like that." His blue eyes locked with hers, making something kick in Sam's heart.

Something that had been dormant for a long, long time. Were those...*butterflies*?

"Great," she said quickly, swallowing and trying not to smile.

"Sam, why don't you show Ethan around and give him an idea of what kind of furniture we're working with here."

"Oh, sure, of course." She studied her mom, her

brows furrowing in confusion. "You're not coming? I mean, you know a lot more about the antiques than I do."

"Oh, I think I'm gonna have a little lie-down." She clasped her hands together. "Old bones, you know."

What? Dottie was so not a napper, especially not in the middle of a discussion about restoring her antiques, which Sam often thought she loved as much as—if not more than—her and her siblings.

"You sure? Is everything okay?" Sam asked.

"Oh, yes." Dottie flicked her hand. "I'm totally fine. Just going to head over to my suite and rest for a little. You show Mr. Price around, and I'll be here for any and all questions."

As soon as Dottie turned to walk down the hallway back to the suite where she lived, she glanced over her shoulder, looked right at Sam, and winked.

Old bones. *Sure, Mom.* Sam would have to deal with her mom's pathetic attempt at being a matchmaker later on.

For now, she had to deal with...

Him.

"So..." Sam swung around and smiled at Ethan. "Let's take a furniture tour and show you the prettiest parts of Sweeney House."

He glanced around but his gaze landed on her. "It's all really pretty," he said with an easy smile.

Whoa. He was flirting and she was...not hating that. As they walked, she subtly glanced at his left hand, just out of pure curiosity.

Nope, no ring.

"We can start downstairs, if you want. The lobby has a sizable collection of old furniture that my dad probably had a thousand stories about."

"He did have good stories. Colorful guy, Jay."

She smiled up at him. "He was the best."

"I remember him talking about a clock. Grandfather?"

"Oh, yes, that beastly thing in our lobby. And perfectly named, because it belonged to my grandfather, Jay's dad. Want to see it?"

"So much."

"To the lobby then." She gestured toward the stairway. "So, do you mostly paint furniture? Or restyle it?"

"Honestly, it's kind of whatever I'm feeling in the moment. Usually the piece will call to me in some way. Tell me what it needs."

"Well, I hope that dresser upstairs told you how badly it wants to be blue with clouds on it."

Ethan slowed his step and narrowed his gaze. "Please tell me you're kidding."

"Oh, buddy, I am so not kidding." She chuckled, lifting up her hands. "Welcome to Sweeney House. You're in for a treat."

"Now that, I believe." He held her gaze, his blue eyes looking at her in a way that made her feel suddenly young and noticed and...flirty.

Sam felt her cheeks warm.

She'd felt like such a sad sack of pity and depression ever since Max cheated on her, basically deciding that she was the furthest thing on Earth from desirable.

But here was this man making her feel all sorts of newness with his broad shoulders and talking furniture gig. She liked it.

"I suppose this would be a good place to start." Sam swept a hand in the direction of the massive grandfather clock that sat in the lobby. "Told you it was...something."

Nearly eight feet tall, the clock was made of dark mahogany with a dozen curlicue inlays, three carved posts at the top and so much ornate gold it looked like it belonged in a cathedral, not a beachfront inn.

Ethan stopped dead in his tracks and stared, his jaw loose.

"I know. It's an eyeful," she joked. "Welcome to our version of Big Ben. Hideous, isn't it? Dad always said it was made well before he was, in the 1930s, which might explain why it never ticks and is only right twice a day."

He choked softly. "Samantha, are you...kidding me?"

"Right? It's painful. What can you do with something that awful? Think we could get a few hundred on Craigslist?"

He laughed softly, closing his eyes.

"Okay, *one* hundred?"

Finally, he turned to her. "That clock?" He pointed to it. "Is an original Howard Miller. From the 1930s? Holy..." He took a step closer, putting his hand on the side and lovingly stroking the wood. "Holy cow. I don't think I've ever seen one."

A tendril of excitement climbed through her chest. "It's worth something?"

"If you think ten or twelve grand, maybe more, is something, then yes."

"What?" She literally jumped back. "Are you serious?"

"It needs work, and plenty of it. I can do the wood and I have a friend who's a clockmaker who could make the mechanism work again and—wow." He let out a sigh of pure admiration. "Look at the inlay."

She had, a thousand times in her life, and never once had a reaction like his. "Ten thousand dollars, Ethan?" She whistled. "Well, there's the granite for the new kitchen. Thank you for small miracles."

"You'd sell it?" He looked surprised.

"You want to buy it?" she joked.

"No, but I'd give my right arm to get it in my shop."

"Keep your arm and consider it yours to work on."

"That's awesome." Ethan touched the dusty glass that covered the old, dull pendulum and weights with reverence. "I'll probably strip it and refinish the wood. A challenging project, if you trust me with it. I bet I can make it nice."

Sam got the feeling that this guy made everything he touched beautiful. He seemed like one of those salt-of-the-earth, works with his hands men who had a gift for wood and paint and building things out of nothing.

"Honestly?" Sam laughed softly. "We're all a little scared to touch it. My dad would have a cow if anyone was bold enough to go near it."

"Well, I'd be happy to give it a go. Okay, we have a sky blue dresser and a ten-thousand-dollar clock." He gave her a slow grin. "What else did you want me to look at today?"

With those blue eyes? He could look at her. But she just smiled and gestured toward the hall. "Bedroom furniture, mostly. A few consoles. And one really ragged armoire that I was planning to throw away, but you might say it's worth a few more grand."

He laughed and walked with her. "Cool. This is going to be fun, Samantha."

"It's just Sam."

He slid her a look. "I kinda like Samantha."

Was it possible? Could it be?

After all these years and a terrible marriage and pity and misery and moving back home...

Did Samantha Sweeney...still have it?

Chapter Eleven

Taylor

"Thank you for calling Coastal Marketing. This is Taylor, how may I help you today?"

Taylor squeezed the office phone between her cheek and her shoulder, clattering rapidly on her keyboard to input the notes for John and the CFO, Robert's, schedule.

"Hi, yes..." A woman's voice crackled on the other end of the phone call. "This is Theresa Schultz with the Beachside Boutique franchise."

A client of the firm. Relatively small, a few locations in the area. Big social media push recently to attract younger customers to their line of clothing stores.

"Theresa, how are you doing?" Taylor asked cheerfully, already pulling up the client information file on Beachside Boutiques while she kept the schedule open on her other screen.

"I'm good, I'm good," Theresa answered. "I'd like to set up a meeting for this week, maybe. With Nina and Jose from the design team, and one of the advertising specialists. We're launching a new fall line, so I want to chat about some ideas for promotion."

"Sounds fantastic." Taylor flipped through everyone's schedules, pulling up Nina and Jose from creative, and Craig from online marketing. She quickly scanned their availability. "How does Thursday at three sound?"

"Thursday at three..." the woman repeated, taking a beat to check the date. "Okay, I can do that."

"Sounds good, I've got you down on the books." Taylor typed her name into the schedule quickly.

"Thanks so much. Have a good one."

"You as well!" Taylor clicked the phone back on the hook and turned to her computer screen, taking a moment to relish the sheer organization of the shared schedule and office information cloud that she was running.

In the last couple of weeks, she'd gotten the hang of it here, and was even praised by the team for her little nugget of information on TikTok video formatting.

It was a faster paced environment than she expected, but Taylor was coming to realize that she actually really enjoyed that.

She took a sip of coffee and scanned through the client file for the boutique, envisioning some possible social media ads for the fall line, which from the looks of it, was gorgeous.

Suddenly, the front door opened and two men Taylor didn't recognize breezed in.

Dripping with trendy hipster vibes, one had reddish hair, a beard, and wore suspenders with a button-down shirt. The other guy was taller, with dreadlocks and a bandana, rocking the classic, faded black jean jacket.

Who were these guys? And why were they dressed for...not Florida?

"Hi!" Taylor sat up and smiled at each of them. "Welcome to Coastal Marketing. Can I help you?"

"I'm Brock." The bearded suspender guy smiled.

"And I'm Andre." Jean Jacket gave a friendly nod, flashing a sharp jawline and pretty brown eyes. "We're the owners of Blackhawk Brewing, a craft brewery in Asheville, North Carolina."

"Oh! Of course!" Taylor stood up to shake hands and greet them, instantly remembering having spoken to them on the phone last week. "You're scheduled for a new business pitch at 1:30. It's great to meet you guys."

A craft brewery in Asheville. Okay, now their looks and attire started to make a bit more sense.

"That's us." Andre pointed and laughed softly.

"Awesome." Taylor smiled. "I'll go ahead and let the team know you're here, if you guys just want to have a seat." She gestured at the two white leather loveseats in the entrance of the office.

They nodded and sat down, and she headed back to let John know they'd arrived. Since they were a new client, he'd lead the meeting.

"Hey, Uncle." She tapped on the glass door to his office. "Brock and Andre are here, from that brewery in North Carolina. Prospective clients for a new business pitch."

"Ah." He looked at the computer screen and gave

Taylor a thumbs-up. "Yes. I've done the research on the brewery and asked Matt, Nina, Melissa, and a couple of others from creative and advertising to join us. These guys are opening a Florida location in a few months and looking for some promo for a new market."

"Oh, that's awesome."

If they want to appeal to a Floridian, tropical customer base, they may want to lose the flannels and jean jackets, but Taylor decided it wasn't her place to offer suggestions on wardrobe or anything else to a client.

Taylor glanced down the hall. "The conference room is all ready. Let me know if you need anything else during the meeting!"

"Actually, Taylor?"

She stopped on her way out of his office and spun around on her heel. "Yes?"

"Would you mind sitting in on it and keeping notes? Ideas can fly, even at a Level One potential client meeting, and I don't want to lose track of anything we discuss."

Sit in on a new business pitch? "Sure, I'd love to!"

"Great, thank you." He stacked some papers and tucked his tablet under his arm before heading out of the office with her. "Plus, it'll be good for you to see the early creative process of marketing. It's kind of the 'fun' part." He held up air quotes and shared a look with his niece.

"Fun is my middle name, as we all know."

"You get that from your mother," he joked, heading into the conference room.

She sped through the office back to the front desk,

picked up her laptop to take notes, and invited Brock and Andre to follow her to the conference room.

They were suitably impressed by the ocean view out the solid glass wall, making small talk about Cocoa Beach while they took their seats on one side of a long conference table.

Taylor assumed a seat in the back corner, and got herself situated with a laptop where she could input a detailed account of the brainstorming session.

As the design team employees and advertising people started to fill the chairs, Taylor felt a zing of excitement for the meeting to start.

Creative brainstorming had to be at the heart of the entire marketing business, but Taylor had yet to really see that side of it. She only knew the administrative side, so this was a new layer she was eager to unfold.

Once the team of Coastal Marketing employees was settled and introduced, John easily took the lead to launch the discussion.

"Brock and Andre, we're thrilled to have you here, and congratulations on your very successful business, Blackhawk Brewing in North Carolina. We're delighted to have a chance to replicate that success at your second location in Cocoa Beach. Why don't you start with telling us a little bit about the company, your mission statement, and your marketing goals?"

Andre thanked him and leaned forward, looking around the table. "That's easy. We're a couple of chill guys who like beer and money, and want to sell one and make the other."

Everyone laughed at the ice breaker.

Andre glanced at Brock. "But my partner studies the demographics and is the real brains behind the business."

Brock nodded at the compliment. "Obviously, the Florida demographic, aesthetic, and customer experience is really different here on the beach than it is in the Blue Ridge Mountains. What we need from a local agency is help targeting a Florida-specific market, including both local residents and tourists."

Interesting, Taylor thought as she rapidly typed some notes.

Cocoa Beach certainly wasn't known for its craft beer scene, but there were plenty of young people around who would love that sort of environment. Plus, with the weather, you could operate outside all year.

"And..." Andre leaned back. "We'd love to hear how you all at Coastal Marketing could get the word out to a customer base here. We know the brand could have a different vibe down here, and we're open to anything except changing the logo." He grinned. "My sister designed it, so it stays."

John nodded to Taylor. "Make sure that gets in the notes," he said to her. "We don't touch family-generated art."

Everyone laughed, and Taylor marveled at her uncle's skill in keeping the meeting informative but not heavy or dull.

Brock leaned in to add, "But we really want to come out of the gate strong with the opening of this new location in a way that will resonate with the young beach scene here. What kinds of programs and promotion would you recommend, just off the top of your head?"

John nodded. "We'll do a formal presentation next week, but we've got a creative group here." He glanced at his team. Instantly, Nina, an account exec, chimed in.

"I got one," she said. "How about a tropical beer, exclusive to Cocoa Beach? You guys could start brewing a beer that's, I don't know, orange-flavored or something. Hit the Florida market a little better."

Taylor tried not to wrinkle her nose at the thought, and kept her face focused down on her computer screen.

Brock and Andre didn't seem too thrilled with the first idea, but they shrugged politely.

The creative director, however, nodded at the idea. "We could partner with a local orange grove to make the beer? You know, somewhere inland?"

Really? Taylor didn't see how that would appeal to the beach market.

"We could hold a contest..." Melissa said, frowning as she formulated a thought. "Winner gets to name a new beer. Lots of social media potential with that."

"The orange beer?" Tommy asked.

"Possibly!" Melissa shrugged.

"Okay, different direction here..." Another creative team woman named Kelly added in. "We run a Facebook event, and one commenter gets free beer for...I don't know, a year. Six months."

Nina pointed at her. "That could be fun."

Taylor diligently wrote down the ideas, doing her job

and keeping quiet, a task that was becoming increasingly harder every second.

"Well," John cleared his throat. "We can definitely do a *Florida Today* feature in the newspaper, bring reporters and photographers to the grand opening."

How did these suggestions just continue to get more and more outdated? Taylor loved and respected everyone at this company, but it felt like this particular project wasn't exactly in their wheelhouse.

"I've got it." Tommy clapped his hands together. "A direct mail campaign. Postcards, designed by us, aimed at Florida residents and locals. They have discounts, specials, upcoming events...a mail campaign."

Did he just say...*postcards*?

Taylor nearly winced as she reluctantly typed the idea, which seemed like it would have been a wonderful marketing tactic, if you were targeting retirees. She couldn't even remember the last time she checked her physical mail.

It was killing her not to say something—not to jump in and talk about how they needed to run a younger-based social media campaign, maybe bring in an influencer, get it on Instagram, TikTok, even a Snapchat account...

But that wasn't her job, and it wasn't her place.

Brock and Andre shared a look, and Taylor kept her internal cringe to herself. These guys were hip, dripping with trendiness and swag, and they were not responding to Coastal Marketing's traditional, conventional, and slightly outdated marketing tactics.

But she was in no place to judge a very successful local company that Uncle John had started from nothing. Clearly, their strategies worked for them, although Brock and Andre were definitely younger and more, well, *millennial* than their typical clientele.

"I think"—Nina pressed her hands on the table—"what we need to consider here is an event. A big, well-planned, well-advertised grand opening event that would attract a lot of locals in your target demographic and really put your name on the map right off the bat."

Brock scratched his beard and nodded. "We definitely want to do an opening celebration or something similar, that's true."

"Oh!" Melissa lifted a finger. "We could have the mayor come and do a ribbon cutting."

A ribbon cutting? Oh, man.

Taylor sunk down in her seat and shook her head a tiny bit as she typed out these new ideas.

Were ribbon cuttings a thing still? Who was the mayor of Cocoa Beach? If she didn't know, she imagined most people her age didn't either. Or care, for that matter.

Andre shrugged slowly. "I like the idea of an event, I just don't know about the whole grand thing with the mayor and the ribbon and..." His voice trailed off as he slid a cringing look over to Brock. "All of that."

Brock cleared his throat. "I'd prefer an event outside of the location, in case it's tough to attract a crowd. Somewhere the locals are gathered already."

He was right. They needed to get the word out at a

place that would have a ton of young, cool, Cocoa Beach locals—their target brewery market.

"Yeah, I could see that," Nina said, thinking. "A party or a fair or a festival..."

Or a...*surf contest*.

Not just any surf contest, the Ron Jon Invitational, AKA Cocoa Beach's biggest event of the year, with tons of booths and stations and brands.

Of course! They should set up at the Invitational! The timing would work out perfectly with their grand opening, and most of the crowd at a surf contest is young and cool and craft beer drinking.

Not to mention, Taylor had a direct relationship with one of the most famous professional surfers who'd be competing at the Invitational, and something told her he'd be willing to do her any kind of favor while he was in town.

She had to remind herself that she was an administrator. She was here to take notes, not to blurt out an idea.

But...this could really help. Worst case, it got shot down, but whatever. The worst anyone could say was no. Or "Be quiet, you're not on the creative team."

This was too good of an idea to stay quiet.

Taylor took a deep breath, lifted her chin, and held up her hand. "I have an idea."

All heads at the table turned to look at her, some faces confused, some surprised, some...annoyed.

"Taylor," John said cheerfully, gesturing toward her. "Absolutely, go ahead."

Oh, she loved her Uncle John.

"Okay, well…" She moved her laptop aside and focused her attention right on Brock and Andre. "What if you guys set up a booth for Blackhawk Brewing at the Ron Jon Invitational in August? It's the largest surf festival on the east coast and attracts a younger crowd from all over the state, even the country. It might be cutting it close, but I'm sure there are still some slots open for vendors, and that surf contest draws a bigger crowd than pretty much any other local event all year. Plus, a lot of surf fans fit right into your target demographic."

"A surf contest?" Andre lit up at the idea, bringing Taylor a rush of relief and joy. "That would be awesome!"

Brock nodded in agreement, smiling at her. "Totally fits the Florida vibes we're going for."

"Taylor, that's…" John laughed softly. "That's a great thought, and the Invitational would be an awesome start for this brewery. But, just keeping it realistic, there's a ton of competition for sponsorship or an event at the RJI, and Blackhawk doesn't have any brand recognition in the area."

"It's true," Andre admitted. "No one's heard of us here."

"I'm worried…" John pressed his lips together. "The cost of entering the Invitational as a vendor might not be worth it if the booth doesn't get enough attention, you know?"

"We'd need a draw," Brock added. "A major draw, because otherwise, you guys are right. People would walk right past Blackhawk to go to vendors that are more known and recognizable in the area."

Taylor sucked in a breath, knowing this was a card that most definitely had to be played right now. She couldn't keep herself from leaning to the very edge of the chair she was on and smiling. "What if...I could get you a draw?"

Andre frowned, puzzled. "What do you mean?"

Everyone at the table looked at her, and she could feel her heart kick up in her chest.

"What if I could get you one of the top professional surfers competing at the Invitational to come to the booth, sign autographs, give out beer, take pictures with customers...all of that. You could even put his face on T-shirts. It would create an instant Floridian association with the brand that you guys want, and people would be lining up at your booth."

Brock laughed and shook his head. "Uh, yeah, that would obviously be, like, freaking incredible, but I don't think it's in our budget to pay a pro surfer for something like that."

"Sadly, he's right." Andre lifted a shoulder. "Star athletes are not cheap, and as fantastic as that would be, we probably just couldn't swing it."

"What if..." Taylor straightened her shoulders. "What if we could get Kai Leilani?"

"Oh, the Hawaiian guy?" Melissa asked. "He's an amazing surfer. Also cute, so the ladies would line up."

"He's high profile," Tommy added with an arched brow. "And probably comes at a very high cost."

"Taylor, I absolutely love your spirit here," John said kindly. "But budgets are unfortunately always going to be a limiting factor."

"Um, actually," she said, confidence rising as she spoke, "I'm fairly confident that I can get Kai to do it for free."

The room burst with gasps and laughs of disbelief.

"Wait..." Andre stood up now, visible excitement on his face. "Are you messing with us?"

"You better not be messing with us," Brock added, joining him.

"I'm not, I promise." Taylor looked back and forth between the two men, who were now staring at her like she held the keys to a treasure chest.

And, well, she kinda did.

"He's a friend of mine," she explained, her mind flashing to the kisses on the beach, the early mornings spent laughing and walking along the sand with Kai Leilani. "He'll do it for me, as a favor. I know he will."

"Holy crap!" Andre looked around the room, where everyone's expressions were shocked and surprised and happy. "Seriously?"

"Yeah, a hundred percent." Taylor smiled. "I'll call him tonight."

"Hell. Yes." Brock and Andre both gave Taylor high-fives.

"Keep us posted." Andre pointed a finger at her.

"I will, I promise. I'll text you guys as soon as I talk to Kai."

"This is sweet." Andre gathered up his stuff and

thanked everyone in the conference room, while Taylor tried to keep herself from physically floating away in the excitement. "I think we got ourselves a plan."

"We absolutely do." John stood up and shook both the men's hands, sliding Taylor a quick little look of approval. "We'll be in touch."

They said goodbye to the rest of the team and waved at Taylor one more time.

"Thanks, man." Andre headed out the door, turning to look over his shoulder one last time, and pointed right at Taylor. "Whatever you're paying this girl, she deserves a raise."

Taylor laughed and waved off the comment.

John looked proud as he walked over to her to give her a pat on the shoulder. "I'm impressed, Taylor, really. Maybe you don't belong at the front desk."

She swallowed, watching everyone file out of the room and go back to work, suddenly feeling a surge of hope and excitement.

Maybe she didn't belong at the front desk. Or maybe she just lucked out because she happened to know the exact right person to blow this client's expectations out of the water.

Either way, she was riding a high. From the thrill of the meeting, of course, not the fact that she had an excuse to call Kai the second she got home.

Chapter Twelve

Imani

"Look at you, working woman." Erica shimmied her shoulders and gave a friendly grin as she handed Imani a laminated *Kennedy Space Center Press Pass* badge.

Imani sucked in a breath, glancing around Erica's top floor office with low-key giddiness and anticipation. She was back, baby.

She had arrived at the Space Center bright and early, knowing it was the perfect place to start for a feature blog on the Space Coast. After the editors at *TravelBee* saw her resume, they were...okay, be real. They were blown away.

Mark Bennett, the editor-in-chief, basically told her to do absolutely whatever she wanted with her articles, and that they fully trusted someone with her credentials and qualifications to write some masterful pieces.

And Imani knew they were right, but wow. She was seriously out of practice. Today was her first day of research, and she was ready to dive back in. It had to be like riding a bike, right?

"It feels good, you know?" Imani nodded, glancing around, getting her press sea legs. "I'm happy to be here.

A little guilty and worrying about my kids every passing second but...happy." She gave an easy laugh. "I have two and a half hours before I have to go pick up Ellen and Liam from camp, so I fully intend to milk every minute of that on this project."

"I'm proud of you for listening to your heart." Erica placed a hand on Imani's arm. "If anyone understands being called to work, it's me."

"Thank you, Erica. And thank you for getting me this press pass." She fluttered the badge.

"I'm just glad you decided to start at the Space Center," Erica said. "It certainly is a claim to fame for the area, and I'm sure you'll do it justice when you write about it."

"I hope I will. I'm definitely going to be a little rusty on the writing front, but the research was always my favorite part, anyway."

Her sister-in-law opened her arms for another hug. "Well, research away, girl. The Kennedy Space Center is your oyster. And you know where to find me if you need anything."

"Where should I start?" Imani looked out the tall windows of Erica's office, eyeing the massive Vehicle Assembly Building and the view of the launchpad. Holy crap, that was cool.

"Honestly? My favorite part of the Space Center is the Space Mirror Memorial," Erica said. "It doesn't get as much attention as some of the more famous sights, like the rocket garden and the space shuttles you can tour, but the Memorial is a testament to anyone who has given their life for space exploration. It's profound and emotional. I think you should include it in your article."

"I would love to," Imani replied, giving Erica another quick hug. "Love you. I really appreciate this."

"You just have fun, Imani. You're back in the game and you should enjoy the experience."

But...could she? Could Imani really trot around the Space Center making notes for an article, asking questions, taking pictures, living her work life? Did it make her a less-than-stellar mother to be happier here than at home, making dinner and waiting for the kids to get back from camp?

No. It did not. She could do this for herself. It was a small freelance project, and she had every right to work, as much as John did.

"Thanks, Erica." She headed out of the office, into the elevator, and down to the ground floor. Armed with an iPad, a camera, and the voice memo recording app ready to take notes on her phone, Imani was ready.

She strutted through the center, the badge hanging around her neck, reminding her of all those days of her past. The days she spent hopping on ferries and trains and planes, interviewing locals, business owners, people from all walks of life and all places around the world.

She had been important, successful. She had been so deeply fulfilled.

And for a long time, Imani thought motherhood was giving her that same kind of fulfillment. And maybe it was, but she needed this now.

She spotted a sign for the Space Mirror Memorial

that pointed an arrow to the other side of the complex, and she decided to take her sister-in-law's advice and start there.

The hot summer sun beat down on her as she headed down the path, and some groups of tourists took pictures and pointed at the launchpad.

Imani tried to wipe the gleeful smile off her face, but it was nearly impossible as she walked around the building and found a metal gate surrounding a tall, wide mirrored wall.

Created by large panels of solid glass that reflected the sky—of course—the massive black stone wall stood like a testament to bravery and hope. As Imani stepped closer, her breath was taken away and a wave of emotion hit her like an unexpected truck.

"Oh," she whispered to herself, holding a hand to her mouth as she stared straight up at the glass wall and her eyes started scanning it.

Names. There were names all over it, lit up by the sun and each one illuminated from behind the wall.

Her gaze dropped down to the engraved plaque in front of the fence.

NASA's twenty-four fallen heroes are honored at this monument to commemorate astronauts who gave their lives for the pursuit of knowledge beyond Earth.

Imani took in a shuddering breath, and closed her eyes for a moment to pay respect to astronauts.

Erica was right, this was powerful. And as fascinating as the launchpad, VAB, rocket garden, and full indoor museum and explorations center were, this memorial stirred something inside of her.

Imani quickly whipped out her iPad and started typing out notes.

"Standing in front of this sacred ground, I suddenly became overwhelmed with a heavy sense of melancholy, aching for the lives of people I'd never even met. The Memorial also elicits a sense of hope, somehow, a sense of achievement and honor for those who made the ultimate sacrifice.

"The Space Mirror Memorial reflects the light of the sun, creating an almost heavenly glow around the names of the honored astronauts. This monument is a must-see for anyone who longs to feel a powerful new kind of attachment and understanding for the magnificence of the Space Center."

Finally, her fingers stopped flying across the glass screen, and she clicked the lock button on her iPad, feeling like she could sit down and write this piece right now, she was so inspired. And she hadn't even seen the rockets yet.

With a bounce in her step, she headed back toward the main area to take a look around the Vehicle Assembly Building and hopefully get some pictures and, if she was lucky, an interview.

Imani felt charged—her body was buzzing with an untouchable confidence that seemed to radiate off of her skin.

This was going to be a fantastic piece, and she was certain she could showcase a unique and fresh angle while describing the special, rare, and wonderful beauty of Florida's Space Coast.

Her braids bounced around her shoulders, which were held high as she walked to the Vehicle Assembly Building, flashing her badge to the security guard, who nodded and gestured for her to walk right in.

Oh, yeah. Imani was back. Imani was *so* back.

Designed to assemble the spacecrafts that her brilliant sister-in-law helped design, the VAB was over five hundred feet tall, and only one story. Standing in this massive, open room with the highest ceiling she'd ever seen, Imani looked straight up, all the way to the top.

"Wow," she whispered.

Imani had been to the Space Center before, but never with an eye for writing research. She'd never fully immersed herself in it, or let herself be so inspired by the science and technology required to take mankind into space. She ached to get that across in her writing.

The place was bustling with engineers, mechanics, tech people, workers, and...

Whoa, what? Was that an *astronaut?*

Imani spotted a man in a white space suit, holding a helmet tucked underneath his arm, talking to a small group of tourists. He was maybe mid-thirties, good-looking, and doing the PR thing today, gladhanding with the guests.

She *had* to interview him.

"Excuse me!" Imani waved a hand and gave a smile to the man, rushing over to get his attention as he headed out of the VAB. "Hi, there."

"Hello, ma'am. You want a picture?"

"Yes, but I'd also like to do a very quick interview." She held up the press pass. "I'm a travel writer doing a feature on Florida's Space Coast. I was just wondering if I could maybe ask you a couple of quick questions?"

The guy ran a hand through his hair and gave a handsome smile. "Sure, I got a minute."

"You *are* an astronaut, right?"

"Nah, I just play one in the movies."

She drew back. "Wait, seriously?"

"I'm kidding." His dark gaze glimmered. "I'm an astronaut."

"Do you always walk around in a space suit?"

He laughed heartily. "Only when I'm on duty to talk to tourists. Once every six weeks. Oh, and when I go into space, which is rare but fun."

Imani smiled and offered her hand for a shake. "Imani Sweeney, by the way. I'm with *TravelBee*."

"Captain Clay Hanson. Pleased to meet you, Ms. Sweeney."

"Okay, then." She pulled out her iPad to jot down some notes, the familiar zing of this job flying up her spine. "Captain, what was your most recent mission with NASA?"

"I flew with the *Raven* 7, about eighteen months ago."

"Really? My sister-in-law actually engineered that launch."

"Your sister-in-law?"

"Yes, Erica Sweeney-Armstrong. She's heading up

the engineering team for the Eagle launch now. She's a rocket scientist." She laughed. "Which probably doesn't impress you."

"On the contrary. Without those people doing their jobs, I couldn't do mine." He gave a sweet smile that probably brought tourists—female tourists, anyway—to their knees.

"So, anyway, I just wanted to ask you a little bit about—"

Was that her phone? It was buzzing in her pocket with an incoming call. Whatever it was, it would have to wait.

"Everything okay?" Clay asked with a tip his head.

"Yeah, sorry, it's just..." She dug through her purse and silenced the call without even looking at the name. This moment was too important. She'd wanted this for too long to step away from it for a phone call. "Nothing. I know you joked about it being an every-six-weeks duty, but how do you feel about meeting tourists, and what would you want to say to get more people here?"

It was, after all, a travel article.

"I absolutely love meeting people and letting them know that astronauts are just like them."

"Only fearless and brilliant."

Clay laughed. "Oh, sure. Put that in your article. But also add this: we love to talk to the kids. Nothing is better than seeing that light in their eyes and knowing you might have planted the seed for a lifelong dream." He broke into a wide smile. "It's the best part of the job."

Seriously? Her phone was buzzing again?

Of course, Imani's mind instantly flew to an emergency of some sort, but she quickly reminded herself that that was extremely unlikely, and everything was probably fine, and *dang it,* she was allowed to have one day for herself.

"Sounds like someone's trying to reach you," Clay teased, nodding his head toward her loudly vibrating purse.

She shook her head. "I'm sure it's nothing. I'm sorry."

"You positive?"

"Yes, it's fine. Anyway, the tourists. The kids, it's fun! Is that mostly what you—"

There it was again, buzzing over and over again, just enough to let Imani know for a fact that, whatever this was, she couldn't ignore it any longer.

"I'm so sorry, Captain." She held up a finger and fished the phone out of her purse. "I'm sorry, I really appreciate your time, I just—"

Her eyes fell to the name on the screen. John.

Why on Earth was he blowing her phone up like this? He knew where she was. He knew she was working. He knew how important today was for her.

"I'm sorry, I...I have to take this." She stepped away and pressed the phone to her ear. "Hey, what's up? I'm in the middle of interviewing an astronaut at the space center!"

"Imani, where have you been?" He sounded...mad? That was rare for her steady and calm husband.

"I just told you, I'm working." She pushed her hair

back and pressed the phone to her ear. "What's going on?"

"Ellen's camp said they tried calling you three times."

Her heart flipped. "Is she okay?"

"She's fine, but apparently she's sick or has a stomachache or something and wants to go home. I'm packed with meetings all day. I need you to get her."

And suddenly, Imani's rocket launch fantasy came crashing back to Earth.

She wasn't a career woman. She was the mother of three kids who could need her at any given moment. Who was she trying to kid? She couldn't just go off and be the badass travel writer she used to be.

"I'll go, I'll go," she promised John. "No worries."

He shouldn't worry, because the kids would stay at the top of her priority list, and that meant today was over. Ellen was sick, and Imani had to go be a mom.

Trying to swallow the resentment and frustration, she quickly said goodbye to Captain Hanson and headed back up to Erica's office to return the press pass.

Imani did not want to hold any bitterness in her heart, but seriously? She wanted one day. One little freelance article. That was it.

"Hey, thanks again." Imani knocked softly on Erica's office door and handed her the badge.

"You're done already?" Erica's eyes widened. "Dang, girl, you're quick."

"No, actually, I'm not done," Imani said on a sigh. "But I have to go."

"What? Why?"

She pressed her lips together and shrugged. "Ellen has a stomachache and has to be picked up from camp."

"Oh. I'm sorry, hon."

Imani shook her head. "It's fine. I just wish I could go more than a literal hour without being needed as a mom." She laughed dryly. "Too much to ask, I guess."

Erica's eyes darkened for a second and she glanced away. "I hate to use the word jealous, but...I'd give anything for Jada to call and say she *needs* me."

Imani paused for a moment, perspective hitting her like a train. "Oh, Erica. I'm sorry."

"No, don't be, please." She waved a hand and smiled. "I totally understand how you feel."

"Jada is going to come around, I know she is." Imani placed a hand on Erica's arm and gave it a squeeze. "Give it time. You should bring her here!"

"To work?" Erica angled her head.

"Yes!" Imani laughed. "You work in a really cool place, she'd have a blast. Plus, it would probably help her feel a little closer to you to see what you do. She'll think it's awesome."

"Really?" Erica asked softly. "You think so?"

"Definitely."

"Okay, I'll do that." She nodded brightly. "Love you, girl. Give Ellen a kiss from me. Hope her stomachache is better."

Imani gave a wave. "Will do."

As she headed down to the ground level and walked back out to her car, she wondered whether it would be possible to "have it all," as the magazines used to say.

Probably not.

Could she really not have this life anymore? Was it going to be this impossible to do both? Lots of families had two parents working. She wasn't asking for a lot.

Maybe she could find a balance. She'd have to. She was not ready or willing to give this up again.

Chapter Thirteen

Erica

A Take Your Daughter To Work Day sounded like a brilliant and fun way to possibly connect with Jada on some level. Erica had felt like she'd made progress, tiny bits of progress, but she was still waiting for that "mom" feeling.

She ached to be needed and wanted and loved by this girl, but could not seem to find that spark, that *bond* that would make them feel like family.

And she knew it took time—enough people had been reminding her on a literal daily basis to be patient—but Erica was not one to sit around and wait. She was, and always had been, one to take action, take initiative, and make it happen.

So today, she was determined to have a breakthrough with Jada, to feel like a real-life mother-daughter pair by bringing her to work for the day.

She had plans, of course. She was going to show Jada some basic math on her engineering CAD/CAM platform, conveniently weaving in education. Then, they were going to walk around the Space Center, because what kid didn't love that?

And later, Erica was going to introduce Jada to her

coworkers and teammates...as her daughter. Because that's what she was. And it was about time they both started acting like it.

The day was flawlessly formulated to create a new closeness between them, Erica was certain.

"So, this is my office." Erica gestured around at her top-floor, all glass, head engineer workspace.

Jada slowly walked around, running her hand across the huge desk right in the middle of the room. She looked bewildered by the three sleek, expensive computer monitors all running highly advanced drawing and engineering software.

"And look." Erica walked over to the side of the room, pointing her finger out the window. "You can see the launchpad from here. 39A."

"Really?"

Okay, that got some attention.

"Yeah, check it out. There's even a rocket on it right now, because this is an active launchpad used by SpaceX." Erica crouched down to meet Jada's eye level, and they looked side by side through the glass at the launch complex, where the tall, white Falcon towered above the ground, ready to head to outer space.

"Can we see it fly?"

"This one, the Falcon 9 SES-24, is going up in two days, which is why it's already in position. I bet I can get us some front-row seats for the launch, if you want."

"Cool." Jada wandered back around the big office, studying everything closely and carefully, like she was in a museum full of glass.

"So, this is pretty much it. Pretty nice, huh?" Erica asked, hoping to spark some sort of newfound connection or interest in Jada.

But she just nodded. "Yeah."

Pulling teeth, that's how it felt. Like she was watching someone else's kid.

"Come over here." She patted the extra chair she brought in to sit right next to hers at the big desk.

Jada walked over and sat in the seat, curling her slender legs up underneath her.

"Okay, so this is actually pretty neat. Do you want to see how we design rockets and their engines?"

Jada shrugged, her eyes flashing.

"I promise it's cool." Erica tapped on the keyboard and fiddled with the screen, pulling up a big, empty CAM grid where she could input specs and blueprints to create a rough model of an engine.

Jada just stared at the screen.

"As we come up with the different formulas and specifications, we put them in, and this software turns it into the plans for a real-life rocket." She wiggled her brows and gave Jada a friendly nudge. "Neat, huh?"

"I guess." Jada looked at her, her blank expression appearing like she couldn't care less about the building information modeling system.

"We can even do math, too," she said cheerfully, pulling up the code box. "Okay, so if I have a base wall that's three hundred feet tall, and eighty feet long..." Erica quickly typed in those numbers. "How do you think we could find area of that?"

Jada huffed out a sigh. "I don't know."

"Okay. We can try something else."

Erica could feel herself getting anxious and frustrated, but she knew she had to push past it. Jada was going to have a fun day, darn it.

"Okay," Jada said on a breath.

"Want to know something crazy? A rocket engine needs eleven thousand pounds of fuel per second!"

"Wow." Jada chewed her lip. "That's a lot."

"It's a ton. That's two million times the rate that fuel is burned by a car. So, a gallon of rocket fuel costs about a dollar and sixty cents. Based on that, we could calculate how much money per second it costs to fly a rocket. You want to?"

"Uh, no, not really." Jada looked around the room, twisting her lips.

Erica leveled her gaze, accepting the reality in front of her that was getting increasingly harder to deny. "You're not interested in engineering and math, are you?"

She looked up at Erica, giving her an apologetic shrug. "No."

"Noted." Erica stood up suddenly and grabbed her purse, swinging it over her shoulder. "It's definitely not for everyone."

And the whole "getting ready for school in the fall" thing was an issue Erica was just going to have to tackle another day.

She'd just earn Jada's love and trust first, and then help her with academics. It seemed like a good enough strategy, although Step One was proving to be harder than designing a darn rocket.

"I'm really bad at math," Jada admitted, as shy and closed off as ever. "I kinda hate it."

Erica let out a breath, her heart tugging with sympathy for this girl, the constant reminder that she was never given a real chance.

"No one hates math. Some people just can't see its beauty."

Jada blinked at Erica with wide eyes and...was that a hint of sassiness in her expression? "Actually, a lot of people hate it. Like me. And I think Sam does, too."

Erica couldn't help but laugh. "They just don't understand it. You can't hate math, it's deeply integrated into the entire world around us. Sam just thinks she hates math, but she doesn't realize how important and wonderful it is."

Jada just crossed her arms and looked Erica right in the eyes. "Well, I hate it."

Maybe diving right into the highly advanced computer-aided design software was a little ambitious.

"Gotcha. So let's go walk around." Erica gestured toward the door. "The Space Center has tons of things to do. There're attractions and games and rockets and all kinds of cool activities."

"Okay." Jada got up and followed Erica out of the office.

They headed down the elevator and through the lobby of the building. The whole time, Erica filled the air with chatter about the rockets and the old space shuttles and how she felt the first time she walked into this place.

She knew Jada didn't care, but...maybe she would eventually. Or maybe she cared and was too afraid to show it.

"We can walk through the rocket garden," Erica mused, leading her through the gateway into the main tourist areas of Kennedy. "And then inside, there's all kinds of stuff. Games, simulations, and oh! You can even sit inside the Mercury Capsule. The real one! Would you like that?"

"Sure." Jada seemed to perk up a bit at this, and Erica figured she might be onto something with the traditional Kennedy tourist route.

After all, it was a third grade field trip to this very place that sparked her initial fascination with outer space. Maybe it could do the same for Jada.

"Yikes, busy day, huh?" Erica craned her neck to look through a long, long line of visitors waiting to enter the center.

Jada recoiled a little, glancing around nervously.

"Well, good thing we don't have to wait in line." Erica lifted a shoulder and smiled, taking Jada's hand and weaving through the crowd to get to the front.

She was going to love this.

Jada squeezed Erica's hand tightly, her body language looking tense and worried as Erica guided her through the hordes of summer tourists filling up the main outdoor areas of the Space Center.

It would be better once they got inside.

"Come here." She ushered Jada to the entrance, showed her ID badge to the employee working the door, and walked right inside. "You good?"

"Um..." Jada nodded. "Yeah."

"Okay. That air conditioning feels nice, wow. It's a million degrees outside!" Erica fanned herself and looked around. "Where do you think we should start?"

Jada looked around, her big brown eyes darting from one corner to another.

Large groups of people filled the space—snapping pictures, rushing to the attractions, filling the spaces in between with lines and crowds and business.

"It's slammed today, but nothing we can't manage, right?"

Jada didn't say anything, but her eyes grew even wider and her expression grew more fearful than usual.

"Come over here. There's an antigravity simulator." Erica waved a hand and led Jada down the hall through the main corridor. "It shows you what it feels like to be up in outer space! That's pretty cool, right?"

Jada looked like she was breathing a bit heavily, and didn't say a word as she followed Erica.

"Jada, sweetie, what's wrong?" Erica leaned down and lowered her head to study Jada's worried face.

She just shook her head. "Nothing," she said, voice barely above a whisper.

Didn't seem like nothing, but Erica knew she still needed to keep the day going and follow through on the plans.

"Okay, if you're sure," she said hesitantly. "Let's go this way."

As Erica guided Jada into another section, a large crowd of nearly thirty kids—a summer camp, she guessed —rushed toward them in a big group.

They were rambunctious and wild and loud, and Jada immediately darted away and hid herself by pressing up against the wall, visibly upset.

"Oh, my gosh, crazy kids." Erica stepped over to her. "It's packed in here, I know."

Jada nodded frantically.

She swallowed and tried to get a better look at Jada's face. "You're not really loving this either, are you?"

Jada shook her head rapidly. "There's a lot of people and...I don't like big crowds like this." She wiped her hair out of her face and stared up at Erica.

Good heavens, she was freaking out. "All right, let's get out of here." She put her arm around Jada and guided her through the crowd, feeling protective and confused and worried about the little girl.

"You okay?" she asked when they escaped the throngs of people.

Jada nodded, but her expression was pained and that kind of broke Erica's heart. Yes, she wanted so badly for Jada to love this place like she did, but...who was she trying to kid? Jada was not integrated into her life, not at all.

And the last thing she wanted to do was upset Jada.

"Okay, we'll just get back to my office," she said

brightly. "Maybe we can go back on a day when it's not so slammed."

"Yeah, I think that would be better." Jada walked quietly next to her as they headed back up the elevator to Erica's office. "I'm sorry," she muttered softly.

"Huh?" Erica turned quickly to the side, not sure if she'd just heard that correctly.

"Sorry. For being scared. I just don't like when there's that many people. It just makes me all freaked out." Jada walked back over to the chair next to Erica's and sat down in it.

A new ray of hope rose in her chest as Erica rushed over and sat down next to her, tilting her chin to level her gaze with Jada's. "Oh, Jada, it's okay. You don't have to say sorry. Crowds can be overwhelming. All of this, to be honest, can be overwhelming."

"I've never..." She toyed with her shoelace. "Been anywhere like that before."

Erica's eyes fluttered shut as she leaned back in her desk chair. "I keep forgetting that."

Maybe one day Jada would tell Erica more about her past. Maybe Erica could help her heal. That was the hope, anyway.

"You're not really much of an extrovert, are you?" Erica asked her, with a hint of playful lightness in her voice.

Jada stared at her. "I don't know what that is."

"An extrovert is someone who really likes being around other people. Someone who likes big parties, and making new friends, and loves doing social things. The opposite is an introvert, which is someone who prefers to be alone or just with a few close loved ones. Introverts feel better when they can recharge by themselves, and extroverts feel better being with other people."

"I think..." Jada continued messing with the shoelace. "I think I'm the inter...whatever. I'm that one, I think."

Erica smiled. "I think that's probably true."

"Is that bad?" Jada asked, worry in her eyes.

"Not at all," Erica answered quickly. "You want to know something about me?"

"What?"

"I'm actually kind of an introvert myself."

Jada furrowed her brows, looking skeptical. "You are?"

"Oh, yeah. I sit in this office and do nerdy math on my computer all day long. And if it were up to me? I'd hardly want to interact with anyone. I have to, because it takes more than just one person to design rockets, and now I'm used to working with others, and I even enjoy it. But believe me, there is nothing wrong with wanting to be alone. Or with a few people you love. You know?"

"Yeah." Jada nodded, seeming to understand.

"So, Miss Self-Proclaimed Introvert, I'm guessing going out there and meeting all of my coworkers is not exactly high on your wishlist for today, is it?"

Jada shook her head, giving a half-smile. "Um, not really. I'm sorry."

"No, it's completely okay. Maybe instead, we can—"

Suddenly, the phone on her desk rang. "One sec,

hold on." She held the phone to her ear and shot Jada a smile. "This is Erica."

"Hey, it's Roger. We need you in the main conference room. There's a dispute about the characteristic velocity needed for the orbital transfer on the Eagle plans."

That again? Seriously?

"Roger, I...I said I was in my office today, not available for meetings. I have my...daughter with me."

"Erica, we're launching a manned rocket to Mars here. We need you in the main conference room. Now."

On a defeated sigh, Erica put the phone back on the hook. "Listen, I have to go deal with something. See? People. They're the worst, aren't they?"

Jada giggled softly.

"I'll be back in half an hour, tops. Oh! Here." She turned to face one of the computer monitors and clicked on a couple of things, pulling up a file. "There are some games on this computer, actually. They're educational, but I don't know."

Jada made a face that was entirely less than thrilled.

"I'm sorry. I'll be right back, I promise."

Erica grabbed her tablet and laptop and headed out of the office to the main conference room.

While she sat around the table with all the other engineers on the project and Roger, the project manager, her mind was doing orbits of its own.

Did Jada feel abandoned, in that office all alone? Maybe this whole day was a lost cause. How was it possible that Erica couldn't find one single thing to connect with her on? A common interest, a mutual passion...anything that could bond them together?

She knew she was supposed to be patient. She recognized that. But she needed to see some evidence that it was all going to be worth it. She needed to know that, at the end of this, she'd have a daughter.

A daughter who *needed* her.

"Erica?" Roger pressed, sounding irritated and impatient. "Your thoughts? Have you doublechecked the calculations of the laminar flow?"

Oh, crap.

She cleared her throat and quickly scanned the diagram and formulas and numbers on the projector screen, her brain racking over laminar flow. Yes, she had calculated it multiple times.

"Uh, yes, I...I did, but I can check it again."

"Please do. And get back to me with it," Roger ordered, his narrow gaze lingering on her as she breathed out a microscopic sigh of relief.

The meeting dragged on for forty-five more endless minutes spent going over numbers and plans that Erica could have analyzed and calculated and perfected in a third of the time, had she just been by herself in her office.

Whatever. She'd get to that later. As wrong as this was for an aerospace engineer at NASA, rocket science just wasn't her first priority right now.

When the meeting finally broke, she beelined down the hall to get back to her office.

Would Jada be mad, having been left alone? She

might feel ignored. That was the last thing Erica wanted. She wanted today to be special and memorable...a big bonding experience for them to share. She thought this day could bring them closer to that intangible connection, but all it had brought so far was...

Disappointment.

Erica tamped down the harsh reality and swallowed the lump in her throat as she headed back into the office, braced for Jada to be angry or hurt or back to total silence.

But what she walked into was a total surprise.

"Oh." Erica blinked, her eyes falling to Jada, relief washing over her as soon as she saw the girl.

Jada was on the small gray loveseat in the corner of the office by the window. Laying flat on her stomach with her feet kicking in the air, she looked calm and relaxed and...happy.

As Erica inched closer, she saw that Jada was holding a pencil in her right hand, and had a notebook of graph paper in front of her.

She was sketching.

Erica's mind instantly flashed back to the first night Jada spent at her house. She had a notebook. She had been drawing that morning when Erica came in. Having been so preoccupied with the initial shock and fear and overwhelming craziness of it all, she hadn't even noticed.

"Oh, hi." Jada whipped around quickly. "I'm sorry. I found this notebook and it didn't look like anyone used it, since you do all your stuff on the computer. But I only used one page. And I can tear it out," she added quickly.

Why was Jada always so afraid of getting in trouble?

Erica wouldn't care if she spraypainted the walls, for crying out loud, as long as she had a smile on her face.

"That's completely fine." Erica assured her, walking over to join Jada on the loveseat. "And you're totally right, I can't remember the last time I did any of my work on paper. So, the notebook's all yours."

"Oh, okay. Cool. I like the paper." Jada nodded, pushing some hair away as a half-smile pulled at her delicate face. "I was worried I stole something by accident."

Erica angled her head, her eyes skimming the notebook that Jada was covering with her arms. "Can I see what you drew?" she asked.

"Oh, sure." Jada shrugged and moved aside from the paper. "It's stupid. It's not even good. I've drawn other pictures that are way better. This one is just..."

"Jada..." Erica felt an unexpected twist of emotion in her gut as her throat thickened.

Jada had sketched Launchpad 39A, complete with the SpaceX Falcon 9, its boosters, and a stunningly accurate replica of the control tower. The drawing was remarkably detailed, thin pencil lines sketching out a beautiful scene of the view from Erica's office window.

Jada had added her own touch, too, filling the sky behind the rocket with big, beautiful flowers and vines and leaves, shading in the petals and darkening the outlines.

The drawing was alive—vibrant and intricate and beautiful.

Erica drew back, looking at Jada in an entirely new

light, as if yet another piece of her endless puzzle had
been unlocked.

Jada was *talented*. Artistic. Creative. She had nothing
but a pencil and a view and she made something that
nearly brought Erica to tears.

"This is absolutely beautiful," she said on a soft
laugh, shaking her head as she continued to admire the
drawing. "I mean...I had no idea you were so artistic."

Jada looked up at her, frowning. "You really think it's
good? I'm really not the best at drawing, I just love it."

"I beg to differ." Erica chuckled and held up the notebook, smiling at it. "You're certainly the best I've ever seen."

"Really?" Her eyes widened as her brows raised up,
and suddenly Erica got the feeling that this girl had never
been told how amazing she was.

No wonder she hated math—she was right-brained
through and through. And she was fantastic.

"Really." Erica smiled, handing the notebook back to
her. "Can I keep it?"

"This?" Jada tapped the sketch, looking stunned and
confused. "You want this?"

Erica nodded with assurance. "Can you gently tear it
out?"

"Um, okay." Jada softly tugged at the edge of the
graph paper, pulling the page with her drawing out of the
notebook and handing it to Erica.

"Thank you." Erica took the paper and walked over
to the big wall behind her desk.

On the wall were two framed degrees—undergrad

and grad school—and a picture of her and Will on their wedding day.

Erica snapped a piece of Scotch tape off of the dispenser on her desk, held Jada's drawing against the wall, and taped it down.

She stepped back, placing her hands on her hips and smiling at it. "There. I love it."

"You want *that*...on your wall?" Jada arched a brow, that tiny bit of dormant sassiness coming through once again.

"Are you kidding? I love it. It reminds me of how passionate I am for my job, how beautiful and incredible it is. Plus, it'll always make me think of you. Jada, you have a gift. And I mean that."

A smile snuck across her face. "Thanks. Too bad they don't give good grades for drawing in school."

"Hey." Erica crouched down, meeting her gaze. "We'll worry about school later, okay?"

And she would. Because right now, Erica was more than happy to ride the high of finding out something new about her daughter. And not just anything—a passion. A hobby. A seriously amazing talent that humble little Jada had been hiding.

She liked to draw. And she was brilliant at it. And that was how she expressed herself. As Erica started putting these pieces together, she could feel a big, fat layer of the daunting Jada onion getting peeled back.

And nothing in the world felt better.

"Thanks for sharing this with me." Erica sat down on

the loveseat next to her. "I'm sorry today didn't really go as planned."

"That's okay." Jada tucked her knees to her chest and rested her chin on them. "I never got to draw a rocket before, so that was cool."

As Erica looked at the sweet, beautiful profile of this girl, she couldn't help but think of how wrong she'd been going about this whole thing.

She'd been trying to connect with Jada in ways that someone could have connected with her as an eleven-year-old. Academics, math, school, space stuff, games... but none of that was *Jada*.

Jada was entirely her own person, and Erica would just have to keep getting to know her, one small victory at a time.

"Jada." She turned to her. "Can I ask you something?"

Jada nodded. "Mm-hmm."

"Are you...happy here, living with us? Is this good for you? Are we...good?" She laughed a little at the silliness of the question, but she genuinely wanted to know what on Earth was going through that girl's mind so badly, it was worth asking.

Jada just stared at her, taken aback by the blunt question.

"It's okay if it's still all new and scary, I just..." She sighed. "I want you to love being with us, and eventually feel like a part of our family. I know it takes time, and I know you've been through a lot. I'm hoping you'll tell me more about your past as time goes on, because I'd love to know you even better. But I want you to take your time. I just want to be sure that you're...good. And this is going okay for you."

Jada thought for a long, long time, staring straight ahead. As the wheels of her brain turned round and round, Erica could feel her heartbeat kicking up.

Oh, man. She was going to say no. She was going to say she misses her mom and can't stand it here and she'll never feel like a part of the family.

Erica shut her eyes for a second and braced for that disappointing but understandable response.

"Well..." Jada said, twisting one of her dark curls in between her fingers. "No one's ever put any of my drawings on the wall before."

"Oh..." Erica tipped her head, not fully knowing how to interpret that.

Jada turned suddenly, looking right at her. For the first time since Erica had met her, all of her hair was completely out of her face, and her bright eyes and sweet smile were finally completely visible.

"I can see you're trying really hard, and you want me to have fun and be happy," Jada said softly, sounding a heck of a lot older than she was. "And I'm...getting there. I promise. Thank you."

"Of course." Erica pressed her hand to her chest. "I just want you to feel at home and get comfortable here."

"I know it doesn't really seem like it but...I'm trying, too. I just get kind of scared sometimes, and..." Her voice trailed off. "I don't know if I miss my mom or if I hate her. My real mom, I mean."

Erica had no idea how to tackle the "real mom" issue, but she hoped that with time Jada would heal and trust and love Erica like, well, a real mom. "Oh, sweetie, I know. It's okay. You have every right to feel all of those things, and you know you can always talk to me about it, even if it's hard." Tears stung behind Erica's eyes, and she reached out for Jada's hand, giving it a squeeze. "We have our whole lives to figure this out. Together."

Her eyes darkened for a second like she might not fully believe that, but she didn't snatch her hand away from Erica's touch.

"Okay." She smiled, meeting Erica's gaze with a sparkle in her expression that maybe somewhat resembled trust or closeness.

"So, we're good?"

Jada sighed and gave a fake eyeroll. "As long as you don't make me do any more math."

Erica rolled her eyes. "Honestly. Who doesn't love math?"

"Um, me."

They laughed and, wow, that felt so good.

Chapter Fourteen

Sam

As Sam strolled down the hallways of Surfside High School, she was flooded with nostalgia and flashbacks of her own days as a student there.

She could picture studying in the library at a table in the back—okay, not *studying* exactly, but desperately cramming for a test she'd forgot she had. Or coming in early in the morning for extra help from her Algebra teacher because...ew, algebra. Had she ever used that one time in her life? Never.

She could vividly remember walking down these halls, books in hand, laughing and chatting about football games and weekend plans with, well, the very woman who was standing beside her now, twenty-six years later.

"Thanks so much for coming with me, Annie." Sam smiled at Annie Hawthorne, who'd quickly become her closest pal in Cocoa Beach since they'd rekindled their long-lost friendship after two decades of distance.

In a sudden panic about being a single school parent for the first time since, well, ever, Sam had asked Annie to join her for the orientation at Ben's new high school, since it was their alma mater.

"Of course! Are you kidding?" Annie flashed those big eyes and bright smile, which Sam had seen next to her in these very hallways so many times before. "I'm just happy your brother let me sneak away from work for an afternoon."

Sam raised a sassy shoulder. "He does what I tell him."

Annie flipped some of that signature strawberry blond hair. "It's just fun being back here, isn't it?"

"It kind of is, actually." Sam laughed softly. "We had a blast in high school together."

"Oh, did we ever."

"The hours and hours and hours of math tutoring." Sam groaned and dropped her head back with laughter. "How did you put up with me?"

"Because you did my makeup for parties and introduced me to boys, remember?" Annie nudged her playfully. "It was a fair tradeoff."

"And yet, here we are." Sam gestured out in front of them at the long hallway lined with lockers and red and white tiles on the floor.

"I'm still completely single," Annie said. "And you're still completely bad at math."

"Also completely single," Sam reminded her. "Time is cruel, isn't it?"

"Hey." Annie smiled. "We may have both had our fair share of life beating us down, but

all of it led us here. To being like sisters again.

Walking these halls, laughing about the past. It's not all bad, you know?"

It certainly was not. And despite the heartbreak and betrayal Sam had endured these past several months, the light at the end of the tunnel was getting brighter by the day.

"Speaking of men..." Annie raised a brow. "And not the evil kind. I want to hear more about this smokin' hot furniture dude y'all are hiring to help with the inn! From what you told me at lunch, it sounds like he has the hots for you, lady."

"Oh, please." Sam waved a hand, feeling her cheeks blush. "Yes, super cute, but maybe just a flirty guy. I think. I mean, I don't know. I'm nowhere near ready to even think about the possibility of dating, but...I can't lie. The attention was nice. I couldn't even remember what it was like to feel young and cute like that."

"Heck, yeah, it was! You deserve it. You *are* young and cute. And, look, I know you're still grieving from the unspeakable behavior of He Who Shall Not Be Named, and I completely get that. But don't hide away forever, Sam. You're too much of a catch."

"Forty-three, waiting on a divorce, and living at home with my mom..." Sam fake-choked in her throat. "Truly a catch. Why are men not lined up to date me?"

Annie couldn't help but laugh. "Oh, please. Go easy on yourself, you're awesome. And who knows? Maybe this Ethan guy will be the one who gets you back out there."

Sam swallowed, knowing there was a very slim

chance of anything happening between her and the unexpectedly handsome furniture guy with the callused hands and messy blond hair.

But she couldn't deny that he had been very attractive. And he'd seemed interested. Maybe Annie was right. The world kind of felt like Sam's oyster right now, filled with newfound freedom and tons of possibilities.

"Okay." Sam looked down at her phone, scrolling through the teacher orientation schedule that Ben had sent her for today. "We met Mrs. Dawson for AP English Lit..."

"She was sweet," Annie added. "Not like that horrific lit teacher we had. What was her name?"

Sam looked up with wide eyes, gasping at the shared memory. "Oh my gosh, Mrs. Hitchinson. Oh, she was horrible."

"So unbelievably mean. Remember when she told me that my essay on *Moby Dick* sounded like it was written by a third grader?" Annie laughed and shook her head. "What did we call her? Witchinson?"

Sam cringed. "Pretty sure it was something worse than that."

Annie laughed. "Okay, what's next on Ben's schedule?"

"Ah, your favorite!" Sam smiled at her math whiz of a friend. "AP Calculus, Room 502."

"Aw, my old home away from home," Annie cooed, holding her hands to her chest as they headed down the hall.

"And my personal hell, but hopefully Ben will fare a bit better than I did."

"He will," Annie said. "And besides, between me the accountant and your sister the rocket scientist, he's got some tutors around, ready to help."

"Another generation of Sweeneys learning from the Annie Hawthorne Book of Calculus." Sam smiled and shook her head. "How poetic."

"It is, only Ben can't pay me in lip gloss and boy band posters like his mother did," she teased. "Which is the only form of currency I accept."

They both laughed as they found their way to the very familiar Room 502, swinging open the classroom door and heading inside.

"I'm getting PTSD already," Sam joked, eyeing the big poster of the dreaded unit circle filling up one of the side walls.

Annie gave a playful eyeroll. "Oh, come on. Math can be fun."

Sam slid a look to her friend. "Please don't ever use 'math' and 'fun' in the same sentence again."

"Personally, I think math and fun are actually synonymous." The unexpected, somewhat familiar male voice startled both women, making them whip around to look over their shoulders.

Sam blinked in surprise and confusion as she stared at the man standing in front of her and Annie.

Holy...what? It was...he was... "Wait a minute, I know you." She waved a finger and laughed softly. "Ethan Price? The carpenter? You're also the..."

"AP Calculus teacher." He laughed awkwardly.

Sam studied him for a second, taking in his significantly upgraded look. He'd traded out the old white T-shirt for a nice button-down and smooth khaki pants, and it appeared that he'd shaved since then. Somehow, he looked just as good as he had in the work clothes.

His *other* work clothes.

Oh, snap. He was *Ben's math teacher*? How was that for the universe having a good laugh?

"You never mentioned you're a teacher," she said.

"You never mentioned you're a mom," he replied with a half-smile, his face looking a little younger and less weathered with a clean shave.

Sam glanced at Annie, who looked considerably entertained by the bizarre coincidence, and Sam figured she'd picked up on the fact that he was, indeed, the *hot furniture dude*.

The awkward tension sent a warm wave crawling up Sam's cheeks, but she shook it off and looked right at Ethan, er, *Mr. Price.*

"What a small world," she said on a laugh.

"That it is." He glanced at her, something flashing for a brief second in his eyes.

Something that almost read as...disappointment? Well, who knew, maybe it was. Now that they'd both learned he was Sam's son's teacher, any more flirtation or butterflies or even whispers of attraction were completely and totally off limits.

Maybe she was a little disappointed, too. But it didn't matter. It wasn't like she really even knew the guy at all.

He just didn't strike her as a calculus teacher, that was for sure.

"Well, welcome to my class..." He gestured for them to take seats at some of the desks and join the few other parents who had made their way into the room.

"Thank you. Oh!" Sam held her hand out toward Annie. "I'm so rude. This is my dear friend, Annie. We actually went to school here together, a hundred years ago. Annie, this is Ethan Price, the..."

It didn't take more than a nanosecond of eye contact between the two women for them to both telepathically communicate exactly who he was.

Ethan reached out and shook her hand. "Nice to meet you, Annie."

As he turned to walk up to the front of the classroom and talk about whatever there was to talk about in a calculus orientation, Sam glared at Annie as they sat down at two adjacent desks.

"That's him," Sam mouthed with exaggeration.

Annie snorted. "Yeah, I gathered," she whispered back.

"He's Ben's *teacher*." Sam kept her voice low as Ethan greeted some of the other parents, shaking hands and talking to them with that charming smile.

"So?" Annie arched a bow. "He's cute." She mouthed the word, making Sam laugh and roll her eyes.

"Welcome, everyone." Ethan clasped his hands together, posed in typical male teacher wide stance, his eyes flickering to Sam. "This is AP Calculus, with juniors and seniors. I'm Mr. Price, and I'll have the pleasure of making your kids' lives miserable for the next nine and a half months."

As he gave his spiel about curriculum and teaching philosophy and early morning homework help, Sam leaned back in the hard plastic chair and looked at him.

She watched this man who came to the inn, sized up the ten-thousand-dollar grandfather clock, and gave her butterflies for the first time in years stand up there...and talk about the beauty of math.

Calculus. Seriously? Not woodshop or something? Sam thought calc teachers were nerds. Or softspoken geniuses like Annie.

Not bold, crafty, carpenters who eyed her up like she was, well...young. And attractive. And not in the midst of a pathetically tragic divorce, living at home at forty-three.

Of course, that was before he knew she had a sixteen-year-old kid he'd be teaching for the next year. He probably wouldn't have been quite as...friendly. And neither would she.

Sam couldn't be thinking about having a fling or a crush or a...date. She wasn't even fully divorced yet. And even if she were ready to think like that—which she was not—Ben's teacher was firmly and strictly off limits.

When Ethan finished up a presentation that Sam totally missed, she took a deep breath and walked up to his desk as the other parents meandered out of the room.

Annie slid out the door of the classroom, giving Sam a knowing glance and leaving the two of them alone.

"So." She pressed her hands on the teacher's desk. "I guess I'll be seeing a lot of you, then, with all the projects at the inn and now..." She gestured around and laughed softly. "This."

"Well, I was hoping to see quite a lot of you." He smiled, his eyes crinkling. "I just had no idea it would be in the school car line."

She laughed and held his gaze for a second, feeling firmly like there was a mutual understanding of *off limits*, regardless of the attraction sparks that may be there.

"Are you, um, married?" he asked, a little awkwardly, but Sam appreciated the transparency. And the apparent respect for marriage, which not all men had.

"Divorced. Well, soon to be." She tapped her wrist where a watch would go. "Any day now. What about you?"

"Divorced as well," he said, making her heart sink.

"Oh. I'm sorry."

He tipped his head. "Happens to the best of us, doesn't it?"

"Do you have kids?"

"None of my own, but..." He waved a hand at the twenty-five empty desks that filled the classroom. "I've certainly got no shortage of them."

Sam laughed and nodded her head. "So AP Calc and antique restoration. You're a jack of all trades, huh?"

He tilted his head and raised a shoulder. "The two actually aren't that far apart. You'd be shocked how much math I use in furniture building."

Sam shuddered. "I can't even think about it. Paint color is more my strong suit."

"I'm sure you have excellent taste."

"Well..." Sam held out her hand and straightened her back, meeting his gaze. "It was wonderful to meet you *again*, and I'm sure Ben's going to love this class. Actually, I'm not sure of that. In fact, he'll probably hate it, but he's going to think you're cool, so that counts for something."

"Oh, I'll make him love it." He shook her hand, flashing one more handsome smile that was just playful enough to bring a couple of those forbidden butterflies back to life. "I'll see you around, Sam."

Aw. No more "Samantha." Too bad. She'd liked the way he said it.

After she said goodbye, she headed out, and squeezed her eyes shut as she reached the hallway. When the door shut behind her, Annie caught up with her. And they broke into gales of laughter like...well, a couple of schoolgirls.

"What a crazy coincidence." Annie chuckled.

"Completely bizarre. I mean, Annie, the guy I met the other day did not give off math teacher vibes. Not even close."

"Well, he gave off cute vibes, and he was looking at you the way I look at a fresh batch of cupcakes, and don't pretend you didn't see it."

Sam waved a hand dismissively. "He's Ben's teacher. End of story."

"More like *beginning* of story," she insisted. "You told me when he came by the inn that you two had a...a banter. Chemistry."

"That was before I knew he was, and I repeat..." Sam

turned to her with wide eyes, accentuating every syllable. "Ben's *teacher*."

"So?"

"So that makes anything beyond a professional and cordial friendship completely and totally off limits. Besides, I'm not even fully divorced yet."

"I know. I'm sorry." Annie put a hand on Sam's shoulder.

"Oh, it's fine. I just wish the process took less time. I hate still being tied to Max in any way. I did drop Parker, though. I'm officially just Sam Sweeney again."

Annie nodded understandingly. "Suits you much better. And you know. It'll be over and done with soon enough."

"Gosh, I hope so."

"So this 'professional and cordial friendship,'" Annie held up air quotes as they walked through the halls of the school. "Is Ben going to think it's weird that his calc teacher is working with you and Dottie on the inn?"

Sam shrugged. "Not if we don't make it weird. And besides, I looked up some of his stuff online. What he can do with antique pieces?" She shook her head. "It's amazing. He's really talented, and he's exactly who we need, especially because the stuff at the inn is so, so deeply important to my mom. We can't give that up."

Annie nodded. "I hear you. Well, you and Mr. Price better get really comfortable with each other then."

Yes. But not too comfortable.

Chapter Fifteen

Taylor

Ever since the tragically embarrassing day when Taylor poured her heart out to Kai Leilani, admitting she had more feelings for him than she'd ever had for anyone and he responded with, "I'm leaving tomorrow," she'd been treading lightly with their conversations.

Even though she always knew he'd go back to Hawaii eventually, Taylor had thought they could ignore his inevitable departure and at least enjoy the thrill of falling in love and being together while he was here, training for the Ron Jon Invitational. But circumstances got in the way, and Kai had to move back to Hawaii two months earlier than anticipated because his dad needed knee surgery. Kai needed to help his mom run their sugar cane farm, a five-generation family business that had deeper roots than an oak tree, and he didn't hesitate to go.

Something that would always and forever tie Kai to Hawaii, and keep him far, far away from Taylor.

They'd talked, phone calls and texts, and he'd even sent her a letter in the mail with some photos, which felt very vintage and whimsical.

They were not in a long-distance relationship, but

they were definitely more than just friends. Taylor, in fact, had no idea what they were or what kind of label to use or if there was any security at all in giving him her heart.

So...she didn't. He certainly had a piece of it, and that she couldn't control, but she threw herself deeply into her new job at Coastal Marketing. Her newfound love for the job and her young, budding career was the safest place for her heart right now.

Taylor paced around her bedroom in the cottage, which she'd slowly made a home since she'd moved here with her mom and brother at the beginning of the summer.

She'd hung some pictures of her and her friends and family, added festive twinkly lights all around the bedframe, and set up an endless supply of toys and perches for her beloved cat, Mr. Minx.

Letting out an audible groan, Taylor flopped down onto her bed, looking at her phone, hating the fact that calling Kai gave her a wave of nervous jitters.

No jitters. No giddiness. None of that was welcome. This...was a work call.

Although it certainly didn't feel like one, especially because it was almost midnight and she was in a pair of pajamas and thinking about the kiss they'd shared on the beach before he left.

Oh, those eyes. That hair. Those lips.

Focus, Tay.

Despite the intoxicating charm and wonderful,

fleeting romance that surrounded Kai in her mind, this was an opportunity to really make a splash at Coastal Marketing.

If she could swing this, get Kai to help spread the word about Blackhawk Brewing at the Invitational and use his status and symbol as a Floridian idol to blow this client out of the water, she could seriously prove herself in the company.

Taylor had learned quickly that the marketing and advertising industry was an exciting and fascinating beast, and she really felt like she could have more to contribute than just answering phones and scheduling appointments.

And now, her big break was right at her fingertips. All she had to do was call...her ex. Ish. The man she still completely adored. And could hardly stop thinking about. Or dreaming about.

"Mr. Minx." Taylor rolled onto her back, coming face to face with her very sleepy and slightly annoyed fluffball of a cat. "Is this a bad idea?"

He purred and rubbed his face against her cheek, always good for comfort if not guidance.

She checked the clock again, figuring it was about six p.m. in Hawaii. If he wasn't surfing or still out working with his mother, he'd answer.

"Okay, here goes nothing," she said on a sigh, clicking the Call button next to his name, stroking Minx's ear for support.

After two rings, that deep, familiar voice came through the other end of the phone call.

"Taylor Parker, what a surprise." Kai sounded like he was smiling, and Taylor could hear waves crashing and a breeze blowing in the distance.

"Hey, you. I can call back, if you're busy. Sounds like you might be out at the beach."

"I'm actually just finishing up training for the day. Besides, passing up a chance to talk to you would be a terrible mistake." He chuckled. "You're hard to reach these days, Tay."

Was she?

Her heart tugged. "Well, you know, the time difference and this new job...it's been crazy."

She could picture him so vividly, the Hawaiian sunset out on the horizon as he shook out his long hair, damp from surfing. He probably had his board tucked under his arm and one of his usual black wetsuits on.

"I miss you," he said it so easily, so simply, so naturally.

She missed him, too. Desperately. But how could they just say that to each other? What was the point? Just calling and saying, "I miss you" for the rest of their lives, because they could never actually be together?

Still, she ached a little, having fallen so hard and fast for Kai that he left a pretty gaping hole in her heart that day.

"I miss you, too, Kai." Her voice was soft, and she sat up on the bed, holding Mr. Minx close against her thigh.

She looked out the sliding glass door on the side of her bedroom that led directly to the beach, thinking about those quiet early mornings she'd spent with him when she first moved here.

Oh, what she'd give to walk out there and watch him surf again.

"How's the farm?" she asked brightly. "And your dad?"

"The farm is the same as it's been for two hundred years. Big and green and an endless amount of work." He gave a dry laugh of resignation. "But my dad's doing well, though. The knee replacement didn't get him down too much. He's already back on his feet. Well, using a walker. Slowly, and a very small bit at a time. But he's good."

"Well, I'm glad to hear that. Are you..." She thought for a second about this next question, not entirely sure she wanted to hear the answer. "Are you happy to be home? Enjoying it?"

Kai let out a long sigh. "Honestly? Not really. I mean, don't get me wrong, I love Hawaii. My heart is on these islands with my family and my home. It will always be a really big part of who I am. But I..."

Taylor paused, holding her breath as she waited for him to finish.

"I feel like I'm meant for more."

"You are," she said, without even thinking about it.

"And I don't mean like fame or stardom or money. I love being a pro surfer, it's my passion and dream come true. But...I don't know. I can't really get my head around the idea that I'll never live anywhere besides the islands. It seems so small compared to the rest of the world."

Taylor swallowed the hope that crept up her throat.

"I understand," she said softly. "But who knows what could happen, right? You have your whole life ahead of you, and you're so successful..."

"I know what could happen," he said dryly. "I know exactly what's going to happen. If there's anything that's completely certain in the entire world, it's that this farm is staying in the family."

Taylor let out a sigh, wondering if the disappointing reality of that would ever stop stinging so much. "You deserve to be happy."

"I am happy. I get to travel enough as a surfer so, you know, like my dad says—I'll get it all out of my system."

She laughed softly. "I think we both know that's not true."

"How is that new job, by the way?" he asked, lightening the mood. "Better than bartending, I hope?"

"Oh, a million times better," Taylor said on a soft laugh. "I know I'm still just an administrative assistant, but I already feel like I'm having some good ideas and making an impact."

"Why does that not surprise me even a little?" Kai teased. "You're brilliant. I'm sure they all see it."

"Well, I'm not so sure about brilliant." She flopped down on the pillows, her initial nerves and tension completely disappearing. "But I could... I don't know. It's still so new, but I could really see myself having a career in this field. It's fascinating and fun. Plus, working with clients is a blast."

"That's awesome, Tay. I'm so happy for you. I know you're going to crush it."

"Thanks. That means a lot." She looked out the window again, as if she was waiting for him to walk up to her room with that wet hair and surfboard. "Actually, that's kind of exactly what I wanted to talk to you about."

"Wow, so you didn't call me just to chat because you miss me like crazy?" He gave a mock gasp. "I'm hurt, Tay."

Taylor laughed and rolled her eyes, shifting on the bed and snuggling up with Mr. Minx. "I did, and I do... but there is this work thing."

"Really? What's up?"

"Okay, we have this new client—they're a craft beer brewery based out of Asheville, North Carolina."

"So they're hipsters."

She snorted. "They practically invented the term. Anyway, they're opening up a second location of their brewery here in Cocoa Beach, and they came to Coastal Marketing because they want to really target the Floridian customer base and change their branding to fit the tropical, beach scene."

"Okay, makes sense," Kai said. "I imagine a craft beer place might do well in Cocoa Beach. Outdoor...laid-back...near the water."

"I think so, too, but they need to get their name out there. Also, their company is so strongly associated with North Carolina and the mountains right now that it doesn't feel nearly tropical enough. But...I had an idea."

"Ah, did you now?" Kai asked playfully.

"So, you know the Ron Jon Invitational at the end of August?"

"You mean the biggest surf competition in Florida that I go to every year and have won three times? Yes, I'm slightly familiar."

She smiled at his wry sarcasm. "Okay, so I was thinking they could set up a booth at the Invitational, showcasing their expanded brand. Selling beer, T-shirts, merch, whatever, and hitting that Florida local market as hard as possible."

"That would be awesome," he replied. "RJI is massive, and people come in droves. It would definitely get the name out there."

"Exactly."

"But it's pretty competitive. That would be my only concern, just that there are so many food trucks and drink stands and local booths everywhere. You'd have to get a prime location and it's probably super expensive."

Taylor took a deep breath and sat up in her bed. "That's sort of where you come in."

"Okay," he said slowly, laughing with confusion. "You know the athletes have nothing to do with the event planning, right?"

"I'll handle the event planning. I was actually wondering if you would maybe...come hang out at the Blackhawk booth, when you're not surfing. Meet customers, give out beer, sign autographs. I mean, let's face it Kai, it would draw a line three miles long if people found out you were there. It would put the Black-hawk name on the Florida map, and create an instant association with a tropical, beachy, Cocoa Beach icon: you."

He was quiet and Taylor could feel her heart rate picking up a bit.

"So...what do you think?"

"I think..." He said slowly. "I think it's genius."

"Really?" She got up off the bed and started pacing around, too excited to stay still. "Oh my gosh, I am so happy to hear that."

"I never even would have thought of that, but it's brilliant, Tay. No one's ever had an athlete at their booth at the Invitational. At least, not that I've seen."

"Well, I imagine most pro surfers would be seriously expensive to acquire for something like that."

"I'll have you know I fully intend to charge you in the seven-figure range for using my name, image and likeness." He could barely get through the sentence without laughing.

"Yeah, you can discuss that with the secretary at the ad agency. Oh, wait—that's me. And there's no budget to pay you."

"That's fine," he said, sounding so close, not a country *and* an ocean away. "I'm happy to help, seriously. It honestly sounds like a blast."

"Thank you so much, Kai. This is going to be amazing for the client, obviously. And it could be my chance to prove myself at the agency. It could be the first step in a marketing career for me."

"I'm so proud of you, Tay."

"I really appreciate you doing this for me."

"I would do anything for you. You know that."

Taylor's eyes shuttered as she leaned her back against the sliding glass door, pressing the phone to her ear.

Anything? *Anything except move to Florida.*

The words echoed through her head, even though she knew full well how impractical and silly and selfish they were.

"I know," she whispered, sliding down the glass a little, bittersweet chills running across her skin.

"Hey, I gotta run. Nightly farm duty calls and I can't leave it all to my poor old mama."

Taylor smiled. It wasn't fair that Kai had to be the sweetest and most genuinely good-hearted man she'd ever met.

It was his own selflessness that would keep him from her, and that sucked more than anything.

"Of course, go help her," she said. "I really appreciate this."

"Absolutely, Taylor. We can talk more about it as the Invitational gets closer, just make sure your company locks down a vendor spot."

"Oh, yeah. I'm already on that."

"Of course you are." He sighed softly, as if he didn't want the phone call to end, and neither did she.

"And, hey, the Invitational is only, like, a month away now," Taylor said. "So I better get planning."

"Well, I'll see you in a month, then. I can't wait."

She felt her cheeks warm. "Me either."

What would it be like the first time she laid eyes on Kai since he'd gone back to Hawaii? Would she feel as strongly as she had before? Would she be able to keep her walls up and her heart guarded?

Or would she do exactly what she wanted to do and fall right into his arms and melt away and wish she could stay there forever? She'd have to wait a month to find out.

Chapter Sixteen

Imani

The laptop called to her, so much more interesting than making dinner. From the island, Imani glanced at her desk and felt pulled for just one more look at the article. One more read through of her first published piece in *TravelBee*.

Oh, why not?

Because this was "family time" and not "work time" and she'd sworn she'd keep them separate as she wrote a few articles that shouldn't interfere with anything?

Putting her knife on the cutting board, she walked over to the desk, glancing out the sliders as she passed to see Ellen and Liam kicking a soccer ball in the backyard. Damien was upstairs doing early SAT prep, and John wouldn't be home for an hour at least.

She had time to read it one more time.

So, she opened up her laptop and tapped the link to the *TravelBee* website, clicking on the huge image of the launch pad and the words "The Heart of the Space Coast," by Imani Sweeney.

After submitting her first piece on the Space Center

for approval, the editors decided to publish the piece as a standalone feature, not just a sidebar for other stories, which she'd expected. They called it "captivating" and didn't want it to get lost among the other pieces that were not much more than restaurant reviews and events calendars.

Imani had agreed, of course, happy to have poured her heart into the article, and thrilled to have her work recognized.

Imani took a deep breath, leaned against the side of her couch, and looked out into the backyard, which was bathed in afternoon summer sun as the echoes of her kids' laughter filled the air.

Ellen had the ball and Liam stood in front of the goal and net they'd put up when Liam started soccer. Somehow they'd incorporated a bat and the seven-foot basketball hoop into their game.

She smiled at the two of them, marveling as she watched her sweet, beautiful, talented kids play in perfect peace and harmony.

Why wasn't that enough for her anymore? Why did she feel this burning and overwhelming desire to have something outside of this family? Something that was only hers?

She scanned the article again, thinking about how it was such a small-time, minor website essay compared to the massive international travel pieces she used to write.

But still, it was exhilarating to see her words in print again. She'd missed the thrill of knowing other people were reading her words and reacting to them.

On the kitchen island, her phone vibrated, and she walked back to pick it up, seeing the name of Kristen McManus on the screen. Well, speak of the devil. It was her new editor at *TravelBee.*

"Hey, Kristen. How are you?" Imani answered, carrying the phone back to the laptop.

"Imani Sweeney, you are officially my favorite person."

Kristen, who had to be in her early thirties and was full of spunk and drive and fun, had been a pleasure to work with and had made Imani feel so valuable, even on such a small scale.

"I am?" She laughed with confusion. "Why is that?"

"Um, hello?" Kristen practically sang the word. "You went viral. Your piece about Kennedy has had more hits, shares, and retweets than any article since we started running this blog in 2018. Girl, you are a gift!"

Wait...really?

Imani shook her head as she processed what Kristen was saying. "I did? People really liked it that much? It was such a short piece, I didn't think—"

"Oh, please. You don't have to do the humble act for me. I'm all about confidence, and, Imani, you should be basking in it right now. Look at the email I just sent you."

Unable to wipe the smile off her face or the joy from her heart, Imani opened a new tab and clicked on her email account, reading the message that had just come in from Kristen.

It was a tracking report, comparing "The Heart Of

The Space Coast" to their next five highest-rated and most-shared pieces on the blog.

"Oh...oh my." Imani held her hand to her mouth as she read over the numbers.

"'Oh my' is right," Kristen replied. "Your feature has gotten more hits than our second-best article by more than a five-times margin. It's amazing. You're amazing. People really responded to this."

Laughing at that, she walked into the family room and dropped onto the sofa, realizing her legs were shaking from the news.

"Wow, I'm so glad it did so well," she said, smiling. "I hadn't written in many years, and all of my previous stuff was very traditional...in travel books and physical magazines and New York-published works. A trendy, online travel site, well, I wasn't sure I'd fit. I thought I might have been too old, so I'm so happy to hear I'm not."

"You should officially never doubt yourself again, because our readers love your voice and your personal connection to the area. It really spoke to people. And you are not old!"

Imani laughed off the compliment. "Well, some days, you know..."

"You're young and vibrant and intelligent," Kristen continued, undaunted. "You know, when I saw your resume and your experience in the travel writing industry, I knew you were way out of our league. I understood that you wanted to stay local and be a mom and have a career, but I gotta say, I'm kind of shocked someone as talented and qualified is you is staying so small scale."

"You know, it was really just more of a fun side project for me. I'm a full-time mom, Kristen. This was just a little work that was good for my heart. I've had my epic career days, and they're behind me."

The reality of those words hurt more than it should have.

"But writing for *TravelBee* is exactly what I needed," Imani added brightly. "I can't believe it's gotten such a great response."

"Well, I'm thrilled to hear you say that you enjoyed writing for us, because we want you starting your next piece, like, tomorrow."

"Tomorrow?" she asked on a laugh. "I guess I had the impression the assignments would be few and far between. I didn't think you'd want anything else on the Space Coast for the rest of the summer. I know we'd talked about covering the art festival in the fall when my kids are back in school."

"Imani Sweeney, do not break my heart right now. I simply will not allow you." Kristen laughed. "We have worked so hard to get this website on its way to becoming one of the top travel blogs on the internet, and having your voice on our pages is going to be the thing that takes us there."

This. This was exactly what John was worried about. He knew she wouldn't be able to stop at just one measly little website feature. He knew it, and deep down, she knew it, too.

"So, what did you have in mind for the next piece?"

she asked, a strange mixture of guilt and excitement leaving a bitter taste on her tongue.

"Obviously we want you writing some more features on the Space Coast area. Yes, the art festival, and maybe something on the pirate's museum in a place called... Sebastian Inlet."

Sebastian was a half-hour away. Doable. Maybe she could take the kids to the museum for a day and...yeah. She could do that. She could stay local and be a mom and a travel writer. As long as it was without the *travel* part.

Plus, the kids would be back in school in a couple of weeks. She could write and research during the school day, and be back on full-time mom duty the second 3 p.m. hit. It was more than doable.

"I can probably do that," she said softly.

"Excellent," Kristen said quickly, as if she never really expected pushback. "And we are also mapping out a big Gulf Coast series, you know, Tampa, St. Pete, Naples, even the panhandle areas like Destin. We want to showcase some tourism spots that aren't oversaturated or watered down. Then we could do the more popular places, like Sanibel Island or Key West. You'd be so beyond perfect to write those pieces. We know you could just go to the Gulf Coast and find the heart and soul of it, like—"

"Oh, Kristen, I can't..." Imani sucked in a breath. "I can't be traveling."

"It's not that much travel! It's all Florida."

"Spoken like a person who lives on Long Island," Imani joked. "The Panhandle is a rock-solid eight hours away, and Key West is a full-day trip." She couldn't do that, could she? She had to be here for John and the kids.

"Start with a weekend," Kristen urged. "One weekend away. You can't take one weekend away?"

"I..." Imani shut her eyes and leaned back on the couch, shaking her head. "I need to think about it, Kristen. I wasn't intending to really dive back into a travel writing career. I just thought I'd...freelance part-time. Minimal part-time."

"You're too good for that, and frankly, we think you're going to be the anchor writer of a whole new *TravelBee* expansion. Please, Imani, you cannot say no to this."

Yes, she could. A serious career in travel writing was not in the cards with kids, even if it was only to the other side of the state. But she already knew about the tiny little town near Destin called Rosemary Beach, and how quaint and lovely and undiscovered it was. She'd start there and bring it to life, talking to locals and unearthing the jewels hidden on the cobblestone streets.

"I really believe with a writer of your caliber, *TravelBee* could rival *Lonely Planet* or even *Wanderlust* for eyes on the internet. And eyes mean ad dollars. Didn't you say your husband owned an ad agency? He'd know what internet marketing makes."

But she didn't write for the money; she never had. She wrote so people could read the pictures she painted, feel the essence of a setting, smell the local food, and want to escape to another place.

Oh, she missed that feeling.

"I have to talk to my family, Kristen," Imani said. "I can't make this decision without them."

"I understand. I do." Kristen didn't sound too much like she understood, but she was polite. "Just please seriously think about it, Imani. We could build something together. But we need you."

She blew out a long breath. "I'll think about it."

"Don't think too hard," Kristen said with a soft laugh. "Follow your heart. And your talent. Because, dang, girl, you can write."

"Thank you."

"All right, keep me posted. I'm off to a layout meeting. Ciao!"

"Bye, Kristen."

Just what Imani needed—more to think about. And this time, she knew what John was going to say. There was no way she would be able to travel to other parts of the state for work when the kids were at their busiest ages and depended on her for every last little thing.

And he'd be right.

Not to mention the work she'd be doing was really more for fun than anything. *TravelBee wasn't* a major player in the game, so the minimal pay for her freelance work was about the last thing on her mind.

She had the privilege of being able to stay home with her kids...and now she wanted to throw that away?

Maybe she didn't have to decide right now. Kristen had said that they wanted her to continue locally in the Cocoa Beach area before they moved to the Gulf Coast, so she could stay local for a while.

Imani clicked over to the article one more time, scanning the comments section, which had already nearly doubled in quantity since the last time she checked it.

Wow. It really was going viral.

Comments like *My son is obsessed with rockets, this article made me book a trip to Florida for his birthday!* and *I love the personal connection here, this writer is making me want to be her friend.*

She didn't want to give this up. Not again. She'd spent fifteen years supporting John's career and his business. Couldn't she get just a tiny molecule of that time?

"Mom! Mom!" Liam yanked the sliding glass door open, breathless.

"What is it?" Imani was up in a flash, Mom Mode Activated. "What's wrong?"

"Ellen fell and hit her elbow. She's bleeding."

"Oh, boy." She rushed out to the backyard, where Ellen sat in a lump on the pavement underneath the basketball hoop, quivering with tears.

"Mommy, my arm."

"Okay, baby. It's okay. Let me see it."

Ellen held out her arm, which had about an inch-long scrape on the elbow and the tiniest bit of blood.

"Oh, no." Imani tsked and shook her head. "Bad news."

"What?" Ellen gasped and looked up with wide hazel eyes, her adorable face surrounded by messy black curls.

"I think they're gonna have to amputate it." Imani pressed her lips together. "Better say goodbye to that arm."

A sweet little giggle bubbled in Ellen's chest, and she shook her head frantically, leaning into her mom's tight embrace.

"No, they're not," she said through the laughter.

"I don't know, El, you might be a lost cause." Imani smiled and tucked Ellen's head under her chin, kissing the top of her hair, which smelled like sunshine.

"You can fix it, Mommy."

"You think so?" She drew back and looked at her daughter, whose gorgeous mixed complexion was a stunning blend of Imani and her husband.

Ellen nodded her head and smiled. "You can do anything."

"All right, let's get you up and clean it off." She helped the girl to her feet and they walked into the kitchen to wash out the scrape.

You can do anything.

Well, Ellen believed in her. Maybe her kids wouldn't resent her for wanting to explore her career again, but admire it. Wouldn't that be setting a good example for them to follow their passion and their hearts? A person certainly could do that and love their family and be there for them.

The whole time she cleaned out the cut, applied a layer of Neosporin, and slapped a Band-Aid on it, Imani thought about going to the Gulf Coast to travel and write about it.

You can do anything.

She darn well could. And being a mom didn't mean

she had to give up other parts of her life if she didn't want to anymore.

She knew she had to talk to John, but they were going to make this work. She deserved it, and she, as Ellen put it, could do anything.

"It would just be a weekend or two. Minimal, really." Imani paced around the bedroom, knotting her fingers together as she anticipated the fight that was already starting to brew.

With the kids in bed, it was quiet and the day was done as she'd broached the subject with John. Based on his expression as he sat on the edge of the bed, running a hand through his hair, it wasn't going all that well.

"Imani, I don't understand where all of this is coming from," he said. "You had an amazing career, wasn't that enough? What about our kids? Aren't they enough?"

"Of course they are!" she shot back, swinging some braids behind her shoulder as she crossed her arms and dug for composure.

She'd never said her kids weren't enough for her, and she hated the accusation. It wasn't that they weren't enough, it was that she wanted more than just being a mom. She wanted something for herself, something that was hers. Something she desperately missed.

John's business was his baby, so couldn't he understand that?

"Why do you need to work?" he asked. "And travel? We don't need the money."

"I miss it, John." She sat down next to him and leveled her gaze into his eyes. "I've been feeling so lost and empty. Not because of the kids, but because I miss my old self. I lost the woman I used to be, and I want to get her back. I don't see why I can't do that and be their mother and your wife all at the same time. Millions of women do it."

He looked skeptical as he leaned his elbows on his knees, taking a deep breath. "Our kids have the world's busiest little lives. They rely on you every minute of every day. So do I. You're raising them to be wonderful, good, amazing people, and we need that. They need that, Imani. They need *you*."

She inched closer to him, lowering her tone to really emphasize how deeply she meant this. "John. I have absolutely no intention of not being there for our children. Not in any capacity."

"But, inherently...work and travel, it will take you away. It requires time. You'll be home less. A lot less."

"I can make it work," she insisted.

"Not with weekends on the other side of the state," he ground out, making her wonder if he'd heard anything past "weekend in the Panhandle." He turned to her, hurt in his eyes. "You agreed, Imani. You agreed with this the day you got pregnant with Damien. What changed? Where is this coming from?"

"Agreed? To what?" She pushed back, irritation firing up her spine. "I agreed to support all of your dreams and goals while I drive a minivan and pack lunches and go to every activity and sport and event known to man while doing nothing—*literally not one thing*—for myself?"

The echo of her words hung in the air, having their intended effect. John let his shoulders sink with a long exhale as he let the moment pass in silence.

If there was one thing about John, he hated conflict. The peacemaker, the mediator, the oldest and only son of the Sweeney family who always calmed everyone down—that was John.

Imani loved that about him. She adored his lack of temper and always knew he would be a steady rock for her.

But right now, even the most composed man she knew was getting emotional about this. And, frankly, it scared her a little bit.

Was he really that vehemently opposed to her having a small career on the side of being a full-time mom? Did he value her own passions that little? The thought stung, a lot.

"You agreed," he said slowly, "to give up work and be a stay-at-home mom until the kids were all out of the house. You agreed that I could run my business and build it up, and you would look after the family. That was the deal."

"The *deal*?" She practically spat out the question. "John, I'm allowed to have dreams outside of mother-hood. That doesn't make me a bad person. We're together because we love each other, not because we made a deal."

"Okay, okay." He held his hands up defensively. "I'm sorry. That was the wrong way of putting it."

Yeah, it was, but Imani held her tongue this time. She truly didn't want to fight any more than he did.

But he needed to listen to her. He needed to hear her. He needed to respect her as much as she respected him.

"I promise it won't change anything," she said for what had to be the tenth time. "Not anything significant."

He looked at her, those deeply familiar blue eyes hitting her with both guilt and frustration. "I knew this was going to happen. I knew it would never just be one article. It was the start of a whole new path for you, and you're not going to get off of it. Not again."

"Don't you want me to be happy?" Imani asked, her voice wavering with emotion.

"Why *aren't* you happy? I just don't get where this is coming from, I thought everything was good. I want to understand. Please, help me understand."

"I don't know," she said, standing and pacing to collect herself. "But I do know that you have a whole life outside of this house. You have an office and employees and colleagues and goals and projects and passions and deadlines and a life. A *world*. Something that is wholly and completely yours." She turned to him, fisting her hands as the realization became clear to her.

"And I have supported every last step of that for you," she added on a whisper. "All the while seeing my life shrink smaller and smaller and disappear into nothing but playdates and sports practices. And I love our kids, more than anything. And I love you. But I also love...me. And I matter, too."

She turned away so he didn't see a tear fall, feeling the weight of those words and thoughts leaving her shoulders and settling into the tense space between them.

"Yes, you do, Imani." He got up and reached for her hand. "I want to see you happy. I just...I have a bad feeling about this. The kids are so busy and they need you. And you know that I can't do this without you. I'd crumble."

"John. You and the kids do need me." She leveled her gaze. "You need me to be me. To be my best self. And the closest I felt to truly myself was when I went to the Space Center and wrote that piece. I felt like me again."

He shook his head. "I'm trying so hard to understand, but to be honest, I'm struggling."

She nodded. "I'm not sure I understand it, either. But I feel this way, and it's very real. I promise you, I will still be an amazing mom. Nothing is going to change. I can handle this. We can handle this."

He looked at her for a long time, and she wished so badly to see a glimmer of hope or certainty or something that wasn't total concern and doubt in those blue eyes.

But they were, undeniably, swimming with something she'd never seen when he looked at her, not once in all their years together...doubt.

He doubted her. Well, she didn't doubt herself. She could do this, and she would.

Chapter Seventeen

Erica

The clock was ticking, and the beginning of the school year was now only a couple of weeks away. And while Jada still felt mostly like a walking enigma, Erica seemed to have made some headway as far as their relationship.

Once she found out Jada loved to draw, she bought her several sketchbooks and nice pencil sets, and Will set up a desk for her by the window in her room. This lit Jada up more than anything had so far, and her genuine "thank yous" even led to a hug.

Or, Jada's version of a hug, where she kept her arms crossed and allowed Erica to embrace her.

She'd take what she could get.

But now that a level of comfort had been established, Erica was certain it was time to buckle down and focus on getting Jada at least somewhat up to speed on school-work and academics.

"Are you sure this is necessary?" Will asked, cleaning up some dishes from dinner while Jada was upstairs taking a shower. "A reading lesson on a summer night?"

"Babe, she has to go to school in a matter of weeks." She looked sternly at her husband, taking the wet platter from his hand and drying it with a dish towel. "I know it's not fun and it's not going to make her happy, but it's what she needs to focus on right now."

"I know, I just feel like..." He rinsed some utensils, shook them out, and leaned down to put them in the dishwasher, his gaze lingering on Erica. "She's finally getting to a good spot with us, you know? She's finally starting to open up."

"A little bit," Erica agreed, leaning against the countertop. "But we've still got such a long way to go."

"The drawing stuff helped."

"It did. Thank you for the desk."

Will flashed her that bright smile, stepping over to wrap his arms around her. "Thank you for discovering our daughter's secret passion."

"I'm glad I discovered it, that's for sure." Erica let out a sigh. "I just know that she's going to get so frustrated and discouraged if she gets to school and can't keep up. I could see it in her eyes, that first night she told us about it. She's terrified, Will."

"I know she is." He shut his eyes and blew out a breath. "I know."

"So the only way to alleviate that fear, or at least attempt to, is to arm her with a little bit of academic preparation."

"Says the queen of academic preparation herself."

She rolled her eyes and stifled a laugh.

"I just think it's going to make her hate us, and all of

that progress we've made will be gone when she thinks we're going to sit her down and make her spend hours doing the one thing she expressed that she can't stand."

"Will." She leveled her gaze on her husband. "There's a time to be a friend, and a time to be a parent. We have to be parents right now, and that means getting her ready for school."

He studied Erica for a long moment, a smile pulling at his handsome, chiseled face as he angled his head. "How'd you get so wise?"

"My sister told me that, actually."

"I'm so glad to see you and Sam getting close again."

"It really is nice," Erica agreed.

She headed over to the dining room table where she'd set up reading exercises, a textbook, and printed out some worksheets and comprehension quizzes.

"Okay." Erica let out a deep breath, straightening some of the papers and laying out a few colored pencils in a perfect line. "This is going to be fun, right?"

Will hung up the dish towel to dry and walked into the dining room to join her, giving her a playful wink. "I'm sure you'll find a way to make it fun."

She hoped he was right.

Suddenly, little bare footsteps padded down the wooden staircase, and Erica looked up to see Jada in one of the new T-shirt and pajama pants sets she'd bought her.

Her long hair was still wet, hanging around her shoulders but out of her face. Jada smiled a little as she walked down, but then her gaze quickly fell to the dining room table.

She looked particularly sulky, which didn't give Erica much hope for how this reading lesson was going to go.

"What is this?" Jada asked, an edge of nerves in her voice.

Erica took a deep breath, and reminded herself over and over of what Sam had said. She had to be a mom right now, even if it made Jada upset. This was what would be best in the long run, as she had to go to school. She had to.

"Okay, so I thought we could do a little reading."

"I don't like reading," Jada said quickly, shaking her head and backing away.

Will stepped forward, placing a firm and steadying hand on Erica's lower back. "I know it's not your favorite thing, Jada, but your mom and I want to help you get ready for school in a few weeks here, and we think—"

"She's not my mom!" Jada's tone escalated.

Erica winced, the words hitting like a blow to the throat.

She was particularly volatile today. She must *really* hate the idea of schoolwork.

"Jada, it's our job to take care of you and help you get set up for the best life possible. And in order to do that, we need to see where you are as far as academics are concerned, and help you catch up, since you haven't had a fair chance to stay in school." Erica kept her tone calm and steady, even though her heart was racing.

"No..." Jada shook her head frantically. "I don't want to. Please, can I just go upstairs and draw?"

Oh, God. How was this already such a dumpster fire? She hadn't even sat down at the table yet.

Erica shuddered to think about what it was going to be like trying to get Jada to go to school.

"How about this." Will crouched down, meeting Jada at eye level. "You do some of this reading with us for half an hour, and then you can go draw all you want."

Jada looked around, her initial anger quickly fading and turning into sadness and fear. Her big brown eyes darted across the room, as if she was looking for an escape.

"Hey, it's okay." Erica stepped toward her, placing a hand on her narrow shoulder. "There are no grades or scores or tests. We just want to get started."

"I can't, because..." Jada's voice caught, and she looked up at Erica, her eyes wide with fear. "Because you're going to think I'm stupid. I can't do it."

"Jada, sweetie." Erica shut her eyes and placed both hands on Jada's shoulders, looking right at her. "We would never, ever think that. Don't you get it? We think you're awesome exactly as you are."

"And you're not stupid," Will chimed in. "You haven't been to school consistently your whole entire life. You speak two languages, for crying out loud. That's a heck of a lot more than I can do!"

This got the tiniest semblance of a chuckle from Jada, but her demeanor was still dark and dreary.

"What do you say?" Erica jutted her chin toward the

dining room. "Give it a shot? Ten minutes, see how it goes?"

Jada sniffled, pushed her hair away, and shrugged meagerly. "I guess."

"All right." Will clapped his hands. "Let's do it."

The three of them sat at the end of the table, Jada at the head and Will and Erica on either side.

Jada shifted around in her seat, clearly uncomfortable.

Erica and Will shared a look of solidarity, his eyes reassuring her that she had backup on all of this, and it was okay if it didn't instantly go perfectly.

"Okay, so this is a passage about elephant seals." Erica gently turned one of the reading worksheets and pushed it in front of Jada.

"My favorite animal," Will chimed in.

Erica laughed. "It is? Who knew?"

Jada swallowed nervously and looked down at the paper, chewing her lip.

"Why don't you try and read some of it out loud to us?"

"I'm really slow," Jada said, shaking her head rapidly.

"That's okay," Will assured her. "We aren't in any rush here, kid."

"He's right." Erica nodded. "Not going anywhere. And I know this is not what you want to be doing, and it seems really awful right now, but I promise it's going to be worth it when you go to school."

She visibly shuddered at the word.

"We're here for you." Will looked at Jada, as strong

and steady for her as he always was for Erica. "We got you every step of the way."

Jada nodded, pushed some hair out of her face, and took a deep breath. "Okay." She fixed her gaze on the paper. "In the f-freezing waters of Ant-ant..." She shook her head frantically.

"Antarctica," Erica helped gently.

"That's okay," Will added. "That's a tough one. Keep going."

"Antarctica," Jada repeated slowly. "The world's la... largest seals make...their...home."

Every word was a struggle that appeared to cause poor sweet Jada physical pain.

She was not stupid. She just hadn't been given a chance. Erica would have to show her that. This girl needed, more than anything, someone to believe in her.

"You're doing awesome." Erica grinned.

Jada swallowed and continued, one irritated, impatient word at a time. "These are south...south..."

"Southern," Erica suggested.

"Southern..." Jada stopped, staring at the next word with a look of discouraged anger. "I don't know it."

"Try sounding it out," Will urged.

Jada gave a frustrated sigh. "El...ele...pant."

"Elephant," Erica said. "You know..." She held her arm up in front of her face and waved it around, mimicking an elephant's trunk.

"Yeah. I know what an elephant is, I just don't know how to read." She crossed her arms, leaning back in the seat and getting more and more upset with every passing second.

"You do know how to read, Jada. You're reading right now."

"I'm not reading!" she shrieked, startling Erica and Will. "I can't do it. Just admit that I'm stupid and leave me alone!"

"Jada, please." Erica felt her tone rising, frustration and hopelessness gripping her throat. "We are trying to help you learn. You're doing great."

"You really are," Will added, reaching for her. "This is a fourth grade reading level and you're crushing it."

Jada sat frozen in her seat, her lower lip quivering a little. "Fourth...grade?"

Erica shot Will a look. "Yes. We thought we'd start there for a baseline, and then we can work our way up to—"

Jada glared at her. "I'm *this* bad at reading fourth grade stuff, and you expect me to go to *sixth*? I can't! And everyone is going to make fun of me and I'm going to fail everything! And just wait until I try to take a math test..." Her voice was thick with emotion and fear.

Erica looked at Will, desperate for answers and guidance and help, but he looked just as lost and uncertain as she was.

This was completely uncharted territory for both of them.

How could Erica help this girl? How could she possibly walk her through this terrifying and overwhelming and difficult season of life and end up on the other side with a daughter who adores her?

It seemed hopeless and impossible.

And right now, it felt like all of the progress and growth she'd had with Jada was completely and totally gone. She wasn't just afraid anymore. She hated Erica.

"Jada..." Erica drew in a slow breath, closing her eyes and digging for answers. "Can you just try to keep going on the passage?"

"No!" Jada shoved the paper away from her, a tear falling down her cheek. "Don't you get it? I'm not *like* you." Her voice faded and quivered and broke. "I'm not a booksmart math whiz who gets good grades. I'm not going to some fancy, smart-kid college, and I'm never going to be able to be rich and perfect like you guys. I'm different, and you're never going to think I'm good enough to fit in here."

With that, she stood up, wiped tears from her cheeks, and ran straight upstairs, slamming the door to her room without another word.

Erica just sat completely still, disappointment and heartache washing over her like tidal waves.

How could Jada hate her so much? How could she not see that she *was* good enough, she just had to try a little bit? Didn't she understand that Erica and Will wanted to give her a good life, and show her that she was capable of doing amazing things?

Maybe Jada didn't want any of that. She sure as heck didn't seem to want love and support. She rejected it, harder than ever tonight.

"Honey..." Will reached across the dining room table and took Erica's hand, giving her a sympathetic glance.

Erica shook her head and shut her eyes, fighting the urge to cry or scream or, worse, question whether this was the right decision.

She couldn't even think it, let alone say it out loud, but the thought nagging in the back of her brain was undeniable.

Was she sure she could go through with this? Would Jada ever love her?

"Just give her some time. She'll come around," Will said softly.

"No." Erica shook her head, standing up suddenly, pushing her chair in under the table. "No. I'm not going to give her any more time to sulk and pout and act like she hates the two people who are doing everything imaginable to make her happy. Just because she's adopted doesn't mean we should have to spend our life walking on eggshells."

"I know, I know." Will nodded, running a hand through his hair as he sighed deeply. "But this is all still new."

"I'm going up there."

"Erica." He leveled his gaze. "Are you sure that's a good idea?"

"We're adopting her, Will. Not looking after her, not fostering her, not giving her a place to stay. *Adopting.*" The word tasted bitter on her tongue.

Will just swallowed, leaning back in the dining chair and glancing off to the side.

"I am going to talk to my daughter, and try to make her understand that we want to help her. We want to... love her."

And maybe someday, they would.

Will clearly knew better than to try and argue with Erica right now, and she let determination fuel her as she marched up the stairs.

"Jada." She knocked gently on the outside of the door to the guestroom. "Can I come in?"

"Go away." The words were muffled, as if Jada had her face buried deep in a blanket or pillow.

Erica took in a shaky breath. "I'm coming in, okay? I just want to talk to you."

Jada just groaned.

Erica slowly opened the door and peered in, seeing that the room was completely dark except for the nightlight.

Jada was lying under the covers with her face in the pillow, curled up in a ball. She'd clearly been crying even more, from the tear stains on the pillow case.

Could Erica get through to this girl? She didn't know, but darn it, she was not a quitter.

"Just go away," Jada mumbled, pressing her face even harder into the pillows.

"Jada, please talk to me." Erica sat on the edge of the bed. "I know you don't like doing schoolwork, but I promise you, you're not doing that badly. I mean, with a little practice your reading could be up to speed in no time. And I'm sorry if I've pushed you too hard. I tend to, well, overachieve."

Jada just breathed heavily, refusing to look up at Erica. "It's not just the reading," she murmured.

"What?" Erica drew back. "Oh, sweetie, I know math is bad, too, but that's where I can *really* help you," she said with a hint of playfulness in her voice.

"No." Jada turned, finally revealing a bit of her damp, flushed face. "It's not just the school stuff."

"Oh." Erica swallowed. "What is it, then? Is it about your mom, or...something else? You can talk to me, Jada. I know you think you can't but you can. I really, really wish you would."

"I'm..." Jada's voice turned to a whimper, and her eyes were wide and scared. "Bleeding," she barely squeaked out the last word.

"What?" Erica frowned with confusion. "Are you hurt? Did you cut yourself? Let me see, we can fix it right up."

"No, not bleeding like that. Bleeding like..." Jada threw her hands over her face like she just wanted to disappear right then and there. "Somewhere else. I've never had that before."

Oh. *That* kind of bleeding.

Erica let out a soft breath, holding her hand to her mouth and feeling, well, a bit relieved. Jada had gotten her first period, which completely and totally explained how angry and freaked out and shut down she was.

Did she want her real mom right now? Probably, but Erica didn't have time to wallow in that. This was her chance to love this girl, and be there for her.

Whether or not she could admit it, Jada needed her.

"Oh, sweetie." Erica offered a kind smile, reaching her hand out and gently setting it on Jada's back. "Do you know what that is?"

"I think so." She sniffed, wiping her nose as she lifted her head a little. "It's my first one."

"Oh my heavens. Well, no wonder you're all upset! Here, let's get you to the bathroom. I can give you something to use, okay?"

Jada nodded reluctantly, standing up and following Erica to the bathroom across the hall.

"Here." She pulled out a little pink cardboard box from the back of the cabinet, and showed Jada how to open up a panty liner. "I'll wait outside, and just holler if you need me."

"You'll be right there?" she asked, blinking.

"I'll be right here."

Erica stepped out of the bathroom and into the hallway, closing the door to let Jada have privacy.

Oh, the poor thing. She was embarrassed and scared and needed a mom.

After a couple of minutes, Erica heard the sink run and then Jada slowly opened the bathroom door.

"All good?"

"Yeah." Jada nodded and sighed with a little relief. "I was just freaking out. I thought I would be older when that happened."

"It can happen at all different ages." Erica guided Jada back to the bedroom and sat down on the bed with her, side by side. "I'm glad you told me."

"I'm glad I told you, too." Jada smiled, clearly more

relaxed and comfortable than she had been. "Sorry for being so mean to you guys downstairs."

"Oh, honey. You were scared and didn't know what to do! Don't apologize." Erica placed a hand on her leg. "I'm sorry for making you read about elephant seals. I had no idea."

Jada snorted a little, tucking her knees up against her chest. "That's okay."

"Well, I think I should probably say something about what this means as far as...your body changing."

Jada just stared blankly at her.

"It means, well, you're getting older. And you're becoming a woman. A beautiful, smart, very talented young woman. And there are going to be other changes and things that feel new or weird or even exciting."

"Really?"

"Oh, yeah. But we can cross those bridges when we get to them." She nudged Jada.

"I was just so embarrassed, I didn't know what to do."

"I know, it's okay." Erica smiled. "You want to hear about my first one? Because it was a whole heck of a lot worse than yours."

Jada nodded, staring at Erica. "Yeah."

"I was at Disney World."

"Yikes."

"Major yikes. Even worse, I was with my dad and my brother, John. Mom had taken my sisters, Julie and Sam, to a different part of the park, but my brother and dad and I wanted to go to Tomorrowland, and we'd all agreed to meet back up later. So, it was just me and the boys. And...white shorts."

Jada's jaw dropped. "No!"

"Oh, yeah. I was hysterical. I've never been so mortified in my life."

"What did you do?"

Erica smiled, nostalgia chilling her at the memory. "I told my dad. He took off his shirt and gave it to me to tie around my waist, like a makeshift skirt kind of thing. And he walked around Disney shirtless."

"Wow." Jada shook her head. "That's a lot worse than how it happened to me."

"It was. But it's all completely natural and normal and, quite literally, happens to every woman on the planet."

Jada nodded, brushing her hair back.

"So, you feel any better?"

"I feel a lot better, actually."

Erica felt her heart soar at those words. "I'm glad. And don't worry, I won't make you do any more schoolwork tonight."

"Can I ask you something?" Jada looked up at her.

"Sure. Anything."

Erica waited for a question about womanhood or periods or feminine products, preparing herself to give the best answer possible without making Jada uncomfortable.

"Did you want a baby?" Jada picked at the bedsheet. "Like, when you were asking the adoption agency for a kid, were you hoping it was, like, a little baby?"

Now that? She was not prepared for.

"Well...I don't think we had any idea what to expect. We just knew we wanted to be parents, so badly."

"You couldn't have a baby?"

She pressed her lips together and shut her eyes. "We tried for a long time, but I went to a doctor and she told me it was really unlikely because of a medical thing."

"That's sad," Jada said softly.

"It was, for a while. But then Will and I decided we wanted to adopt a baby—or a child," she added quickly. "Because we wanted to have a family. So we went to the adoption agency and told them we want to love and care for whatever kid in the world needs us."

"Do you..." Jada's voice was barely audible. "Do you wish you got a baby instead?"

The words hit Erica like a moving train, the weight of them pressing down on her hard.

"No," Erica said, surprised at how honestly she meant it. "I got you. You're all I need."

Jada's eyes flickered with surprise as she looked up at Erica through those thick, dark lashes. "Really? You're sure?"

"I'm positive, kid. I think we need each other."

Jada twisted her lips, finally lifting her gaze up to meet Erica's. "I think so, too. I hope you weren't sad. When you found out it was me, instead of a baby."

"Jada." Erica turned to her daughter, taking her face in both hands. "You are so unbelievably wanted in this house. Don't ever think for one second we would have rather had anyone else in the world become a part of our family."

"I didn't..." Jada's brows furrowed together and her lip quivered. "I didn't know I'd ever have a real family."

"Well, you have one now." Erica sniffed, feeling mist in her eyes.

"You promise you weren't sad? You promise you don't wish you got a baby?"

Erica shut her eyes, almost laughing at how genuinely she could and did promise that. "I swear, Jada. You're my girl now. We'll always have each other, and that's all I want."

"I'm never going to see my real mom again, am I?"

Erica paused, sucking in a breath as the question smacked her across the face. "Honestly, Jada? No, I don't think you're going to see her for a long time."

Jada just nodded, staring down at the carpet for a long time. "Well, then I adopt you, too."

"Huh?"

She turned to Erica and placed a hand on her arm, an act that required bravery, since Jada was still getting used to any kind of physical affection. "I'd like to stay. I want you to be my mom."

"Oh..." Erica's throat squeezed shut and her voice grew thick with emotion. "It would be my honor to be your mom, Jada."

Jada smiled. "Good. Because I need one."

Erica hugged her daughter, tight and hard and for a long time. Jada didn't pull away or fight it, she just leaned into her.

"You know what else I think we need? Some girl time. With ice cream sundaes and a good movie."

Jada lit up, gasping with excitement. "With fudge?"

"*All* the fudge."

"Okay!" She hopped up and followed Erica downstairs into the kitchen, where Will was still sitting at the dining room table, reading something on his phone.

"Hey, babe." Erica smiled at Will, her eyes wide with happiness and a big, major, unexpected Jada victory.

He instantly put the phone down at the sight of the happy girl, drawing back in surprise and confusion. "Hey, you two..." He drew out the words slowly, looking back and forth between them.

"We're making sundaes and watching a movie," Jada announced, walking right past him into the kitchen like she...well, like she *lived* here.

Will stood up, staring at her with astonishment. "Are you now?"

"Yup." Jada opened the freezer. "Girl time."

Erica nodded, sliding Will a playful look. "Girl time," she repeated.

He chuckled, holding his arms up defensively. "Well, I will leave you guys to it, then." Before he walked out of the room, he caught Erica's gaze.

She gave him a massive thumbs-up, and he nodded at her, beaming with pride.

"Jada, have you ever seen *The Sisterhood of the Traveling Pants*?"

"Nope." She shook her head as she pulled out the tub of vanilla ice cream. "It's a movie about pants?"

"Kind of..." Erica cocked her head and laughed. "It's a must-see. A rite of passage, if you will."

"Okay." Jada dug into the ice cream container, then suddenly put the scooper down on the counter and walked over to Erica.

Without hesitation, Jada put her arms around her, and for a brief second, pressed her head against Erica's chest. "Thank you."

Erica could hardly speak or think. This moment was way too good to be true. "Of-of course, sweetie."

Jada pulled away and went back to her ice cream. "I think you're..." Jada paused to consider this. "A really good mom."

"Thank you, Jada. That means a lot."

Erica could practically feel her heart folding in half. Although there was still a long way to go, for the first time since she met Jada, she felt like...she loved this little girl.

She loved her amazing sketches and her sweet little laugh and the way she approached everything with caution and thought. She loved that Jada had a tough exterior, but was actually vulnerable deep down.

She loved watching Jada open up and become part of her family and life, and she couldn't wait to love her daughter forever and make a million more memories together.

Chapter Eighteen

Sam

"Keep it coming. Yup. All the way to the top, don't be shy, sister." Erica waved a generous hand as Sam poured her a hefty glass of rose, sliding it across the countertop to her.

Sam smiled and shook her head, pouring a glass each for herself, Imani, Taylor, Dottie, and Annie. They'd added Annie to the Sweeney Girls Night at the cottage, and it felt so right.

"I'm dying to hear about Jada," Sam said. "Tell us everything."

Erica smiled—lit up, actually, taking a sip of the sweet, pink, summery wine. "It's good. It's been...really good. Like...we had a breakthrough."

Sam gasped with joy. "Oh, that's wonderful! You'll have to tell us all about it."

"My girls, my girls." Dottie floated into the kitchen, giving Sam a kiss on the cheek as she handed her a glass. "How did I get so lucky to have you all here together?"

"Someone call Aunt Julie," Taylor suggested, picking up a wineglass and giving it a swirl.

Dottie sighed and waved a hand. "Maybe one day."

"Oh, I've missed this cottage." Annie looked around,

beaming with a big smile as she admired the vast ocean view through the sliding glass doors, the sunset painting the sky orange and pink beyond the horizon.

"And we've missed you," Dottie said, giving her a hug.

"I brought a batch of cupcakes." Annie opened a rectangular plastic Tupperware container, revealing six absolutely gorgeous cupcakes, each with different colored frosting swirls and little candy pearl sprinkles. "Totally bribing my way into your group."

"We take bribes," Sam cracked as she put out some napkins for the cupcakes. "You have a gift, Annie Hawthorne."

"Too much free time by myself is what I have," Annie quipped. "But I hope you all like them. They're vanilla strawberry swirl, a new thing I've been working on."

"Don't mind if I do." Taylor took a bite of cupcake, moaning. "Holy cow, Annie, these are amazing."

"Seriously," Imani agreed, dabbing some icing from her lips with the napkin. "These are otherworldly."

She laughed. "Thanks, you guys."

"You should open a bakery or sell these on the beach." Taylor admired the dessert as she peeled back the paper and took another bite. "These are, like, designer cupcakes. People pay good money for that."

"Oh." Annie waved off the compliment. "I'll stick to my spreadsheets and financial security for now. My cupcakes are just for my loved ones."

"We're so happy to have you, Annie. And your delicious baked goods." Dottie grinned at Annie with love in her eyes. "I can remember you and Sam doing your hair and makeup here before the school dances back in the day."

"We were the cutest." Sam lifted a shoulder and sipped her wine.

Sam led everyone out to the back deck, where they all got situated on couches and chairs and watched the peaceful ocean as they caught up and enjoyed the invaluable connection and closeness of family and friendship.

"All right, who's going first?" Erica glanced around at the women. "I want the details of everyone's lives. I've been so busy lately, I've missed you all!"

"Tell us about Jada," Imani urged, lifting her glass. "You said it's been better?"

"Oh, yes, please fill us in." Dottie grinned. "She's such a sweet girl. I hope she's starting to come out of that hermit crab shell a little bit."

"She actually is." Erica took a deep breath, glancing out at the ocean with wistful hope in her gaze. "We've been getting closer. Bonding, I think. It's a long process and we've still got miles to go, but you know. We're on the right track."

"That's amazing, Aunt Erica." Taylor smiled, tucking her legs underneath her on the outdoor couch. "Has she been making any progress with schoolwork? I know you said she was crazy behind."

"Poor thing," Annie added, having been filled in on the entire Jada saga by Sam throughout the past few weeks.

Erica pressed her lips together, frowning. "No, that's

been a slightly slower progression." She ran a hand through her hair and shook her head. "I know she hasn't had the chance to really learn, well, anything academic. And it's so unfair. But I think if she gets very comfortable at the house with Will and me, she'll agree to go to school, and we can hopefully get her set up with a tutor, you know?"

"That's a good plan," Imani said with a nod. "I can give you the name of Damien's math coach. She's fantastic."

"That'd be amazing." Erica smiled. "You know, if we can get her caught up within a couple of years, she could still excel by the time she gets to high school. Graduate with honors, even, get into a good college. It's still very doable, it's just a long journey."

"Oh, Erica." Dottie practically cackled with laughter, shaking her head. "My Erica."

Erica drew back. "What?"

"You just…" Dottie gave her a warm look. "You just don't know yet, but you will."

"What?" Erica looked around, eyeing the other women to try and read Dottie's vague platitude. "What don't I know yet?"

"Sweetheart." Dottie pushed away a soft, white curl of hair and clasped her hands around the stemless wineglass. "Jada might never make the honor roll. Heck, she might not even go to college. Not the way that you did, anyway."

"I know, I know that. I mean…" Erica stammered, laughing awkwardly. "We're going to help her get there.

We'll give her every resource imaginable, and she'll learn to apply herself. She can go to—"

"Erica, Jada isn't you," Dottie said, matter of fact.

Sam, Imani, Annie, and Taylor all stayed quiet, listening to the inevitably wise, quotable, and brilliant words of the best mother they all knew.

"I know that," Erica insisted.

"And I'm not saying that because she's adopted," Dottie clarified. "I'm saying that because...she isn't you. She's an entirely different person. She likes to draw. She's creative. She likes to paint. She's never going to enjoy math, and probably not reading a whole lot, either."

"But...she will." Erica swallowed. "She has to learn. I'll help her learn."

Dottie just pursed her lips and shook her head, keeping a nearly comical sense of calm in the midst of Erica's stressy and characteristic desire to control and fix and handle everything.

"You will help her, I don't doubt that." Dottie nodded. "But remember, Erica. You're going to reach a point where you stop trying to get her to be what you want her to be, and just love her for who she is."

The profound words pressed on Sam's heart and she glanced over at Taylor, knowing that there was so much truth to that it was scary.

Erica puffed out a sigh and leaned back on her chair. "I know, I will, but I also want her to do well in life and...succeed."

"Success isn't necessarily college, though," Imani added, shrugging. "Jada's so talented, she could end up at art school or something. Heck, John will probably hire her as a graphic designer in ten years."

Erica looked from one to the other, her shoulders dropping with a sigh. "You know, you guys are right—and good motherhood role models. I guess I'm so busy pressing my own priorities onto her, I'm missing the big picture. Loving her for, well, her." She nodded. "And not because she's valedictorian."

"Overachievers are overrated," Taylor teased, arching a brow as she lifted her glass to her lips. "Right, Mom?"

"I wouldn't change you, Tay, you know that." Sam smiled. "Oh! Speaking of Taylor overachieving, tell them about the Blackhawk thing!"

"It's not that big a deal, Mom."

"Um, excuse me?" Sam laughed, shaking her head. "It's a huge deal."

"Yes, it is," Annie chimed in. "All of Coastal Marketing is buzzing about this."

"Taylor here..." Sam grabbed her daughter's arm and gave it a proud shake. "Came up with a brilliant idea for a new client at Coastal Marketing to debut their new brewery location with a booth at the Ron Jon Invitational. And..." She nudged Taylor. "Tell them!"

Taylor rolled her eyes and reluctantly leaned forward. "I'm having Kai come to the booth to bring customers and attention and press. I got lucky, since I know him, but the Blackhawk guys seemed insanely excited, so I guess it's a good idea."

"Oh, quit the humility." Dottie flicked her fingers.

"It's fantastic, Taylor. You're a marketing wizard and you've only been there three weeks."

"I don't know about wizard, but...it's cool." She glanced around and flashed a bright smile. "I'm really enjoying it."

Sam beamed with pride as everyone fussed over Taylor and reminded her how amazing she was, not that Sam would ever forget, even for a second.

"Enough about me, though." Taylor took a sip and slid Sam a look. "Annie can back me up here—my mom has quite a story to share."

Instantly knowing what her daughter was referring to, Sam groaned. "Oh, please."

"What is it?" Erica asked.

Annie chuckled and answered for her. "A bizarre coincidence is what it was."

"I'm intrigued." Imani raised her brows.

"Basically, the guy we hired to restore some of our antiques for the renovation, well, he was...you know." Sam shrugged, laughing. "Attractive, witty, age appropriate. I guess we had kind of a little, I don't know...smidge of a flirtation when he came by for a consultation."

Dottie nodded knowingly. "A smidge," she agreed.

"Sam, that's amazing." Erica laughed. "I'm so happy you met someone."

"Oh, wait until I finish the story." Sam rolled her eyes. "Because the someone I met also happens to be Ben's junior year AP Calc teacher."

"Which"—Annie lifted a finger—"we did not find out until we were standing in his classroom."

"Hah!" Imani tilted her head back. "That's hysterical. What a small world."

"Seriously..." Erica shook her head. "Who would have thought?"

"Not me." Sam took a sip of the sweet rose. "I guess it's nice to know I can be, you know...noticed again. But that particular interaction will not be going anywhere beyond pleasantries at the school and paint color discussion at the inn. It'd be too weird for Ben. Besides, it's way too soon to even consider dating. I'm still not divorced."

Erica huffed a breath. "I hate how long it's taking."

"It is what it is. I'm just focusing on myself and the inn." She reached over to Dottie and grabbed her hand, the two of them sharing a mother daughter moment. "It's bringing me more joy than I knew was possible."

As the women sipped, chatted, laughed and enjoyed each other, the sun went down, and the beach turned silver and gray with nighttime. Palm trees swayed in the breeze and the heat of the sun disappeared, leaving the air warm, tropical, and comforting.

"Okay." Erica lifted a hand as the patio filled with laughter and another bottle of rose. "So we've covered my life and developing parenting skills, which clearly still need some work. We've discussed Sam's next husband—carpenter slash math teacher."

Sam laughed heartily. "Oh my gosh, please."

Erica continued, gesturing at Taylor. "Young Tay's budding new marketing career, Mom—your reno progress. That just leaves you, darling sister-in-law." She turned to Imani, who had definitely been noticeably quiet and keeping to herself tonight.

Sam suddenly wondered if everything was okay. Imani hadn't mentioned her freelance work, hardly brought up her kids or John. Come to think of it, she'd barely said anything at all the whole night.

Everyone turned to face Imani, and the sudden dose of attention made her eyes widen.

"How are you?" Erica asked gently. "How's *TravelBee*? The Space Center piece was amazing. I texted you about how much everyone loved it."

Imani smiled, but something in her expression was weak and forced. "Thanks. I'm glad."

"Honey, what is it?" Dottie angled her head, her thin brows knitting together with concern for her daughter-in-law.

"Oh, it's...it's nothing." Imani flicked her hand and took a sip of wine, looking away as she swallowed.

"Is something going on?" Sam asked. "Talk to us."

"Is it John?" Erica frowned.

"If he's upset you..." Dottie folded her arms across her chest. "He's going to be hearing from me."

Imani managed a laugh, but looked like she was seriously holding back tears. "We just...we're kind of fighting. A lot."

Sam shook her head, completely mystified by the notion of the most perfect, rock-solid American dream couple being anything but flawless and happy.

She thought back, wondering if she'd ever even heard of John and Imani having so much as a disagreement. She drew a blank. They were always happy. Always steady. Always on the same page.

"What happened?" Taylor asked gently.

"It's...it's the whole writing thing. I want to get back into it, I really do. I knew I missed writing, but I didn't actually realize how much." She exhaled sharply. "*TravelBee* wants me to keep doing pieces for them, some of them featuring places in other parts of Florida. Nothing crazy. Apparently the Kennedy article went viral and they think I'm their ticket to becoming a major online travel website."

"Imani!" Erica nudged her. "That's great!"

"Yeah, congratulations!" Sam raised her glass. "Back and better than ever."

"And as you all know..." She tipped her head. "I'm already deep into another piece for them, this time a feature about our very own Sweeney House Inn."

"I am so excited to read your finished work on our little spot, Imani. I know you'll make it absolutely sing." Dottie clasped her hands together. "So, why are you and John fighting?"

"Well, that's the thing. I want to do it. It wouldn't be a ton of travel, and nowhere even out of state. I'd just be going to a few other beach towns and hidden, undiscovered areas, writing about them for this fun, hip, travel blog site, and that's it. A few weekends of travel, max."

Erica shrugged. "It sounds doable, but I've also never had three kids, so I'm probably not the best judge. But I'll babysit those angels anytime."

"Same," Sam said.

"Get in line, ladies." Dottie gave them a stern look. "Grandma dibs."

They laughed but Imani just let out another sigh.

"What we're saying, Imani, is just do it," Sam said to her. "You're a wonderful mom, and nothing is going to change that. Nothing. If you feel like you need this, and it's going to make you happy and fulfilled, do it. Believe me. You deserve to have passions of your own, and that won't take away from how great of a mother you are. Take it from someone who was never even allowed to explore those passions."

Imani gave Sam a sympathetic glance. "I don't know, you guys. I'm certain I could do both, I really am. I mean, it's part-time freelance. It's not like I'm traveling across the globe like I used to. And of course we have a big family of loving babysitters. But John..." She shook her head and slumped down in the chair, her eyes darkening. "He's so traditional, and he's so positive that my absence for two days is going to affect the kids' lives and send him into a spiral."

Erica leaned forward. "Do you think it will?"

"Honestly? Not really." Imani threw her hands up. "Like I said, I can do both. But...we fought about it, and it was the first real argument we've had in years. It makes me wonder...is this worth putting a strain on my marriage? Should I just shut up and forget about it?"

"No," Sam said quickly, and with more fire than she expected.

Everyone turned to face her, and suddenly she felt

very strongly that her sister-in-law should follow her heart and not entirely lose herself in motherhood.

"You *can* do both." Sam pushed some hair behind her ears and set her wineglass on the coffee table. "It's freelance, right? I mean, you can decide how much you want to travel and how much time you want to spend writing. The kids will be in school all day starting in August. Why the heck not?"

"I'm with Mom." Taylor notched a finger at her mother. "You're an amazing writer, Aunt Imani, and clearly this *TravelBee* sees that. You should get to enjoy your talent as a writer and a mother. Uncle John will have to just get over it."

"And he will," Dottie added with a calm, reassuring nod. "John is just like his father. He hates change." She laughed softly. "But he will learn to deal with it and eventually embrace it."

Imani nodded, clearly feeling a bit more at ease with the support of the women who loved her.

"I just feel like..." She sighed. "I can't shake the notion that it makes me a terrible mom, like... why aren't my kids enough to make me happy?"

Erica lifted a hand. "Um, because you're a human, with your own desires and dreams outside of just family? I mean, look at me. I just adopted an eleven-year-old, pretty much out of the blue, and I have absolutely zero intention of quitting my job."

"Your job is important," Imani said weakly.

"You're important," Sam insisted, reaching to take her sister-in-law's hand. "John will come around. You two never fight. I'm sure this rough patch will blow over in no time, and you'll be back to being painfully adorable and obnoxiously perfect."

Imani snorted. "I hope so. It feels like a pretty nasty rough patch. Things have been so tense."

"Marriage ebbs and flows," Dottie said.

"I'm sure that as soon as he sees how not a big deal it is, he'll say he was totally wrong and overreacted and worried for nothing." Taylor smiled at her aunt, her kind wisdom and support making Sam proud.

"Thank you, guys." Imani looked around. "I feel better. I needed this."

"We all needed this." Erica lifted her glass. "To the Sweeney women. And Annie, our honorary sister."

Annie laughed sweetly and raised her glass, too.

"Cheers, my darlings." Sam clicked her glass to theirs and took a sip of wine, wondering how she'd spent so many years pushing all of them so far away.

Now, she'd hold them close, and never take these relationships for granted again.

Chapter Nineteen

Taylor

I t had been a whole week—a full seven days—and Taylor still continued to replay her conversation with Kai over and over again in her head. Despite being up to her eyeballs in planning, managing, and working out all of the details for the branding debut of the Blackhawk booth at the Invitational, even the time-consuming, exciting project wasn't enough to get her mind off of him.

Sigh. She still had it bad, no matter how hard she tried to distract herself. It didn't help, of course, that every loose end of this Blackhawk endeavor led her straight back to Kai—the answer to all of her work problems, and the cause of all her personal ones.

Nonetheless, Taylor was over the moon to be getting a real chance to be in charge of something at the ad agency, hoping to impress Uncle John and the other higher-ups at Coastal Marketing. She'd found a passion in this, and was starting to really discover the thrill of seeing her very own vision coming to life.

The Ron Jon Invitational was rapidly approaching, which meant preparation was in high gear—almost as high gear as the anticipation of knowing she was about to see the only guy she'd ever loved.

For a week. And then it was goodbye again. Forever, probably.

Taylor shook her head and pushed away the bitter-sweet lump in her throat as she navigated down the boardwalk on the beach cruiser that Mom had unearthed at the inn.

The air was gorgeous at this time of day, right around sunset, swirling with salty warmth and just enough breeze to keep you cool. She loved hopping on the teal bike with its precious basket and high handle-bars and taking an after-work ride down the long wooden boardwalk that connected several beach access areas.

The boardwalk was close enough to the ocean that she felt like she could see the water and hear the birds, a perfect place for a long, head-clearing, solitary bike ride. Taylor could be alone with her thoughts and feelings and try to sort out why on Earth this guy had such a tight hold on her.

As she pedaled at a steady pace, she moved along the wooden path, letting the breeze lift her hair and blow it freely around her face. She took a long, deep breath and watched the ocean waves crashing on the sand, wishing that she could somehow separate the memories of Kai from the ocean.

Would she think of him *every* time she looked at the water for the rest of her life?

They had barely dated, after all. Why was she so stuck? Taylor Parker had never been hung up on a man—not once in her life. Especially after Dad cheated on

Mom and revealed himself to be pretty much the worst person on the planet.

She'd decided then and there that men couldn't be trusted.

But something about Kai had been so different. So comforting and exciting and real. He saw her in a way that no one else ever had, and being with him was the perfect balance of thrilling and peaceful.

He'd seemed worthy of trust, and loyalty and...love.

And he still was. He was just gone. Thousands of miles and an entire ocean away, and nothing was ever going to change that.

Taylor puffed out a sigh, knowing that time would heal but wondering how much freaking longer she had to wait for time to do its thing.

He would be here in a week for the contest. Maybe after all of that was over, and they said one last goodbye, maybe then Taylor would be able to fully move on.

Or maybe the wound would be as fresh and raw and painful as it was the day he left the first time.

Taylor decided that was probably enough alone-with-her-thoughts time, and turned the handlebars around to head back down the boardwalk toward the cottage.

Maybe they could get another bike and she and her mother could go together, out here on the boardwalk. Or maybe Ben would like it. Nah. Her little brother was way too cool to ride a bike. Wouldn't be caught dead, probably.

As Taylor cruised her way back to the cottage along

the uneven planks of wood, she thought about all the ways she had changed her life in the past couple of months.

She was thriving in her new role at the agency, Mom was the happiest she'd seen her in years, and Ben was, well, a changed man. Or boy. Or somewhere in between.

Having started to truly and deeply heal from the shattering of her family and, essentially, the loss of her dad, the only thing left in Taylor's life that made her blue was...Kai.

As she pedaled up the boardwalk, she could see the faded yellow paint of the cottage getting closer and closer.

Looking to her left, the surf was glassy and the waves were small. There was no one on the beach except for...

A surfer?

Huh. That was weird. Someone was surfing in the ocean right behind the cottage, and so late in the day. Who would...

"No," Taylor whispered out loud to herself, deciding that if she was having hallucinations about seeing Kai, she seriously needed to get some professional help, because...yikes.

After she stopped riding and leaned the bike against the railing of the boardwalk, Taylor jogged out onto the sand and squinted at the deep blue horizon.

She was not hallucinating, there was definitely a surfer out there.

Quick, elegant, athletic, he moved with the waves,

spraying up water splashes and gliding across the glassy water.

Taylor's heart kicked up as he got closer, even though she knew it wasn't him. It couldn't be. He was still all the way in Hawaii, and he wasn't coming to town for another week.

But...the black wetsuit. The tan surfboard with a dark green design. The...

"There you are!"

It *was* him!

Taylor laughed breathlessly, shock and confusion washing over her like those ocean waves. "Kai? Is that you?" She jogged closer to the water. "What are you... how is this..."

He walked to the shoreline, tucking his board under his arm and shaking out that signature Hawaiian Prince Charming long hair. "Surprise."

"You're..." She looked at him, a good, long look to really make sure her eyes and mind weren't deceiving her.

Nope, it was him. Broad shoulders, tanned skin, sharp, defined features around dark eyes on that unbelievably handsome face.

"You're here," she finally croaked out.

"I am." He walked toward her, running a hand through his hair. "I decided to come for the Invitational a little early. I wanted to surprise you, but you weren't home, so I figured I'd just get some waves in. I knew you'd find me out here anyway."

Of course she would. It's where she always looked for

him, even though she knew he'd never be there. Except this time, he was.

And suddenly, Taylor was overcome with happiness. "You're here!" she said again, running the rest of the distance to jump straight into his arms. He dropped his board and held her tight, lifting her up and spinning her around and making her feel so deeply adored.

"So..." He lowered her back down, running his hand over her cheek, those deep, dark eyes drinking her in like never before. "Do you like the surprise?"

"I..." She shook her head, still in total disbelief. "Yes! Are you kidding? I missed you, Kai. I missed you a lot."

"I missed you more." He leaned forward and kissed her, light and sweet and tasting like saltwater.

She melted into him, practically floating off the ground as she wrapped her arms around his neck and let go of everything that was pressing on her heart during her bike ride.

Yes, he lived five thousand miles away. Yes, he was only in town for a short time. And, yes, she knew this could never and would never become some sort of epic, fantasy love story like in the movies.

But right now, Taylor was wrapped in his embrace, her toes in the sand and the water at her ankles, holding him, touching him for real instead of just in her dreams.

She shut her eyes and let herself lean into the moment, knowing that nothing, *nothing* could take away this tremendous joy she was feeling right now.

"So where have you been? John got you working late for the Invitational stuff?" He asked with a smile as they walked away from the water and sat side by side in the sand, like always.

"Not exactly." Taylor tucked her knees to her chest and leaned her head on his shoulder as the beachside sky turned dark. "I was just..." *Deeply pondering why it's been so impossibly hard for me to get over you.* "On a bike ride."

"So you'll ride a bike but you won't ride a wave?" He nudged her, his strong arm sending warmth up her spine.

"That is so completely different," Taylor said through a laugh.

"Yeah, surfing is a million times more fun."

"And more dangerous."

He raised his brows dramatically, giving her an exaggerated look of disgust. "No way, Tay. You can't fall off a board and break your arm. The ocean will catch you."

"Um." She wrinkled her nose playfully. "I'd be willing to bet that plenty of people have broken an arm surfing before."

"You can't scrape your knee," he teased.

"I'd rather scrape my knee than get bit by a shark." She leaned closer to him, falling into his deep, knowing gaze.

"Ah." He drew toward her, his arm sliding around her waist. "They're friendly."

"Sharks?" She arched a brow and stifled a smile as the space between them got smaller and smaller.

"Yeah." Kai brushed the back of his fingers along her cheek, his lips just inches from hers. "They're misunderstood."

"Is that right?" Taylor laughed and sucked in a sharp breath as she leaned forward and planted her lips on his, because, well, she couldn't wait one more second.

Kissing Kai was like diving into the ocean. Everything went silent and still and moved in slow motion. It created a bubble around them that made the rest of the world feel like it was sealed off, a thousand miles away.

She wished she could live in that moment forever.

She pulled away just enough to catch his gaze, running her hand through his long hair, still dripping with ocean water. "You're here for...what? Like, ten days, since you came early?"

"Not exactly." His eyes flashed.

"What do you mean? You have to stay through the Invitational..."

"I do, but I need to get back right after. Basically, the minute the competition is over, I'm getting on a plane."

Taylor felt her heart sink a bit. She had been counting on those few extra days after the contest to be with him. Every second was so precious.

"Wow. Well, you came early, but you're leaving... even earlier." Taylor frowned, glancing out at the ocean and the starry night sky above it.

"I know. It sucks." He kissed her cheek. "I missed you so much, Tay. I didn't even realize how much."

Neither did she.

"About a week then. That's what we have until the RJI and you have to go back..." Taylor repeated slowly.

A few busy, hectic, stress-filled days with hardly any

downtime and a whole lot at stake with her career...and her heart.

Kai turned to face her, the sunset casting a warm orange glow on his angular profile. "We better make the most of it, huh?"

Chapter Twenty

Imani

I mani skimmed through her latest finished piece on the *TravelBee* website, brimming with pride at her short and sweet feature on the exciting renovation and restoration of the Sweeney House Inn.

She *had* to do it, and the editors loved the idea. They gobbled up how personal and close to home it was for the author, and also loved that the article showcased a Space Coast gem that was bringing together tradition and modernity in such a cool and unique way.

Not to mention, who wouldn't adore Dottie and Sam? Writing the piece had brought Imani so much joy and fulfillment. Plus, it had been such a fun and easy article; taking only about a week to get to a final draft, she'd flown through it.

Sweeney House deserved all the love and shares and attention in the world.

And...it was getting a lot of that, because Imani's Space Coast travel blogs were continuing to break records for the website.

She fired off a quick text to Kristen, thanking her for yet another cover page feature, and leaned back on the sofa, tucking a throw pillow behind her as she relished the new excitement of her work.

She was back. And the girls were right. John would have to just get over it, and learn to adapt. She craved this too much, she needed it in her life too much to just throw it by the wayside, and Imani was certain that it wouldn't affect her children's lives or happiness.

Only her own, for the better. She'd be a better mother and wife with her own well filled, she was sure of it.

"Okay, that's enough ego stroking," she said to herself with a laugh, closing the laptop and reaching over to set it down on the coffee table.

Yes, things with John were tense, and that weighed heavily on her heart. Her marriage was something that Imani truly never thought she'd have to worry about, but ever since she'd started writing again it had seemed like they were inching toward a serious rough patch.

Ever since she'd applied for the freelance work, John had been distant, preoccupied, and irritable. Tensions between them were high. Really high.

But she told herself over and over that it would pass, and they'd go back to being the rock-solid couple they'd always been. Because a job wasn't worth a marriage, and she knew that.

A vibration from her phone on the table next to her caught Imani's attention, and she leaned over to see who was calling.

Unknown caller, from 916 area code. Expecting a marketing call, she answered brusquely. "Hello?"

"Hi, have I reached Imani Sweeney?" A cheerful

man's voice came through, and Imani tried, and failed, to place it.

"Yes, this is her," she said slowly.

"Imani, it's a pleasure. My name is Jackson Holladay. I'm the managing editor at *Wanderlust*."

She sucked in a sharp breath as a shockwave ripped through her.

Wanderlust? The most famous, fastest-growing, and high-profile online travel guide in the world?

"Oh, hello, Jackson." She cleared her throat and gathered herself, sitting up straight and pressing the phone to her ear so that she didn't miss a single word. "How are you?"

"Doing great, doing great. So happy I caught you. Is it a good time to chat?"

Did it matter? When the senior editor of *Wanderlust* calls and wants to chat, it's always a good time.

"Yes, I'm totally free. What can I do for you?"

"Well..." He chuckled softly. "I know this is going to seem a bit out of left field, so bear with me, okay?"

She twirled one of her braids, curious and intrigued. "Okay, I'm bearing."

"I'll just cut right to the chase. We want you to write for us."

She nearly choked, standing up as the words sank in. "You want...me to write for *Wanderlust*?"

"Yes, we do. We've been following you, actually. Not to sound creepy," Jackson laughed heartily. "But we have. Your pieces in *TravelBee* just blew us out of the water. So, I did some digging and found out that you had yourself quite the reputation as a sought-after travel writer many years ago, for *Fodor's*. Am I wrong?"

She smiled, feeling her stomach flutter. "Uh, no you're not wrong. I wrote for *Fodor's*, back when everything was still hard copy, but I stopped working when my oldest son was born. I hadn't worked in fifteen years, but I saw *TravelBee*'s posting for a freelance writer a little while ago, and it was something I could do locally, so I figured I'd dip my toes back in."

"Well, you've made quite a splash."

She had?

"Your articles have been circulating, old and new. We want you here, Imani. And I'm not a man who takes no for an answer, so please. Hit me with all of your objections and reasons why you can't do this, and I promise you, I'll have a response to every single one."

Imani was so floored she could barely breathe for a second, and she sat back down on the edge of the couch to gather herself.

"What would I be writing about? Where would you want me?"

"California."

She choked a dry laugh. He might as well have said Mars, it was so far out of the realm of reality.

"First, understand that this isn't a lightweight assignment," he continued before she even started to say no. "We're partnering with the tourism board, and they have a massive budget—and I do mean *massive*—and want to create not a feature story, but a whole spinoff section on our site that will be called 'The Golden Coast.' Every week, it will run a new feature of another section of the state, each one with that deep, raw emotional connection you are so good at delivering."

"That's...huge."

"It is, and when it's done, we are going to transform all the writing and photography into a coffee table gift book with your name on the cover. In fact, we're already in discussions with a top New York publisher. This project is going to breathe new life into California, highlighting the rich history, the beauty, the surprises—not typical tourist stuff. Things that have never been done before."

She practically salivated. "Uh, how long would something like that take?"

"We'd give you three months to research and pull together the bones of each story, then you could take another, say, two to four months to do the writing. So only three months of travel, all expenses paid at the finest hotels. We'd provide a photographer and a team to assist you. We want someone who's going to highlight that deep history of California, who's going to bring people here just with the way they describe the sunset at some tiny, local, hole in the wall beach bar. I believe that person is you."

Every word had her reeling with shock and hope and disbelief. "I...wow. I..."

"What do you say?"

Her phone beeped with an incoming call that she ignored, letting it go to voicemail.

"I can't say much, since I'm speechless," she told him.

"First of all, I'm honored. I mean, seriously. Thank you, that's a huge compliment." Imani took in a shaky breath, centering herself. "Three months in California...I just don't think that's at all feasible for me. I have a family, and they need me here in Florida."

"Bring 'em."

"Wow, you really do have an answer for everything," she said on a laugh, still trying to get her feet back down to Earth and process this with a level head.

"Come on, keep trying," Jackson said. "I got all day, believe it or not."

She laughed softly, switching the phone to her other ear, noticing that her palms were sweaty. "You know what, Jackson? I'm going to talk to my husband..."

Who is going to tell me that I have officially lost my mind and not support even the tiniest discussion about this.

The reality hurt Imani's heart. This phone call was a literal dream come true for her, and she had no doubt in her mind that her very own husband would be completely opposed to it.

"Fair enough." Jackson clicked his tongue. "You talk with your family about it, but don't take too long. We want you on a plane in two weeks."

"Two weeks?" She blurted out the question.

"Timing is tight, we know, but this is big and moving fast. Take a day or two to mull it over, but I know you're a professional who knows opportunities like this don't come often."

No, they certainly did not.

The phone vibrated and beeped again, but she didn't recognize the number, so she jammed her finger on the Ignore button. Nothing could possibly be as important as Jackson Holladay and *Wanderlust*.

"Listen, Imani," he said on a long sigh. "Like I told you, give it thought. But not too much thought, okay? It didn't take a ton of digging to discover that you were, and probably still are, extremely passionate about travel writing. You wouldn't have had the career you did if this didn't bring you a lot of joy and excitement."

Her eyes fluttered shut as each word pressed down hard on her heart. Why did he have to be so spot-on?

"You're one of us," Jackson said softly. "Follow your heart, see the world, write about it. That's what we do. And I know you're called to it, or you wouldn't have picked up a freelance job for an online magazine. Once again, am I wrong?"

"You are..." She laughed shakily. "You are quite a mind reader, that's for sure."

Another beeping rang through the phone, and this time she recognized the caller. John.

Imani grunted with frustration and pressed Ignore. No doubt it was him needing something from her, and expecting her to drop everything and do it.

Not now. She was busy.

"Anyway, that's all I got for you," Jackson said. "This

is my direct cell number, so shoot me a text or give me a call back when you've thought it through."

She nodded, sighing with a bit of relief that she'd have at least a small amount of time to actually think about this.

Of course, it was silly and insane. She wasn't going to do it. California? That was crazy. There was no chance. Absolutely no chance.

But, oh...how thrilling it would be. "I'll call you, Jackson," she said. "I promise."

"Looking forward to it. And remember—don't overthink it. You're one of us. Talk soon, Imani."

As he hung up and the call ended, Imani flopped down onto the sofa, laughing to herself.

Was this actual real life? Even though she knew she was going to turn it down, just the prospect of being called and sought out like that made her feel incredible.

She *was* going to turn it down, wasn't she?

Yes, of course she was. California was way, way too far and even though this was a dream opportunity for her, traveling and working like that wasn't her life anymore. Leave in two weeks? The kids would just be starting the school year.

She had to focus on her family and being a mom. This was supposed to just be a side project. But...wow. They wanted her. They'd looked at her canon of work and *hand selected* her for this position.

Turning that down was going to sting a little. More than a little. It was going to shatter her.

Breaking her out of a rabbit hole of thoughts and

possibilities, her phone started buzzing again, over and over.

"Oh, crap," she said out loud, grabbing the phone as she realized she'd completely forgotten to call John back.

As soon as she looked at the screen, Imani's heart rate kicked up, this time for an entirely different reason.

She had four missed calls from John and three from another number.

Frantically switching right back into Mom mode, she called John and he picked up right away.

"Imani," he answered, his voice sounding nervous and anxious and...mad.

"What's going on?" she asked, nerves spiking.

"Where are you? Where have you been?"

"What do you mean?" She stood up to pace. "I'm home, I was on the phone with someone. What happened?"

"The zoo has been calling you, calling both of us, actually."

"The zoo?" Her mind shot straight to Ellen and Liam at camp and the unknown number she'd been ignoring. "Are they okay?"

"Evidently, Ellen got bit by a spider or something and her whole arm is swollen and red. The counselors have been begging us to get a parent out there. They don't know if she's allergic or needs medical attention or something. It could be serious, Imani."

"Oh my gosh!" She frantically ran to the front closet, threw on the nearest pair of shoes and snagged her purse off a hook, throwing it over her shoulder and darting out to the car. "I'm sorry I didn't see the calls, John. I was—"

"It's okay, just please get there." He sounded disappointed and worried and very much like it was not okay. "I'm nervous about it."

"Me, too. I'm going to get there as fast as I can."

"Please," he replied. "Keep me posted. I was trying to get out of these afternoon meetings and was ready to get in the car myself."

"No need, I'm on my way, and I'll keep you posted." Imani ached for her poor baby girl, knowing that if this spider bite was bad enough for the counselors to call her and John, it wasn't nothing.

Imani sucked in a shuddery breath and forced herself to focus on the road. She'd gotten so caught up, so distracted by this shiny new possibility that she ignored her phone and her baby needing her.

But she was going now, laser focused on the road and the steering wheel and getting to her youngest as fast as humanly possible.

No more ignoring calls.

It wouldn't happen again. Her kids came first. They always would.

Was she a terrible mother for getting so caught up she couldn't be bothered to answer her phone? Was she an even more terrible mother for actually being tempted by this California job?

"Okay, she's down." Imani tiptoed out of Ellen's room, gently shutting the door after three full bedtime stories before their youngest finally drifted off to sleep. "And the swelling on the bite is practically gone."

John hardly looked up at her from the hardcover book he was reading, laying in bed up against a tall pillow and the headboard. "Thank goodness. I'm glad you were able to get there. I hope she wasn't too upset waiting."

Imani let out a deep sigh as she went into the bathroom and wrapped her braids up in a silk sleep bonnet and brushed her teeth. "I think there may have been just a tiny smidge of classic Ellen drama involved today," she said, knowing her sweet and adorable daughter was a bit prone to exaggeration...the stomachache, the knee scrape, the bug bite.

She also knew that John was definitely less than thrilled with her right now, although being the nonconfrontational peacemaker that he was, he didn't say anything. Not yet, anyway, but another blowout seemed inevitable.

They had kept it cool all through dinner and the evening, never, ever wanting to fight in front of the kids. But now, the kids were all in bed, the tension was palpable and it was clearly time, yet again, for the world's most perfect couple to have it out.

"John." Imani slid into her side of the bed. "I'm sorry, okay? I should have answered the phone."

"Yes, but it's fine. Things happen," he answered without turning to face her. "This just...really isn't like you, Imani. And it's got me worried."

She squeezed her eyes shut. "I feel absolutely awful. You know that. I don't know how many other ways to say that I feel bad and I screwed up. Can't we just let it go?"

He finally turned and looked at her, and those blue eyes that were normally the most comforting place in the world for Imani looked stormy and unwelcoming. "It's not that. I'm just concerned about you. You're distracted and distant. This is more than just the world's most-on-top-of-her-game mother having some...issues. You're changing, and it scares me."

Imani swallowed, leaning back against the headboard and pulling the silky comforter up around her chest. "I just made a mistake, that's all. I should have answered the calls."

He looked at her, quiet for a long minute. "Because you're completely preoccupied. With work."

He wasn't wrong. But was loving her job—one she was so good at that the top editors in the world sought her out—that bad? Really? He was being unreasonable, but she knew he didn't see it that way.

"I wasn't working," she said slowly.

"Honey, please. Ever since you went back to work and started writing again, you've been completely distant and busy. It seems like you're always wishing you were somewhere else. It sucks. For me and the kids."

Emotion gripped her throat, and she willed herself to keep it together. "That is not true."

"What were you doing this afternoon?" he asked gently. "I'm really not trying to yell at you or accuse you, Imani. I want to know what's going on with you, because all of this is so out of character. It's worrisome. I don't think you've ever ignored a call when the kids are in someone else's care. You just aren't yourself lately. I want to fix it and I don't know how."

That was John, all right. Determined to fix everything all the time. She loved him for it, but she didn't agree that she hadn't been herself.

Why did she feel more like herself than she had in... years? And how could she possibly explain that to him without a fight, or worse?

"I, um..." She lowered her tone, staying as calm as possible to avoid this inevitably escalating. "I got a phone call."

"Okay." He studied her, his brow furrowing. "From who?"

She chewed her lip, looking him right in the eyes. "Jackson Holladay. The senior editor at *Wanderlust*."

John's jaw fell slack and he wiped his palm over his face. "Oh my God."

"Yeah." Imani nodded. "Big time."

"What did he want?"

"He wanted me..." She met his gaze again, jitters zipping up her spine. "To write a piece for them, a feature on the entire coastline of California. It's not just a feature, though, it's a—"

"California?"

"Yes. It will run for a year on the site, in conjunction with the tourism board, and they'd turn the whole thing into a coffee table book, professionally published and..." She squeezed her eyes. "They want me to spend three months going up the coast of California to do the research."

John turned straight ahead, his jaw visibly clenching as he processed the atomic bomb of shock. "Holy cow."

"Yeah." She laughed dryly. "I know. I was floored. And that conversation was happening and I got wrapped up and he was kind of a chatterbox and I was, of course, hanging onto every word and...I messed up."

He pinched the bridge of his nose with his fingers, shaking his head. "California..."

"I know. I mean, it's nuts, right?" She shrugged and leaned back. "I couldn't believe it. I felt like I was dreaming. When the book is published, my name would be on the cover as the author."

"I mean, this isn't a serious thing, right? This is crazy, Imani. You can't..." John glanced at her, and she searched his face for even a hint of a smile, but there wasn't one. "I don't know what to say."

"You could try, 'Congratulations'," Imani replied, her voice breaking a little.

She turned away so he couldn't see her start to cry.

"Imani, are you actually considering this?" His voice was a soft whisper. Not angry, not frustrated. Almost...scared.

Was she?

She had written it off as soon as she got off the phone with Jackson. But what if she was too quick to say no? What if this really was the opportunity of a lifetime?

She inhaled sharply to answer and then paused, truly having no idea what to say. "I don't know." Imani shook her head, feeling more conflicted than she ever had in her life.

"Imani..." He inched closer to her, his eyes wide with astonishment. "You're thinking about this."

"Of course I'm thinking about it. It's a freaking dream opportunity for me."

"It's three months on the other side of the country away from your family."

"He said you guys could come with me," she replied quickly. "All of you."

"We could *what*?" John ran a stressed-out hand through his hair. "Imani, the kids are about to start school. And a million extracurriculars. I have a business that I have to run. Here. In Cocoa Beach. Our *home*."

She drew back, her heart pounding. "I know."

"We can't just pick up and move to the other side of the country. I..." He shook his head. "I just don't understand. I'm trying to understand, but I just...I can't. What changed?"

"What about me?" The words spilled out, fiery with emotion before she even had a chance to pause and think them through. "What about my dreams? What about the fact that this would be a once in a lifetime thing for me, and you don't even care?"

"You had an amazing career." His tone rose now, too. "I thought that all your dreams came true, and that being a mom was your dream now. I thought that was all you needed. Why did it change?"

"Why can't I have both?"

He shut his eyes and clenched his jaw with frustration. "You really want to do this job, don't you?" The words broke as they fell from his lips.

Pain and guilt pounded on Imani's heart as she studied the man in front of her.

She took in a slow, shaky breath and lowered her voice to a whisper. "What if I did want to?"

"Because...we need you here. I can't survive without you, and the kids..." He gave a dry laugh. "You know I would completely crumble without you. We all would. You're my rock, I...I need you."

"You're not losing me, John. Plus, I never said I was going to do it for sure," she insisted.

"But you want to."

"Of course I do."

He let out a sharp exhale and turned away from her, silent for a long time before he said, "I don't know, Imani. Maybe you should go. Maybe we need a break."

She drew back with shock, her breath leaving her lungs. "*Seriously?*" She whimpered the question, feeling as lost and hopeless as ever.

Her heart cracked in half as she turned away and flicked off her bedside lamp as tears poured down her cheeks.

Chapter Twenty-one

Taylor

"And the winner of the 2022 Ron Jon Invitational in Cocoa Beach...finishing with a perfect twenty-point heat...Hawaiian native Kai Leilani!"

The announcer's voice boomed through loudspeakers all across the beach, and the droves of crowds erupted in cheers as Kai hopped to the stage and accepted the over-sized trophy.

Taylor beamed, clapping her hands and cheering as she squeezed her way to the front of the massive cluster of people, watching Kai hold up the gold cup with his right hand, pumping a victorious fist in the air.

Gosh, he looked good up there. And he surfed like the pro that he was, catching five waves in his last heat and a perfect score.

"Woo! Go, Kai!" she shouted, still riding the high of her own personal victory—the roaring success that was the Blackhawk Brewery booth at the Invitational.

Kai's presence, along with his warm demeanor and willingness to take about a billion selfies, brought the longest line of any vendor at the entire contest to Taylor's well-planned and effortless Blackhawk event. They had sold hundreds of beers, T-shirts, and other merchandise, and Brock and Andre had been floored with the popularity and success of their debut promotion with Coastal Marketing.

The day had consisted of a steady stream of guests, lining up all the way around the block to try some new beer and take a picture with the soon-to-be winner of the Ron Jon Invitational. It was a win-win for everyone involved, and Taylor felt like she was on a cloud as she took a lead role in coordinating the entire timeline of the event.

That cloud started to turn a bit gray, though, as bittersweet sadness crept over her.

As Kai took photos, kissed his trophy, held up his surfboards and signed some more autographs, the looming and all-too-familiar heartache of saying goodbye became more and more present by the second.

They'd spent all day together at the booth before he had to compete, and Taylor had been so distracted and consumed with putting on this Blackhawk event flawlessly that she hadn't given herself a chance to be sad.

She'd just enjoyed every second with him, laughing together as he posed for pictures, and bringing fans to meet him, and sharing tastes of the surprisingly delicious craft beer from Asheville.

It felt smooth with him. It felt easy. It felt...like they were a couple.

But that feeling was fleeting, and Taylor knew it. Any second he would kiss her goodbye, get in a car, and head to the airport. And this time, he wasn't coming back for an event. For...any reason.

She swallowed the pain of that truth as she finally made her way to the front of the crowd of fans, and locked eyes with Kai.

He lit up the second he saw her, stepping away from the fans around him to jump off the dais and hustle toward her.

"Congratulations," she said through a laugh as he wrapped his arms around her.

"Congratulations to you, Miss Marketing Queen," he teased. "Your booth was a complete hit. You killed it today."

"Okay, first of all…" She placed a hand on his strong shoulder, his wetsuit still damp from his record-breaking surf. "You literally just won the RJI, so I think *you* killed it today. Not to mention the fact that the Blackhawk event was only a real success because everyone wanted to take a picture with the one and only Kai Leilani."

"Eh." He waved a humble and dismissive hand. "I was just a small piece. You put together the puzzle, Tay."

"Well…" She smiled, feeling her cheeks warm as she got closer to him, smelling the saltwater on his skin. "Thank you. I had a lot of fun with you. You were amazing, both on the waves and at my booth."

"I had the best time, too. Seriously." He wrapped his arm around her shoulders and slowly guided her through the crowd, finding a place behind a local news truck that was a bit more secluded so they could talk.

And say goodbye.

"Come here," he said, pulling her close as they escaped the crowd and craziness of the massive event.

"What?" Taylor laughed, her eyes beaming as she looked up at him, every fiber of her body buzzing with love and desire.

"I wanted to make sure we had a chance to properly say..."

"Goodbye," she answered for him, nodding and shutting her eyes. "I knew it was coming."

"I hate it as much as you do." He placed a hand on her cheek, gently running his thumb across her skin. "Actually, I think I hate it more."

"Nobody hates it more."

Kai leaned down and pressed his forehead against hers, taking a deep breath and holding her so close she could practically hear his heartbeat. "I don't want to say goodbye to you, Taylor. Every second I'm with you...I'm so happy. And I thought surfing was all I ever needed to be happy, but now I'm starting to think it's not enough. I'm starting to think I need you, too."

She tilted her head up to meet his gaze, smiling softly. "Maybe you're just getting greedy."

"Heck, yeah, I am." He laughed.

"Kai..." She bit her lip. "You live in Hawaii, and that's not changing."

"Ever since I went back to the islands, all I can think about is how much you'd love it there. How happy we could be...surfing, hiking, adventuring all the time. I started to see Hawaii how it would look through your eyes—through us together—and it was incredible."

Taylor drew back, blinking with surprise and confusion as she tried to process what exactly Kai was insinuating right now. "What are you..." She sucked in a breath. "What are you saying?"

He took her face in his hands, holding her tight as he lifted her chin up and leveled his gaze.

"Come with me."

"W-what?" Her lip quivered as she blinked back with shock.

Was he serious? No, surely this was a dream and any second now she was going to wake up in her sweet little room at the cottage with Mr. Minx purring by her feet, realizing she'd had another pathetic Kai fantasy.

But she shut her eyes and opened them again, and she was still here. With the August sun beating down on them, hidden behind a news van in the beach parking lot.

And Kai appeared to be dead serious.

"You heard me." Kai smiled and planted a quick kiss on her forehead. "Come to Hawaii with me. Live there with me, just for a little while if you don't want to make it permanent. I know it sounds insane, Tay, I know. But...the way I feel about you, the potential we have here, I'm not willing to let it go. Come on. My car is pulling in any minute to take me to the airport. Just come with me, just jump." He laughed, pulling her closer. "Why not?"

"I...I..." she stammered, pulling away as she shook her head with total astonishment. "I don't even know what to say. Kai, I can't just...leave."

Could she?

What would she be leaving behind, besides an administrative desk job and a room at her grandmother's cottage that would certainly still be here when she came back.

And Mom, of course. She'd be leaving Mom. But ever since they got started on the inn renovation and Sam had really become closer than ever with Dottie, she didn't need Taylor as much.

Mom might even want her to go. Follow her heart. Follow love. Do something crazy and free and fun for once.

"Tay..." Kai glanced down at his phone. "Car's here. What do you say?"

"That you're crazy and I can't...not now, anyway. I have to pack and say goodbye to everyone and...I need to bring my cat."

"Okay, okay." He pushed a strand of her hair back. "How about this? You get your stuff together, pack up little Minxy, say goodbye to your family, and meet me out there. I fly you into Maui in a week, and..." He dipped his head low, sincerity and excitement radiating from him. "We start our own adventure. What do you say?"

Everything in her wanted to scream, "Yes!" and leap into his arms and start planning her new life in Hawaii. But that was the impulsive, reckless, falling in love side of Taylor Parker that seriously lacked rational thought and logic.

Taylor knew, even in the heat and thrill of this moment, that she couldn't ignore reality, and a decision this massive and life-changing would require a bit more thought and consideration.

"I want to," she said breathlessly. "I just...I need to—"

"Think about it," he finished for her, glancing down at his phone again. "Please do. I have to go now. My driver's waiting for me..."

"I'll think about it. I promise."

As if she'd be thinking about anything else.

"Good." Kai wrapped his arms around her one more time, kissing her with enough passion and love and intimacy she could have melted into a puddle right there in the parking lot. "I'll see you, Tay. Hopefully very soon."

"Goodbye, Kai."

Kai reluctantly drew back, walking away as he flashed one more smile over his shoulder. "Don't think too hard!"

"I won't!" Taylor stood on her toes and waved goodbye to him, wondering if this goodbye might end up being very, very temporary.

She could be with him again, for a long time. She wouldn't have to say goodbye, and they could make a thousand memories in one of the most beautiful places on Earth, and she didn't even have much here, and—

"Taylor! There you are!" Uncle John's distinct voice boomed from across the parking lot, yanking Taylor right out of her state of shock and excitement and wonder.

She quickly gathered herself and turned to see him striding toward her, with Brock and Andre—the Black-hawk Bros, as Kai had called them—walking on either side of him.

Uncle John looked liked he was on a mission, and this probably wasn't the best moment to drop an "I might be moving to Hawaii" bomb. Besides, she needed to actually think about it.

Didn't she?

"We've been looking everywhere for you!" Andre offered an effortlessly cool fist bump that Taylor attempted to match with a laugh.

"Sorry, I was just saying goodbye to Kai. He had to head back to Hawaii."

"Already?" John frowned. "That's a shame. I wanted to give him a proper thank you for how much he helped out at the event today."

Taylor smiled. "I'll let him know."

"Good, good." John rubbed his hands together, glancing at both Brock and Andre before nodding his head back toward the vendor area. "Taylor, mind if we steal you for a bit? There's something these guys and I want to run by you."

"Sure, of course." She followed them back to the Blackhawk Brewing booth, still trying to shake off the thrilling haze of her last words with Kai.

As they reached the shade of the booth, some people had already started cleaning up and breaking down the setup, but there were a few chairs still standing in the corner, and she, Brock, Andre and John all sat down.

"So..." Taylor rubbed her palms up and down her thighs, glancing at the three men. "What's up?"

"First of all..." Uncle John cleared his throat. "It's no secret that today was an incredible success."

She breathed a sigh of relief and smiled.

"We were a little wary of this idea at first, you know."

John raised his brows. "A vendor booth at the Invitational was certainly not in our usual repertoire of promotional marketing strategies for a new brand. But you, Taylor, brought a fresh perspective, a youthful, creative eye and used your resources to put on one of the most successful promo launches we've ever done for a client."

"We just..." Brock jumped in, running a hand over his slicked back hair. "We couldn't be happier with the amount of customer outreach and exposure we got here today."

"And Kai Leilani?" Andre added with a laugh of disbelief. "You got the literal winner of the contest to be the face of our beer today. That was killer."

Taylor smiled, blushing at the compliments. "It all came together really well, everyone was awesome. I mean, you guys are great salesmen, and the beer, I have to say, is fantastic."

"We love the humility, Taylor." John chuckled. "But, please, take the credit for this. The entire thing was your idea, and you deserve it."

She sucked in a breath. "Well, thank you."

"Which is why..." Andre lifted his brows, giving a big, wide smile as he shared a look with Brock and then turned back to face Taylor. "We want you to run our account at Coastal Marketing."

She shook her head, not sure she'd heard right. "Me?" Taylor laughed nervously, wondering if her body could physically take any more surprises today. "You guys know I'm admin. I work at the front desk and have never managed an account."

"Yeah, we know," Brock said. "But Andre and I'd never brewed a drop when we came up with the plan for Blackhawk. We love your energy and ideas. The rest you can learn from the team around you."

John leaned forward, patting Taylor's arm. "I would like to offer you a full-time position as an account executive at Coastal Marketing. And your first client is Blackhawk Brewing."

Taylor held her hand to her chest, laughing with shock and wide eyes as she drew back. "I don't...I don't even know what to say. Thank you, Uncle John."

"It's unprecedented for someone to move up this quickly within our company, but these guys here"—John gestured at Brock and Andre—"think you're an advertising superstar in the making. And so do I." He smiled. "I'm very proud of you. Congratulations."

Her heart folded, and suddenly she literally felt like she was being pulled in two different directions. Hard.

Did he realize she hadn't said yes? Of course not, because turning down this job would be *insane*. Almost as insane as moving to Hawaii.

Taylor forced a laugh, but suddenly felt a little dizzy and sick. "Right, of...of course. Thank you. Wow, thank you so much."

It was the ultimate head-versus-heart decision, and Taylor had never truly known which way to go.

She let out a breath, shaking her head and trying not to appear distressed over this.

She should be completely overjoyed, but how could she be? Because now...she had a reason to say no to Kai.

A real, smart, tangible, logical reason why she could not and should not move to Hawaii right now.

That was crazy. And this job opportunity was amazing.

But then there was Kai...and he was so totally worth doing crazy things for.

Chapter Twenty-two

Erica

"See? You're getting it!" Erica smiled with encouragement as she gave Jada a high-five, having finally finished the long section of fraction problems they'd been working on since Erica got home from work.

Jada had been spending the workdays at the inn with Dottie, who promised to try and incorporate some schoolwork, but probably focused more on curtain patterns and paint color.

Erica couldn't complain. Jada was integrating deeply into the family, and there was no better place for her to be while Erica was at work.

"I guess so." Jada shrugged her shoulders as a familiar smile glimmered on her face.

Erica had been seeing a lot more of that smile lately, and every time it brought her even more joy and peace than the time before. "Don't sell yourself short, Jada. You're making huge strides."

Jada exhaled and pushed her hair out of her face, tucking her legs underneath her in the dining room chair. "Thanks."

"So, how are you feeling about school next week? Ready to take on sixth grade?"

She looked up nervously, her eyes wide and her smile gone as quickly as it had appeared. "I don't know. You'll still help me, right?"

"Are you kidding?" Erica nudged her. "Of course. I know you're not going to be completely caught up for a while, but I've already talked with your teachers and they know your situation. They're going to work with me to keep tutoring you and getting you up to speed. Jada…" She placed a hand on her arm and leveled her gaze. "Everyone wants you to succeed, and everyone wants to help."

She let out a shaky breath and nodded. "Okay."

"And I have a surprise for you." Erica grinned.

"What is it?"

"I got you into art class for your elective this semester."

"You did?" Jada's whole face lit up, the bright sparkle in her eyes making Erica want to shout with victory. "I thought you said it was full."

"It was, but I made a couple of phone calls and they added a seat for you."

"I get to take art?" Her smile was in full force now.

"You get to take art."

"That is going to be so much better than math," Jada said on a laugh, shaking her head as she looked back down at the fraction worksheet.

"Speaking of which, we can be done for tonight."

"Thank goodness."

"Why don't you head upstairs, pop in the shower and get some jammies on, and then we can watch the next episode of *Gilmore Girls*?"

"Okay!" Jada climbed out of the chair and darted upstairs, her long, thick curls bouncing behind her with each step.

Erica leaned back and took it in for a second, basking in the joy of her growing and evolving relationship with the girl who felt more like a daughter every day.

They weren't without their challenges, but Erica was starting to deeply adore Jada, and they'd developed a bond and a trust and a uniquely special kind of relationship that Erica cherished.

"All smiles tonight, huh?" Will came around the corner from the kitchen, offering Erica a glass of wine and a big thumbs-up.

"She's doing great." She accepted the wine and took a sip, then gave Will a little kiss of gratitude. "She's really smart, Will. No one has ever told her that before, or given her a chance to show it. She's picking this stuff up. It's amazing."

"Well, she's got a great teacher."

"Oh, please." Erica laughed as Will wrapped his arm around her waist and pulled her in for a hug.

"We're not doing too terribly bad at this whole parenting thing, are we?" he asked with a playful wink.

"You know...I think we're kind of getting the hang of it."

As they chatted and caught up on the progress at the inn, Erica's work on the Eagle launch, and, of course, endlessly talked about Jada, Erica realized it seemed like a long time had passed, and she was still upstairs.

"Do you think I should check on her?" she asked, glancing up toward the staircase. "It's been a while and she hasn't made a peep."

Will shrugged. "I'm sure she's just drawing or something, but go ahead."

Erica nodded and headed toward the stairs, a strange sense of uneasiness rising in her throat as she walked down the hallway and opened the door to Jada's room.

She gasped softly and rushed over with concern as soon as she saw Jada, curled up on the bed, crying. Hard.

"Oh my gosh, Jada." Erica sat right down next to her, gently touching her arm and wondering what on Earth could have possibly happened. "Are you okay? What's wrong?"

"You..." Jada's voice waivered and her lip shook. "You lied."

"What?" Erica's heart kicked. "Sweetie, what are you talking about?".

"You said..." She sniffled, glancing away from Erica and avoiding eye contact. "You said you didn't want a baby still. You said that I was enough and you were happy you got me."

"I am," Erica answered quickly, so beyond confused by what was happening right now. "I meant every word, and that hasn't changed."

"Yes, it has, because you still want a baby. That's what those mean." She pointed to a small white cardboard box sitting on the end table in her room.

Erica's gaze darted to the box. "What are you..." As she studied it, she realized exactly what was going on.

They were pregnancy tests.

"Oh, Jada." Erica's heart dropped as she turned all of her attention back on the girl. "Just let me explain that to you, okay?"

"You're gonna have a baby like you've always wanted." She wiped a tear from her cheek. "And then what about me? You won't care about me anymore. You'll have a newborn instead of a stupid sixth grader."

"No, you're wrong." Erica's voice rose and emotion tightened her throat. "Jada, those are old, they're from a long time ago."

"And...and...." Jada inhaled shakily. "You said I was enough, but you lied, because you're still trying to have a baby. So that you can replace me. Because you never wanted me in the first place, you wanted that." She looked over at the box again and shuddered with a sob. "I knew I was right that you wanted a baby."

"Jada, please listen to me, okay?"

"I did listen to you." She looked up at Erica, her giant brown eyes sullen and hurt, that sweet, tender little soul clearly aching to be loved. "I believed you when you said you didn't wish you got a baby instead. But now I know you still want one, and then you're gonna forget me."

"That would never happen."

"But it's what you really wanted." Jada recoiled even further away. "And now I know, so can you please just leave me alone."

"Jada, listen—"

"Please," she whimpered, turning away and pulling the blanket over her face. "I just want to be by myself. I'm an introvert, just like you taught me."

Erica's heart tugged hard as she shut her eyes and dug for patience and composure. "Okay," she said reluctantly, knowing it was important to respect Jada's need to be alone, and they could talk this out later.

She got up, took one long look at Jada in the bed, and slipped out the door.

"Honey." Will grabbed her as soon as she got to the bottom of the staircase and crumpled in his arms. "What's wrong? What happened?"

Erica took a deep sigh and the two of them walked over to the living room sofa and sat down. "She found a box of pregnancy tests in the bathroom, back from when we were trying to conceive."

"Oh." Will frowned, not entirely understanding the significance of that right away. "Okay...what happened?"

"Well, evidently she has decided that means we want a baby, and we're going to have one and forget about her."

"What?" He shook his head with disbelief. "That's crazy. I hope you told her that's crazy."

"Of course I did. But she's convinced we wanted a baby from the adoption agency instead of her, and she's got that in her head and it's killing her."

He paused for a long time, leaning back onto the sofa and thinking hard about the enigma that was their daughter. "Well, that obviously struck a nerve with her, okay? She struggles with feeling like she's not enough, and maybe she's scared to get too comfortable and get hurt.

She feels betrayed thinking we're trying to have a baby, because to her, it means she's not enough."

"But she is enough, and I don't know how else to tell her that."

"I think it might just be one of those things that takes time." Will placed a reassuring hand on Erica's thigh. "And patience. Your favorite."

She laughed dryly. "I want to go explain it to her, but she begged me to be left alone."

"Then let her be for now. I know you want to solve every problem the second it arises, and I adore that about you. But Jada has a lot of complicated emotions and I think we need to give her a little bit of time to gather herself before we try to go in and explain things to her."

"Okay. You're right."

"Good. She'll be fine, she'll know she overreacted, we can tell her that we have not lied about a single thing, and everything will go back to how it was, okay?" He gently grabbed her chin and tilted her face up to meet his eyes.

"Okay." Erica chewed her lip, worry rising in her chest.

"Come on, let's throw on a show and kill some time. Let her have a bit of space."

She nodded and turned to face the television, wrapping a throw blanket over her legs.

Will found something on TV to watch, but Erica couldn't calm her mind enough to focus on anything but Jada.

She wanted to go up there, but she also wanted to give her space to breathe. Will was right, finding the tests in the bathroom clearly triggered something in her, and she'd been hurt badly by it.

Patience, as always, was a challenge, but Erica tried to persevere.

"It's been almost an hour..." she said slowly as soon as whatever HGTV special he'd found had ended. "Don't you think I should go talk to her?"

Will lifted a shoulder. "I think she'll probably be ready to talk now."

Thank God.

As soon as Erica stood up to head upstairs, there was a knock on the front door that startled her.

This late? Who was here?

"Someone at the door?" Will asked, walking over to join her as she headed through the entry way to the front door.

"Yeah, probably one of my insane siblings who have no sense of boundaries whatsoever," Erica quipped with an eyeroll and a laugh as she swung open their heavy, wooden front door.

But the person standing on their front porch was most definitely not a Sweeney.

"Abigail?" Erica drew back, her heart skipping a beat as she realized the adoption agent from Space Coast Family Connections was standing in front of her house. At ten o'clock. Unannounced.

That could not be good.

Abigail pursed her lips together and gave Erica a look that bordered on disappointed. "Hello. I'm so sorry to be coming here so late."

"What's going on?" Will walked over to the entryway and placed a hand on Erica's back. "Everything okay, Abigail?"

"Actually...no." Abigail's eyes flashed.

Erica craned her neck to see in the driveway behind her, where she could make out the same big, black SUV that had dropped Jada off at Sweeney House a couple of months ago. It was pouring rain, pounding down onto the pavement.

What was happening?

Nerves prickled across Erica's chest as she took a steadying breath and waited for Abigail to explain.

"We just received a call from Jada on our twenty-four-hour emergency line." She inhaled, her thin brows knitting together as she looked back and forth from Erica to Will. "And I'm very shocked and saddened by this, but Jada has requested to be placed in a different home."

"What?" Erica croaked out the word as astonishment rocked her to her core. "No...no...that can't be. There has to be a mistake."

"Jada's very happy here," Will added, his voice only moderately calmer than Erica's. "We've made so much progress. Surely this can't be right."

Abigail shut her eyes. "I am very sorry, but it is part of our Children First Policy that if a child tells us directly that they do not want to stay in a certain home, we promise to honor that request. All of our kids are briefed on it pre-adoption, and given the hotline phone number."

Was this seriously all because she found some old pregnancy tests?

Erica felt herself quiver a little as she clenched her fists and attempted to breathe, although her throat was thick and tight. "Can I at least just talk to her? I think she might have gotten a little overdramatic about a disagreement."

"A disagreement?" Abigail's brows shot up. "With the child?"

"Not like a fight or anything," Will jumped in, lifting a hand and offering the first smile of this whole interaction. "There was just a misunderstanding."

"That's all it was," Erica insisted, fear rippling through her so fast she felt like she could melt into the pavement. "Please, let me just talk to her."

"I'm sorry, Erica. I really am." Abigail let out a sigh. "We have to remove Jada from the home immediately, it's our policy. Especially if there's been problems going on and the child claims to feel unloved, we do have to respect that."

"She's not unloved!" Erica exclaimed, losing any shred of composure she was still clinging to. "We love her so much, Abigail. Please, can I just—"

"I'm sorry." Abigail shook her head. "She called us."

With that, Abigail and a couple of men who had gotten out of the black SUV pushed past her and went upstairs to get Jada.

"No..." Erica sucked in a shaky sob, glancing at Will with desperation. "No, they can't take her. Can they? They can't take her."

The world swam in front of her as tears fell from Erica's eyes.

"Maybe we can get her back," Will suggested. "Maybe it's temporary, or if we get a chance to reason with her..."

"You heard her." Erica sniffed, watching the three people from the adoption agency emerging at the top of the stairs. "She requested to leave, it's done."

Her heart plummeted into her stomach as Jada walked down the stairs between Abigail and the men, staring straight down at the ground.

Her sullen face was completely covered by her hair and her backpack was slung over one shoulder, and suddenly it was like none of it had happened. Like none of it had mattered. Like none of it was even real.

"Jada, come on." Erica rushed over to her as they walked through the entryway. "This is crazy, we're adopting you!"

She froze and finally looked up, her red-rimmed eyes tearing Erica in half. "I'm too scared."

"Of what?"

"Losing...everything again. It will hurt so much that I...I just don't want to feel it again."

Erica took a step closer, reaching for her. "Honey, I understand—"

"No, you don't," Jada said, her voice low but strong. "See, you don't have any idea what it's like to love someone, to depend on them, and think they are your...mother and then. Wham. Gone. Just...gone."

"No, I don't, honey, but I will never let that happen to you. You don't have to be afraid."

Will put his hand on Erica's back, but his gaze was on Jada. "You don't," he said. "We are making a promise."

For a moment, Erica thought Jada would give up the fight, but she swallowed and pushed her hair back and looked from one to the other, her dark gaze settling on Erica. "My mother promised, too. She swore she'd stop taking the stuff that made her sick. She said she'd never do anything bad. She told me I wouldn't have to stay in those homes for more than a few days. But every time, *every single time*, she lied."

Erica closed her eyes and let out a breath. "That had to hurt."

"It did. And now...I feel...like this could all get taken away any second. I know it will. You'll have a baby, I won't be so interesting to you anymore, and then..." Tears spilled. "No. I don't want to hurt like that again. I am so scared that if I love you and need you, I'll lose you. I don't deserve...you." She turned to Abigail, who'd watched in silence. "Please, I want to go."

"Honey, you don't—"

"Please! I want to leave!" Her voice echoed through the entryway, punching Erica in the heart.

"Then I have to take her," Abigail said softly. "She has the right to ask to leave. I'm sorry."

Erica swayed into Will, who held her as Abigail opened the door to the pouring rain and guided Jada out, where a summer storm sent sheets of rain onto the front walk.

"No, she can't go!" Erica cried, standing in the doorway as Jada got into the backseat.

"Honey." Will held his arms around her, a sweet attempt to console her but it did nothing to help. "Just let her calm down, we will not give up. We'll talk to Abigail tonight and be at the agency to fight for her first thing in the morning. It'll be okay, I promise."

But it wouldn't be okay. Everything Erica had ever dreamed of was finally there, in her arms and in her life and in her heart. And now...

It was pulling out of the driveway.

"Wait!" She wiggled her way out of Will's tight embrace, and darted down the street.

Her bare feet sloshed in the puddles that covered the pavement, and buckets of rain poured onto her head as she chased down the black car.

"Stop! Please!" She ran as fast as she could down their street, waving her arms like a lunatic in one last, embarrassingly desperate attempt to keep the daughter she loved so dearly.

The red brake lights lit up, and Erica took her chance to jet out in front of the SUV and stop it from moving one more single inch.

Rain washed over her and the car as the windshield wipers swiped rapidly, droplets spraying everywhere.

It was dark and soaking wet and Erica could hardly breathe, but she stood there, feet planted on the road.

"Jada!" she shouted, pushing wet strands of hair out of her face as she choked on a sob. "Jada, please don't go. I'm...I'm begging you."

The front passenger-side window rolled down ever so slightly, and Abigail shielded her face from the onslaught of rain as she looked up at Erica. "I'm sorry, we have to go."

"Jada." Erica completely ignored her, staying put and letting the water practically drown her. "Please stay. Be my daughter."

Erica had to scream over the loud sheets of rain coupled with roaring thunder in the distance and a flash of lightning.

But she'd scream. She'd scream at the top of her lungs out here in the rain all night long if that's what it took.

"Jada, I love you!" she shouted, tears mixing with rainwater as she took heavy breaths. "And I don't care if you're terrible at math." She laughed tearfully. "And I don't care if you're never on the honor roll. I don't even care if you go to school, I really don't!"

The engine hummed and the rain soaked through to her skin and her heart just continued to break.

Erica sniffed, wiping her wet face. "I love you for exactly who you are. My daughter. And, yes, I used to think all I wanted in the whole world was a baby…"

She drew in a shuddering breath as the rain fell in sheets, waiting and waiting for that door to open. Nothing.

"But that was before I knew you. You're witty, and fascinating, and ridiculously mature for your age. And tough. Tougher than any eleven-year-old should ever have to be. All this time I thought I had to teach you everything, you know? Reading and math and all this crap I tried to teach you. But, Jada, you were the one who was doing the teaching. All along. You taught me how to open my heart, how to let go of control. You taught me how to be a mom. And that's who I am now."

Everything was still and silent, muffled by the down-pour and the pumping of Erica's heart in her chest. "That's who I am. I'm your mom. I don't want a baby. I want you."

Erica waited, drenched in rain, as raw and vulnerable as she'd ever been in her life. She wiped her face, wishing, hoping, praying for that back door to open.

A long beat of silence and stillness hung in the air, with Erica's entire heart poured out onto the pavement with the rain.

She looked back at the house, seeing Will jogging out into the downpour to join her.

Erica watched, waited, and ached, until finally she decided she was going to have to give up.

She'd done everything she could. She'd begged and pleaded and tried desperately to get Jada back. But she was in that car, leaving this neighborhood, and Erica would likely never see her again.

Pain dumped down on her as hard as the raindrops as she walked away slowly, defeated, wondering how on Earth she could have been such an astounding, epic failure at motherhood.

"Wait." Will reached them, shaking raindrops out of his damp hair and beelining straight to the passenger side of the vehicle, locking eyes with Abigail through the open window.

Erica watched him, heart pounding.

"Abigail." Will leveled his gaze with the woman as his

clothes got soaked by the weather and Erica stood frozen in place. "When is the absolute soonest we can adopt Jada?"

Erica gasped, stepping forward to join him. "Yes," she agreed hastily. "How fast could we adopt her? Officially?"

"Well..." Abigail shook her head, frowning. "It does take time, and this is a weird situation now since Jada has requested replacement, but..."

"Could you make it happen?" Will asked eagerly, pressing his palms onto the bottom of the window. "Like, as soon as humanly possible?"

"Please, Abigail," Erica said. "We want to adopt Jada now."

"Right now," Will echoed.

"Well..." Abigail shook her head, visibly confused and flustered. "I suppose if all was okay and the child agreed to it, I could pull some strings and expedite the adoption certification, but that would only be..."

"Let's do that," Will said, glancing at Erica with hope in his eyes. "Expedite it, please. That's what we want."

Suddenly, a loud metal click caught Erica's attention, and she whipped around to see Jada climbing out of the back of the car, running into the pouring rain, heading straight toward her.

Jada's backpack bounced wildly on her shoulder as she darted over to Erica, getting completely soaked in the process. "You...you guys want to adopt me already?"

"Oh." Erica crumpled to the ground with relief, wrapping her arms around her tiny, wonderful, ridiculously strong-willed and ever-so-slightly dramatic daughter. "Yes. Yes, we do. So badly."

Will joined them, smiling at her through his soaking wet face. "We absolutely want to adopt you, as fast as possible."

Jada shook her head, rain sticking thick strands of hair to her face. "You're sure?"

"Yes!" Erica and Will exclaimed in desperate unison.

Jada paused for a long time, rain falling on all of them as she studied her new almost-parents, and her eyes widened. "I'm sorry. I'm sorry." She whimpered. "I shouldn't have called them. I was just really mad and upset and then I realized it was a bad idea, and—"

"Hey." Erica held Jada's face in her hands, smiling through tears of joy. "It's okay. I don't care. Just please, don't ever leave again. We want you to be ours."

"Forever," Will added. "Jada, we love you." He crouched down to join them, wrapping one arm around Erica and the other around their daughter.

"I love you guys, too." She sniffled and looked back and forth, water droplets falling off of all three emotional faces. "I won't ever leave again. I promise."

"Jada..." Abigail, who'd scrounged up an umbrella from somewhere in the SUV, stepped out of the vehicle. "Are you sure you want to stay? You make the call."

"Yes." She nodded. "I want to stay. They're gonna adopt me. Can you make it...what was that word?"

"Expedite," Erica suggested, her heart lighter already.

Abigail smiled, happiness flashing from her expression as she caught Erica's gaze. "Good. I'm so glad to hear that. And remember, calling the hotline is a serious matter."

"I know." Jada swallowed. "I'm sorry."

"We'll let it slide this once. I guess we can be on our way then, and we'll leave this happy family to dry off." She notched her head at the car.

"Hey, Abigail?" Erica stood up and reached out to touch the other woman's shoulder to get her attention before she got back into the car.

"Yes?"

"How soon do you think it could be? If you, you know, pulled some strings?"

Abigail paused for a long time, a big smile pulling at her face as she stared down at an unlikely yet wonderful success story. "With a foster care adoption? I can get it done in a week or two, strings pulled."

Erica hugged Will and Jada with the joy of that news. "That would be wonderful."

"The sooner the better," Will added.

"I'll give you all a call on Monday." Abigail nodded before stepping back into the car and driving away down the street.

"I'm sure my mom will want to throw a big party to celebrate," Erica said, putting both hands on Jada's shoulders. "It's not every day we get a new member of the family."

Jada looked up at her, tears in her eyes, her smile as blinding as ever. "Thanks...Mommy."

Mommy. Mommy? Erica put her head back and let

more tears spill. "Wow," she whispered. "I love that name."

"Good," Jada said. "'Cause I really like Jada Armstrong."

"I love that, too." Erica slid her arms around Jada's slender frame, pulling her close. "Nothing and no one could ever replace you, Jada. I promise."

She realized in that moment that she truly would not trade Jada for anything on the planet. She loved exactly who this girl was, and would continue to love her more every day.

And that's when Erica knew, without a shadow of a doubt, that she was finally a mom.

Chapter Twenty-three

Sam

"Have another cupcake." Dottie inched a paper plate with one of Annie's spectacular creations on it toward Sam. "These things are good for the soul."

Sam laughed. "Seriously, what magic does she put in the mix?" She took a bite and groaned, leaning against the counter. All around the cottage, she could see the faces of the people she loved—people she'd missed all those years in Orlando with Max. "This is such a beautiful day, Mom."

"Well..." Dottie grinned brightly. "I just want my new granddaughter to know how excited we are to officially have her in our family."

Sam looked out through the open sliding doors, out to the beach where Ben, Damien, Liam, Ellen, and their newest cousin, Jada, were all throwing around a football, shrieking with giggles.

"We're one Sweeney stronger." Sam smiled. "And Erica's glowing."

"Like a darn lightbulb," Dottie agreed, her eyes misty with pride as they watched Erica laugh and talk with Will and Annie, who had joined the party, her eyes finding Jada every few seconds.

"I'm so happy they expedited the adoption." Sam took another bite of cake, her eyes finding Taylor, the daughter of her own who was not quite in the happiest of ways. "I can't believe they got it done in a week!"

Dottie sensed her concern, practically reading Sam's mind as she placed a gentle, loving hand on her arm. "You're stressing about Tay, aren't you?"

"How can I not be?" Sam shut her eyes, letting out a slow breath. "She might be moving to Hawaii."

"But she might not," Dottie added. "I don't know if Taylor will turn down John's promotion. It's too good of an offer. She said she's still thinking about it, though."

"Mom." Sam leveled her gaze with her mother's. "You and I both know that love makes you do crazy, crazy things. This might be Taylor's moment for craziness. I just...I hate to see her make my mistakes, you know?" She shook her head. "I threw away any semblance of a career to be with a boy, because I thought he was all that mattered, and it left me broken and empty and hollow."

"Well, no offense, honey, but you didn't exactly pick well."

Sam snorted at Dottie's blunt but painfully true statement, shrugging her shoulders. "I know. But I want Taylor to be something besides someone's girlfriend or wife, or even mom. She has this golden chance sitting in front of her, but I worry that she's going to follow in my footsteps and choose the guy over everything."

"Taylor is going to make her own path, her own mistakes, her own decisions." Dottie sipped a cup of punch. "You just have to let her go, and catch her if she falls."

"Like you did for me." Sam turned to her mom, gratitude and love swelling in her chest. "After all those years I spent icing you out, you still caught me."

"And look at us now." Dottie smiled. "And I still haven't said I told you so."

Sam laughed heartily. "I can't believe we're officially closing Sweeney House for renovations next week."

"I know." Dottie shook her head wistfully. "It's all a bit surreal, but I truly am so excited. I'm just not looking forward to breaking the news to the team that they're all going to be out of a job for so long. I'll tell them I'll do everything I can to get them all temporary positions in the local hospitality industry, but who knows if that'll be possible?"

"They're all such great, competent people, they'll be okay."

"I do worry about Bella, that new maid," Dottie said. "She seems to be a bit cagey about things, and I get the impression she doesn't have a lot of money. Sweet girl, too."

"Maybe we can find her something to do during the reno process, if she really relies on the income."

Dottie grinned. "That's a wonderful idea."

Sam looked around the cottage, her gaze catching Imani and John in the corner of the living room, deeply engaged in what appeared to be a stressful conversation. "Everything okay with them?" Sam asked.

Dottie sighed. "I don't know, Sam. Imani going back

to work has really put a stress on their family and their marriage. John doesn't talk to me the way that you and Erica do, but they're having serious problems."

Seriously problems? John and Imani? It seemed completely impossible. Their marriage was a beacon of love and stability and loyalty. They'd never even so much as had a disagreement, at least not that Sam had ever seen.

But this exchange happening in the living room, hushed voices, angry eyes, lots of hand gestures...it didn't look good.

Sam pursed her lips. "I know she's been getting back into writing more and more, and it's been taking a lot of her time. But why would John be so upset by that?"

"He relies on her for every last little thing. He needs her. She's his rock." Dottie shook her head and took another sip. "I think the idea of her having something outside of the family scares him. John couldn't survive one single day without Imani, and he knows it."

Sam wondered, for a fleeting second, if Max ever needed her that much. Sure, he relied on her for handling the kid stuff and grocery shopping and keeping the house nice.

But did he ever really need *her*? Or did he just need her to do stuff for him?

Did John need Imani?

Sam looked back over at Taylor, who was holding her fluffy cat in her arms and was now chatting with Annie. Was her precious girl going to move to Hawaii? Sam would be happy for her if that's what she decided... wouldn't she?

Well, at least Ben looked happy. He was finally out of his casts and all healed up from his accident, and currently teaching Jada how to run a corner route on the beach.

In the midst of all the unknowns and uncertainty and fear, there was family. The piece of Sam's life that had been missing for far too long.

The conversation between John and Imani appeared to get even more heated, and Sam watched as Imani stormed away from her husband, her hands thrown in the air with frustration.

Wow, they really weren't doing well.

"Mom, you are a rockstar for this party." Erica breezed into the kitchen. "Jada's on Cloud Nine."

"Oh, wonderful." Dottie clasped her hands together. "I'm so glad to hear that. She's a wonderful addition to the family."

Erica beamed. "We think so, too."

"Hey, Mom and G-Mom." Taylor flipped her hair as she bounced into the kitchen, seeming light and happy.

"Hey, you." Sam smiled. "Enjoying the party for your new cousin?"

"It's awesome."

"You look..." Sam studied her daughter. "You look like you're glowing. Does this mean you've made a decision on the Hawaii-versus-Coastal Marketing dilemma?"

Taylor pressed her lips together. "I honestly am so

back and forth. The idea of going to Hawaii is so appealing...it's hard not to at least entertain it."

Sam's heart skipped, but she tried not to show her thoughts and fears about her daughter possibly moving many, many thousands of miles away. "I get that."

Taylor sucked in a breath, glancing at Dottie and then back at Sam, her eyes glimmering. "I kind of...maybe want to go. But then there's the promotion at Uncle John's. Which is such an opportunity for me, and he was so gracious to give it to me. I don't want to pass it up."

Sam gave her daughter a steady smile. "Think on it. Talk it over with us. You'll make the right choice."

"I know!" Taylor grinned.

Taylor was a grown woman, and Sam knew that no matter what, she had to support her and love her and pray she didn't make all the same mistakes that Sam did.

Suddenly, there was a loud dinging of a knife on glass, and everyone hushed to look over and see Imani holding up her drink, tapping the side of it as if she were about to make a toast.

"What's going on?" Erica asked in a hushed tone.

Sam just shrugged, and they all turned to see their sister-in-law, who looked visibly upset, trying to get everyone's attention.

"Hey, family." Imani smiled, but it looked strained.

The room went silent, and even the kids stopped playing to come into the house and stand quietly in the living room.

"I have an announcement, and I figured while you're

all here, I might as well just go ahead and share it." Imani took a deep, nervous breath.

Sam glanced at Dottie, who looked as mystified as everyone else.

Imani cleared her throat and continued. "I have been given an amazing opportunity to write for the online magazine called *Wanderlust.*"

Sam gasped.

"No way!" Erica shouted. "Yay!"

Sam didn't know all that much about travel magazines and websites, but everyone had heard of *Wanderlust* and seen their ads all over the internet. This had to be a huge deal for Imani.

Was this what she and John had been arguing about?

"It's really exciting," Imani continued. "So, I will be... leaving," she said the last word with pained reluctance. "For California. Tonight."

"California?" Dottie spat out, shock in her voice. "Tonight?"

"I'm only gone three months," Imani added quickly. "And this was just too amazing of a chance to pass up. So, that's the news!" She smiled awkwardly. "Obviously, we're going to need some help from family, and I know I can count on all of you..."

As her voice trailed off, the air in the cottage was suddenly thick with tension, and no one really knew what to say or do or think.

Imani was...leaving? For three months?

Sam understood that she wanted to get back into

writing, but wasn't that a bit extreme? Was their marriage really that rocky?

She looked for John, catching him just in time to see him sigh, close his eyes, and slip out of the room.

"California?" Erica's eyes widened.

"Three months." Sam shook her head in disbelief.

"I'm gonna go talk to her," Erica said, grabbing her drink and heading out of the kitchen to talk to Imani. "I need to know what's really going on."

Sam swallowed and nodded, turning to Dottie. "You okay?"

"I am." Dottie sighed. "But my son isn't."

Sam's eyes fluttered shut, her heart aching for both her brother and her sister-in-law.

The sound of the door bell broke into the hushed conversation, and Sam turned to her mother. "You expecting anyone?"

Dottie shrugged nonchalantly. "Could be a straggler, who knows."

"I'll get it," Sam said, heading toward the front door to swing it open and...what?

"Julie?" Sam breathed her sister's name in true disbelief that the black sheep of the family—the always-missing puzzle piece—stood right there in front of her.

"Hey, li'l sis." Julie Sweeney's long black hair hung straight down her sides, a tank top baring rail-thin arms covered in tattoos. She still sported her signature little silver nose piercing that she was just cool enough to pull off, and that same effortless confidence that Sam had always envied.

"No..." From behind Sam, Dottie gasped, then practically ran to the door with shaky hands up to her mouth as she took in the sight of her renegade musician of an oldest daughter. "Julie! My Julie, you're home."

Dottie lunged forward and crumpled into tears as she hugged Julie, who laughed softly as her gaze caught Sam's.

"Holy cow, you're here!" Sam leapt toward them and joined the hug, a million questions flying through her mind all at once.

"Julie, Julie, oh..." Dottie pulled back and sniffed in an attempt to gather herself. "What are you doing here? I never thought you'd come back, I...what are you doing here?"

Julie took in a slow breath, her eyes flashing with a kind of fear and uncertainty that looked out of place on the face of someone who was always so wildly assured. "Well..." She looked back at the old, bluish green van sitting in the driveway.

Sam squinted at the sunlight and craned her neck to get a better look at the vehicle.

The front passenger-side door opened slowly, and out stepped a thin, gorgeous, blond sixteen-year-old girl. It took Sam a few seconds to recognize Bliss, Julie's daughter, who was no longer the little kid Sam remembered.

Julie never married Roman, and he clearly was not with them right now, so Sam had no idea if he was even still in the picture.

Had their band broken up? Had *they*?

The questions came a million a minute, but all Sam could do was stare in awe at her long-lost sister and niece.

"Hi, Grandma. Hi, Aunt Sam." Bliss stepped forward slowly, standing next to her mom, looking like the spitting image of her younger self.

"Hey, Bliss." Sam grinned. "You're so grown up, my goodness."

"My beautiful granddaughter." Dottie embraced her and kissed her forehead.

"How long are you in town?" Sam asked quickly.

Julie looked down at her daughter and wrapped an arm around her shoulders. "Well, we're going to be here for...a while, actually."

Dottie drew back. "You are?"

"We need some help." Julie swallowed.

"Of course. Anything," Dottie said.

"We need help...getting this little lady a new kidney."

Bliss swayed a little and looked up at them through sad, tired eyes. "Mine stopped working."

Sam felt her heart plummet as Dottie shot forward to hug her granddaughter.

"Oh, baby Bliss. We are here for you," Dottie cooed. "Whatever you need. Anything, anything at all."

Bliss inched back and gave a wry smile. "Well, it seems I need a kidney since neither of my parents match."

"Then you shall get one," Dottie said with shocking brightness. "Why, I'll give you one of mine."

"It might not be that simple, Mom," Julie whispered. "But until we solve the problem and figure out if we can find a match, she needs stability, a home that's not on wheels, and dialysis. I hope you don't mind us coming here. We just had nowhere else to turn."

"Mind? I'm thrilled." Dottie hugged them both and lifted her arm to bring Sam into the group hug. "We're family, my darlings, and we'll get through anything together."

"Thank you, Mom."

Dottie took in a quivering breath, straightening her back as she held Sam's hand tightly in her own, holding Julie's gaze and visibly fighting tears. "Welcome home."

*Want to know what happens next for the Sweeney Family? Don't miss book two: **Cocoa Beach Reunion** Or sign up for my newsletter to get the latest on new releases and more!*

The Sweeney House Series

The Sweeney House is a landmark inn on the shores of Cocoa Beach, built and owned by the same family for decades. After the unexpected passing of their beloved patriarch, Jay, this family must come together like never before. They may have lost their leader, but the Sweeneys are made of strong stuff. Together on the island paradise where they grew up, this family meets every challenge with hope, humor, and heart, bathed in sunshine and the unconditional love they learned from their father.

About the Author

Cecelia Scott is an author of light, bright women's fiction that explores family dynamics, heartfelt romance, and the emotional challenges that women face at all ages and stages of life. Her debut series, Sweeney House, is set on the shores of Cocoa Beach, where she lived for more than twenty years. Her books capture the salt, sand, and spectacular skies of the area and reflect her firm belief that life deserves a happy ending, with enough drama and surprises to keep it interesting. Cece currently resides in north Florida with her husband and beloved kitty. When she's not writing, you'll find her at the beach, usually with a good book.